Connections

Connections

Patrick A. Ryan

Thurles Books

This edition first published 2019

Published in Ireland by Thurles Books

The moral right of the author has been asserted in accordance with the Copyright and Related Rights Act, 2000.

Print ISBN: 978-1-5272-4818-2

Copyright © Patrick A. Ryan, 2019

This is a work of fiction. Any resemblance to any persons, living or dead, is entirely coincidental.

Internal Design by www.carrowmore.ie

Cover Design by GD Associates

PROLOGUE

1912

The August humidity combined with the gasoline fumes from the rapidly increasing number of automobiles was already creating another hazy Philadelphia day. Nine a.m. Mass celebrated by Bishop Richard Walsh in the side chapel of the Cathedral of Saints Peter and Paul on 18th Street had concluded.

Older, wealthier and more formally dressed Mass goers walked slowly and sedately to their carriages or automobiles parked outside the gate. Others headed for streetcars or for their homes in the local area. A few lingered to chat to their friends.

Nobody noticed the dishevelled man sitting on the ground close by. If they had, they would have assumed, incorrectly, that he was one of those tramps or down-and-out immigrants who often begged outside the cathedral.

Bishop Walsh left the cathedral and was greeting the few people still around when the man jumped to his feet, let out a loud plaintive cry, drew a gun from inside his coat and fired two shots at the Bishop. Both missed and hit the wall of the cathedral.

The Bishop ran back into the side chapel, and the others scattered quickly in various directions. The man made no attempt to flee. He threw the gun away and fell to his knees shouting, "I'm innocent, I'm innocent. He knows I'm innocent."

No one heard him. Then he cried, loudly and bitterly.

When the police arrived, he was lying on his side with his knees pressed against his chest, still in a distressed state.

He did not resist arrest.

1

The town centre was deserted when the Clondore Gaelic football team arrived home by coach. Tommy Walsh swung his kit bag over his shoulder and turned to his friend Dave McCarthy. 'Reaching the final of the county championship mustn't mean much around here. So I suppose we'll just have to win the bloody thing.'

It started to rain as they passed a few customers who were leaving O'Riordan's pub, noisy but cheerful, but they paid no attention either. Dave said, 'Are you coming in for one?'

'Ah, I dunno.' When Dave pulled a face, Tommy added, 'OK, but one means one. I've got a class first thing tomorrow and I have to sort myself out.'

Over an hour later, Tommy headed for his home a few hundred yards away on Barrack Street. He lived with his dad, Frank, on two floors above the family business: Walsh's DIY and Hardware. Tommy had helped his father to build the lean-to sheds in the yard to the side and rear of the shop that increased the storage and the selling space for gardening and building materials. This area could be accessed through the shop or via a laneway to the left of the shop. The laneway was shared with the Garda barracks that had been built for the Royal Irish Constabulary. The little bit of local history Tommy knew told him that this had given the street its name.

The living area was accessed through a dark-green door at street level to the right of the shop. Tommy's bedroom was one of three on the second floor, which also had a bathroom, and the first floor was taken up by the kitchen, which had seen better days, a dining room, which was rarely used, a sitting room, which had been his mother's pride and joy, and a room at the back which was used as an office and a storeroom.

His father, Frank, was drinking tea at the kitchen table with the Sunday newspaper spread in front of him. The smell from the wood-burning stove dominated and mixed with cooking smells, giving the room a welcoming feel. Frank looked up as he said, 'Well done, that was a real tough game.' He nodded at the teapot on the cooker. 'I've made a fresh one. Will you have a cup?'

'Thanks, Dad, I will.'

'And there's cold meat and a few other things in the fridge.'

Tommy poured his tea and went to check what he fancied in the fridge. 'Yeah, we were going well, and it looked easy for a while, but we were lucky to get through in the end. We didn't have a lot of support at the match.'

His dad lifted his head again from the newspaper. 'Ah, they're probably like the Kerry lads.'

'How's that?'

Frank grinned. 'When a Kerry supporter is asked if he's going to the All-Ireland semi-final in Dublin, he may say, "No, but I'll definitely be there for the final." Now that's confidence. So maybe our lads think the same way.'

Tommy laughed. 'Doubt it, but thanks for the compliment.'

'Has the date for the final been fixed?'

Tommy put a plate of food on the table and dropped wearily into a chair. 'Yeah, it's on the last Sunday of the month.'

'That soon?'

'Yeah, and if we win that one we qualify for the provincial

championship, which starts four weeks later at the end of October. But we're trying not to think that far ahead.' He looked over at his dad. 'Are you not eating yourself?'

Frank shook his head. 'I've had my tea thanks.' He glanced at his watch and stood up. 'I must be off, or I'll be late.'

'Off where?' Tommy said with surprise. The newspaper usually kept Frank occupied on Sunday nights.

'I … I'm off out to the pictures.'

'Oh?'

Frank hesitated. 'Yes, with Orla Maguire.' With that, he went out the door and down the stairs.

God, these dates are getting a lot more frequent.

Tommy put more wood in the firebox of the cooker. The heat and cosiness reminded him of his mother's presence and now, eight years later, her absence. He reflected on how much her enthusiasm and business sense must have helped his dad and on how much he must have missed her over the years, in the business, in his bed, in his life. They had shared twenty-four hours a day, every day.

She always seemed to be in good humour. She used the business experience gained in a jewellery and gift shop in Tullamore to persuade Tommy's father to give up the grocery part of the shop because it could never compete with a supermarket.

Would I have preferred if I had been told it was terminal? Did it take longer to get over the shock, the loss? Hard to say. Dad and Mary were protecting me and Deirdre, and no doubt Mam had a big say in it too. Seventeen and thirteen are difficult ages.

He looked at the family photo on the wall beside the cooker and wondered again if it had been taken because his mother had been aware of her prognosis. He avoided asking his dad about these things so as not to remind him of that terrible time, but now he thought that perhaps Dad also needed to talk about it.

The Salvador Dalí print on the opposite wall always intrigued him. It depicted Jesus Christ on the cross as if it was a photo taken from above, looking down on the top of his head, his shoulders and his outstretched arms. Tommy was surprised that his mother had hung such a controversial piece of art in such a prominent position.

Dad never seems to be aware of it, but I'm sure he'd miss it if it was removed.

This led Tommy on to thinking about Orla Maguire. He shook his head wondering where that might be leading.

* * *

Next morning, in the crowded staffroom of the Clondore Community School, the chat was all about the match and the bulletin from the Teachers' Union of Ireland on the proposed cuts in salary. This was Tommy's fifth year teaching Business Studies having started immediately on graduating from University College Galway in 2007.

Being a former pupil, it was strange at first, particularly as he was now a colleague of several of his former teachers. To make matters even more awkward, he also had to deal with the fact that his former girlfriend, Clare O'Connor, was also a teacher at the school. Seeing each other every day had been tough for both of them for the first few months after the break-up, but they were friends again now. Clare and Dave McCarthy had recently become an item, and Tommy was OK with that.

As usual, when school finished he spent an hour or so helping out in his father's shop. For as long as he could remember he had done that. It started with fetching and carrying for his mother, then helping to unload supplies or put purchases in customers' cars and finally to implementing stock control and sales software and taking charge in his father's absence.

Tommy unpacked a delivery of tools, DIY products and giftware and did a bit of general tidying. It pays to keep things under review and maybe we should have some additional shelving or a display platform in the centre of the shop floor, he thought to himself. Then he sighed. What am I like? I should be preparing lectures instead of this stuff. He hated the way the business took hold of him so easily and filled up his thoughts and his time. He always told himself he'd never take over the business or allow himself to be stuck in Clondore. He'd had plans to travel, to see the world, but he'd only made it to Galway and back again.

What do I say or do if Dad asks me to take over the business, putting my plans in a cul-de-sac? How could I avoid disappointing him? He's sixty-three years old, and one of these days he's going to raise it.

That evening, Tommy answered the phone in his bedroom. Daytime calls were usually about the business and were left to his dad. His sister Mary was on the line.

'I heard ye won the match, well done. Don't get a swelled head now.'

'Wait till the final before you start the slagging.'

'How's Dad?

'Dad's fine.'

'Is Orla Maguire still in the picture?'

'Yeah, they're together a lot.'

'I know Orla to see around the town. So, what's the story?'

'I don't know what to make of it really. They went to the cinema on Sunday night.'

'You sound like a concerned parent.'

'Funny you should say that. I was thinking same myself.'

'Explain please.'

'You know, it can be risky to marry too young. Could the same apply to an elderly couple?'

'That's getting ahead of yourself, isn't it?'

Tommy laughed. 'You're right, I'd better shut up so.'

'You're not off the hook yet. How's your love life?'

'No comment. How is that husband of yours?'

'A swift change of subject. He's fine, doing night shifts, which he doesn't like, and there's talk of him moving to the traffic corps. Any contact from Deirdre? How are her studies going?'

'No idea. You'd think she was in London and not a couple of hours away in Limerick. If you can drag yourself away from Dublin, you both should visit together – and soon. I know Dad would look forward to that.'

Next afternoon, Tommy sat at his desk in his bedroom, facing the window and overlooking the outdoor part of the shop and rural County Offaly beyond. Before getting down to work, his eyes rested on the autumn colours in the trees nearby.

As he corrected papers on 'Industrial Relations in a Medium Sized Company', he was amused by the bias shown by a few pupils on the union or the management side. Without checking the author's name he could identify the likely individuals involved. He decided to use this in class the following day, without putting any pupil on the spot. The mix of pupils from all levels of society in the town appealed to him. He regarded this as providing an education in itself, for him as well as for the pupils.

He went down to the kitchen to prepare the evening meal for himself and his dad. It was nothing fancy and fairly predictable. He and his dad relied on Mrs Duggan who came each Monday through Friday, as she had been doing for twenty years or more, to prepare a midday meal and do the cleaning, washing and ironing, making the place look less like a bachelor's house.

Later, he left the clearing up to his dad and rushed away for football training. The post-mortem after such an important match was a painful if necessary part of the sport. The team manager, Sean Maher, did the analysis, supported by some amateur video shots. He mixed the positive and negative in his remarks about individual players. Looking at Tommy, he said, 'Great overall, but on two occasions you mistook the flight of the ball because you got into a tussle with your opponent. You recovered well, but it could have caused us problems.'

Tommy nodded, saying, 'I hear you.'

The usual rumours circulated about team selection and switching positions with Tommy to play centre-field.

God, not this again, I want to play centre-back or not at all. He hoped this was just the start of the mind games, which, no doubt, the managers and coaches of each team would instigate and promote, each one portraying the opposition as superior in every way.

2

The next day, when Tommy entered the shop, Jimmy Walker was placing a delivery of paint on the shelves on the left wall, showing great vitality for a man of sixty-eight. Tall and broad, with a strong square face and a good head of grey hair, if you didn't know him you would guess he was a well-to-do farmer or a retired army officer. He had that physical aura about him.

He gave Tommy a firm handshake. 'Well done yesterday. Ye're now in the final, isn't that just fantastic? Sean, my stepson, is delighted. You know, he captained the team when we last won the final in 1996.'

'Yeah, I know, as team manager he makes great use of all that experience.'

Jimmy, enthusiastic as always, said, 'I've no doubt ye'll win the final now.' He went to help a customer load fence posts and a few small bags of cement in his trailer. When he returned, his coat and hat covered in raindrops, he said, 'That Liam Moran fella must have his First Communion money.'

'Oh?'

'Yeah, he never fails to ask for a discount, even during a clearance sale.'

'So, what do you do?'

'I play him at his own game. I add a bit to the price and then take it off when he asks for a reduction and he goes away happy.' Jimmy was silent for a moment, and then said, 'Have you a few minutes? I need a private word.'

'Yeah, sure.' Tommy was intrigued and wondered whether the reason was business or personal, recalling Jimmy's marriage in his late fifties to the widow, Joan Maher.

'I need your advice about legal matters.'

'I'm not the one you should be asking about that.'

They moved to the two chairs on wheels, behind the counter.

'Well, you know a lot more than I do. It's like this. Joan hasn't transferred the farm to Sean, even though he's been running it successfully for more than twelve years. He has a wife and two young children to think about. He only found this out when he went to the bank to discuss borrowing. I'm now getting the clear impression from him that he thinks I may be behind Joan's decision, or lack of decision. As you know, he's a quiet-spoken man but very determined. I don't want to get on the wrong side of him even if it's not my fault.'

Tommy hesitated for a moment or two, surprised to be given so much family information. He reckoned that Jimmy's lack of experience with property or wills was the reason.

Before Tommy could respond, Jimmy added, 'I reckoned with your college education and your friendship with Sean you're the one to ask.'

'I know nothing about the law. You need to talk to a solicitor.' When he got no response, Tommy added, 'I can understand Sean's concern. Does he have a rival for the farm? What about his younger brother Dermot?'

'I don't see any problem there.'

'Has Joan made a will?'

'Don't know.'

'That's the crucial thing. Wills have caused terrible family rows. You know the variation on the old proverb, "Where there's a will there's a relative."'

'Yeah, I've heard stories about that.'

Tommy felt he was straying into unknown territory but decided he should do the best he could and said, 'She may have made a will but hasn't told anyone. It's perfectly reasonable for you to raise this with her, and, as far as I know, you have the option of renouncing any claim you might have on the farm.'

Jimmy's face brightened. 'That sounds good. Sean would be relieved.'

'If there isn't a will, ask her to talk to a solicitor. My team-mate, Dave McCarthy, only qualified a few years ago, but I would recommend him.'

'Thanks. You have set my mind at rest. Now I'll try to do the same for Sean.'

Tommy, moving his chair backwards, said, 'By the way, do you and Joan go to the movies?'

'Rarely since the cinema here closed. Why?'

'Dad and Orla have gone a few times recently and I thought maybe you and Joan went as well.'

'It must be ten years since our cinema closed,' Jimmy said wistfully. 'As you know, it's now a supermarket. I remember as a kid when it reopened after renovations and installing new equipment. They brought a fellow from Dublin, Harpo the Harpist, to entertain us before the film each night for a week.'

'A film and live entertainment?'

'Yeah, he got the audience to sing and clap along when he played "Deep in the Heart of Texas." We kids used to help him carry the harp, which was as big as himself, from the hotel. Ah, happy days.'

'It's a pity it closed. Tullamore is a long way to go to see a movie.'

'Anyway, thanks for the suggestion. I'll see what Joan thinks.'

Tommy made a move, intending to check invoices and update

accounts, but he sensed that Jimmy had something else on his mind.

Jimmy then said, 'Look, maybe this is none of my business, but it's been on my mind for weeks so I'd better spit it out.'

Tommy could see that Jimmy was apprehensive, so he said, 'Come on Jimmy, let's hear it.'

'Well, retirement is on my mind as well as your dad's so it's about you taking over the business.'

'Jimmy, I'm happy to hear your views, so fire ahead.'

'OK then. Your father wasn't given any choice you know. He wanted to become a bank clerk, but, like you, he was an only son, and when his dad had his first heart attack in 1966 Frank had to leave school early and take over.'

'God, that must have been tough.'

'You didn't know this?'

'I just knew he took over as a teenager but not why.'

'Yeah, he was only seventeen. He had to sink or swim. His father's health never recovered, and he died about seven years later.'

Tommy wondered why he was only hearing this now. 'Was my granny any help to him?'

Jimmy, happy that he had managed to start this conversation, gave a sigh of relief and said, 'No, not really, she hadn't been involved in the business for many years. Besides, she was worn out from nursing your granddad.'

'I'll bet you were a great help to him.'

Jimmy raised himself out of the chair and glanced out the window to check that there wasn't a customer in the yard looking for attention. 'Well, I hope I was. I was there about eight years at that stage. Your grandfather took me on when I was only fourteen. For that and for other kindnesses he showed to me, and before that to my mother, I'll always be grateful.'

Knowing how much Jimmy had contributed to the business, Tommy was a little embarrassed. He looked away briefly and then said, 'Jimmy, thank you for telling me this. It must make me look like an ungrateful sod.'

'No, no, I never thought that. I just felt I should say my piece and leave it to you.'

'I never saw myself running a business. I became a teacher because that's where the university application system took me. Having said that, I do enjoy it, at least for now.'

'You know I want the best for you and for your dad.'

'Of course I do. I'll have a chat with him and hopefully we can work something out.'

Their attention transferred to two customers entering the shop. They both gravitated towards Jimmy, and Tommy had to intervene. Jimmy's parting comment was, 'Look Tommy, I'll get off your back. That stock control and accounting system you introduced has shown how suited you are to the business, so please think about it.'

3

On a very warm August day in DeSales University in Center Valley, Pennsylvania, Anna Novak was taking part in a tryout match for the college intramural soccer team. She liked field hockey as well but felt that soccer gave her the best chance of making the team. The opposition, from a university in Philadelphia, was also on trial, and this was reflected in the physical challenges and the determination to win.

Anna was happy that the game had gone her way with plenty of time on the ball and that she had played well. Whether it was well enough, she thought, only time would tell. From an early age she had been the competitive sporty daughter while Barbara, her older sister, was the compassionate caring one.

When she had showered and returned to the playing area to watch the next trial match, she was thrilled to see her boyfriend, Josh Hamilton, waiting for her. He wrapped her in a bear hug saying, for all to hear, 'Nice job honey – I think you have a great chance of making the team.'

Anna hugged him back and kissed him, aware that her parents and classmates were watching from the stadium benches. She grabbed Josh's hand, saying, 'C'mon, say hello to Mom and Dad,' and she led him up the steps.

'That was great! They'll pick you for sure,' her dad, Peter, said, and her mom, Katherine, gave her a hug.

'Thanks,' she said, beaming. 'Josh thinks so too.'

'Good to meet you again,' Josh said, but his face didn't match his words.

'Likewise' and 'Hello, Josh,' her parents answered.

Anna was surprised that Josh seemed so nervous. He'd met them a few times since they'd started dating back in January.

On their way home, she and Josh stopped for a burger and a beer. They held hands across the table and talked about plans after college. Anna asked, 'Do you plan to go to grad school or will you look for a job?'

'I won't have to look: my dad wants me to work for him. I guess I'm lucky, eh?'

'You sure are, but is it a good idea to work for your father?'

'Well, it's more an instruction than an offer.'

'You'll be staying in this area then?'

'Expect so.'

Anna squeezed his hand as she said, 'I hope I'll be doing the same.'

Josh beckoned the waitress, saying, 'I'll have another beer. How about you?'

Anna slapped his hand playfully. 'You've had two! You're driving, remember?' Why do I have to keep reminding him? She swatted similar disturbing thoughts from her mind like gnats on a summer's evening.

Josh answered in a gruff way, 'OK, let's go then.'

As they left, hand in hand, Anna asked, 'When is your next home game?'

'A week on Saturday. Will you be there?'

'You bet.'

Josh put his arm around her and squeezed her shoulders.

4

Frank was sitting in a paved area cordoned off from the retail part of the yard which contained two small sheds. He reflected that in Liz's time the area was enhanced with potted hydrangeas, heathers and a shrub with a Latin name which she called 'Flame of the Forest'.

It's more like a compound now really, though Tommy likes to call it 'the patio'. It's giving me fresh air and sunshine on maybe the last evening of autumn when this would be possible.

Tommy arrived, carrying a cushion. Frank lifted his eyes from the local newspaper. 'Any news from Deirdre?'

'Nope, not this week nor last.'

Frank tutted. 'She's a terrible one for not calling home.'

Tommy agreed but felt he should defend his sister. 'I expect she's busy with the new college term.'

'I'm glad she has stuck with the course. I was worried about that.' After a pause, he added, 'Well, that's all of you sorted, I suppose.'

There was something about the 'suppose' that made Tommy feel uncomfortable, and he found himself dreading what might be coming next. 'I suppose,' he replied, trying not to sound anxious.

'Mind you, it was a very different world when I finished school,' Frank said. 'We didn't have the choices young people have now. My dad's heart attack decided my career. In those days, not to have carried on the business he started would have been unthinkable.'

Tommy reflected on the conversation he had with Jimmy and began to wonder just how much pressure his dad intended to use. 'I'm not sure how much of a choice I had myself. I sort of feel I became a teacher by accident. I had thought by now I would be living elsewhere, working at something very different. But, sure, there you go.'

Frank nodded. 'Sometimes the best outcomes are unplanned. I felt trapped initially, but I got to love this business and my job. Of course, your mother, God rest her, played a huge role in that change of heart and mind.' Tommy searched for a comment. Frank added, 'You know, I'm sixty-three. I don't plan to retire any time soon, but I need to talk to you about it.' Before Tommy could reply, he continued, 'I know it could be counterproductive to have you here unwillingly. Mary and Deirdre made their career decisions, so where does that leave us?'

Tommy felt the pressure mounting. How do I avoid a commitment and not ruin his plan? 'This must look like I'm thinking only about myself. Let me work on it. I'll try to help you find a solution.' Frank just looked at Tommy without comment, and, as he reached for the newspaper, Tommy added, 'It's been rough on you, losing your father and mum well before their time.'

'Yeah, it's said that such things make you stronger, but I'm not sure I'd go along with that.'

Tommy could see the sadness, the pain, in his father's face and felt under pressure to agree to his wishes. He decided that, short of that, the best help he could give was to get his dad talking about the past. 'I know very little about your dad and nothing at all about your grandparents.'

'Well, where should I start? My dad served his time in a shop in Dublin owned by someone from this area and then set up the business here, and, as he said himself, he learned as he went along. Both my parents had good business acumen, as it would be described today. They certainly weren't afraid of hard work.'

'Was he a hard taskmaster?'

'Most times he had an easy-going manner, but he also had a short fuse, and you needed to watch out for the signs of that.' Frank was silent, reflecting. 'I was reminded about him the other day by Paddy Collins who was home on his annual holidays from Birmingham. When we were kids, Paddy spent a lot of time in our kitchen. One winter's night, Dad told a few of his ghost stories, you know, about banshees, headless horses and the Devil appearing at crossroads. Anyway, Paddy, who lived in an isolated cottage outside the town, was so scared he wouldn't walk home alone. I said I'd go with him until it struck me that I would have to walk back alone.'

Tommy laughed at the thought of it. 'How'd you get out of that one?'

'The solution was that my sister Jean came with us, so we had three on the outward journey and two on the inward. Your grandfather was highly amused. Paddy and I laughed about it.'

'I'd like to hear more of those stories.'

'Would you really? I thought young people had no interest in any of that.'

'Well, that's changing. Anyway, I'd like to know about earlier generations – who they were and what they were.'

Frank leaned forward in his chair. 'If it's family history you're after, your Aunt Evelyn was into that a few years ago. She gave me a file on us Walshes with newspaper clippings, a few certificates, names, addresses, dates. It's gathering dust somewhere, but I think I can find it.'

'Oh? I never heard about that. How far back does the file go?'

'To your great-grandparents' time.'

'I'd love to read it. Maybe there's enough there to create a family tree.' Tommy's show of enthusiasm was more about placating and distracting his father than any eagerness to get involved in family research.

'Haven't a clue about that.'

'I'll have a chat with Joe Dunphy. He gives lectures on the subject. You know Joe, don't you? He's the sales manager in Fitzpatrick's Garage.'

'Yeah, never spoke to him. Anyway, let me know if you have to spend money.'

As Frank turned his attention to the newspaper, Tommy took his cushion and went indoors.

Frank was disappointed but not surprised with Tommy's response. Maybe I should put more pressure on him, insist that he takes over from me, but that has its own dangers – a major risk for the business. Maybe if he had left home, worked elsewhere, he would be more willing to inherit. Maybe he could do that now. Maybe that's the answer.

* * *

All Tommy's free time was now devoted to football training, with sessions each weekday evening, increasing in duration and intensity. The team was now as fit and hopefully as well prepared as it needed to be. On Wednesday night, after the final session, the team was announced: first to the players and then to a sizeable group of supporters and two journalists representing the Tullamore radio station and the *Clondore Chronicle*, the local weekly newspaper.

Tommy was relieved that, despite the rumours and the hype, he was selected to play at centre-back. Well, thank God for that.

I'd hate to be faced with an unavoidable row with Sean Maher.

On Thursday evening, the squad discussed tactics based on an analysis of the opposing team and then had a group session and a short one-to-one meeting with a sports psychologist, a new experience for most of the squad. All was in place for the following Sunday at 3 p.m. in O'Connor Park, Tullamore, against their old rivals, St John's Gaelic Football Club. That club had tasted success more often and more recently than Clondore and were from a rural area much closer to Tullamore and therefore more likely to be supported by the locals.

5

In the Crofton Inn in rural Pennsylvania, the live band was doing its best to get the Friday-night crowd to sing along but was drawing only a half-hearted response. Anna Novak and her friends and classmates, Martha Douglas and Jane Taylor, were part of a large group of fellow students.

Anna said, 'If I go to grad school, I need first to decide if I want to work in sports and leisure management or to cast my net wider. How about you two?'

'Me too,' Jane added. 'But in what? And what kind of job could you get?'

All three reflected on that question. Anna tried to strike a hopeful note. 'I'm not ruling out starting work after graduation. And right now I'm just going to focus on my grades.'

'Here's a better idea,' Martha said. 'The three of us should take a year off and visit Europe.'

'Yeah, yeah, think of all those French guys,' said Jane, and laughter followed.

They listened to a few more numbers by the band and finished their second round of drinks. When the music stopped and they were resuming their conversation, Josh came through the door. Anna went to meet him, took his hand and steered him to a table away from her friends.

As they sat down, Anna noticed that Josh had one too many drinks taken, and the strong smell from his breath was further evidence. 'Good to see you, Josh, how are you?'

'Good, and you?'

'I'm worried about you.'

Josh smiled and mumbled, 'No need, no need.'

'You've had a few beers already this evening. Maybe a few too many?'

'God, you exaggerate. You got it all wrong.'

She took his hand and said, 'Josh, each time we've met recently you've had a few on board. I don't want to have this conversation either, but I cannot avoid it. I hope you can see it's because I care for you and what we have between us.'

He withdrew his hand and didn't respond, leading Anna to say, 'Josh please go home and sleep off the booze. We'll meet next week. I'll text you, OK?'

He left without a word, and with an expression that, to Anna, seemed to show anger and apprehension at the same time, which matched her own state of mind. Is he now headed for another bar? She returned to her friends, hoping they wouldn't say what she was sure was on their minds.

When Anna got home, her mother was in the den watching TV. Katherine was stretched out on one of the large cream-coloured sofas that formed a V-shape in front of the log-effect gas fire. Light from one of the reading lamps positioned behind each sofa set off the opulent dark burgundy carpet giving the room a familiar warm, cosy feel. Katherine smiled her welcome and invited Anna to sit, patting the cushion beside her. 'Did you have a good night sweetheart? How are the girls?'

'Yeah,' Anna said, 'we had a blast.'

'Have you an early start in the bookstore?'

'Yeah, but I'm cutting back for my senior year.'

The chat continued. Then Anna, her head full of Josh, excused herself, saying she'd better have an early night.

Anna found it impossible to think of sleep. Her head was full of thoughts of Josh, all negative, all worrying. What a transformation in a few months. Is it all down to alcohol? Should I have spoken up earlier? What should I do now? She turned out the light, hoping that at work next day she would find some inspiration.

* * *

A week later, when Anna arrived at the booth at the back of Jackson's Diner, Josh was sprawled across the seat. He made no effort to make room for her so she slid along the seat opposite him. She could sense that he had put away a few beers already. His glass was nearly full, but he ordered another and a sparkling water for her.

'How are you, Josh?'

'Fine, I guess. Why wouldn't I be?'

'You know how much you mean to me.'

'Sure do.'

'And you know I'm worried about you.'

'No need, no problem.'

'Did you take a cab home from the Crofton?'

'You bet. See, I know how to take care of myself.'

'I want to help you, to help us. I want to get back the way we were.'

'Look, could we please change the subject? This is becoming a real drag.'

Anna's annoyance took over. She had hoped for a pleasant conversation leading to a meeting of minds, a new start, but she blurted out, 'Look, we need to talk about your drinking. I can't stay quiet about this any more.'

'Ah, typical. You're overreacting. I don't have a problem.' His slight slurring of words said otherwise.

'Except cutting back or giving up.'

He gave a humourless laugh. 'Why would I do either?'

'Because it seems to be taking over your life, and because it's killing us.'

'God, I'm really pissed off with your lectures.'

Two couples nearby were having a noisy, happy time. Anna was annoyed, then envious and finally relieved that her conversation would not be overheard. She took Josh's hand. 'This is painful for me too. I'd much prefer to be talking about anything else.' Josh's reaction was a dismissive scowl. Anna persisted: 'Have your parents talked to you about your drinking? Did they offer help?'

'They don't give a shit about me, and it seems you don't either.'

Anna's hurt was shown in her face, but she knew the remark was intended as a diversion. She let it pass. She sat back, folded her arms and looked straight at him. 'Josh, I don't get your attitude.' He just shrugged his shoulders and glanced around the diner. 'Your parents can afford to send you to counselling, but first you have to accept that you have a problem.'

'You seem determined to give me one.'

Anna sighed. She knew point-scoring would only make matters worse. She put her hand on his. 'Josh, you know that's not fair. I can see that you're hurting, and it's breaking my heart. I don't want to make matters worse – I want to help you. But I can't do that unless you want my help. Will you let me help you?' Josh avoided eye contact, and when he didn't answer, she continued, 'Look, I'll email you websites on counselling. You'll read it?'

'If I do, will that be the end of the lectures?'

'That depends on the decisions you take.'

'Fucking hell.'

'Josh, do you want us to have a future together? It's that important.'

'Ah, shit, I've had enough of this.' He left the booth and headed for the door.

On her way home, Anna's mind was full. Why does he use attack as his form of defence? Why will he not discuss his problem or even admit how his life is sliding downhill? She felt that the only thing she had achieved was Josh's resentment and the worries travelling around her head in never-ending circles.

She put on her smiley face as she entered the den and was relieved that her parents were engrossed with the TV instead of asking questions about her date with Josh.

'Have a look at this,' her mother said. 'It's a rerun of Who Do You Think You Are? on the family history of Martin Sheen. You know, the guy in the movies and on TV? His father's people were from northern Spain, and his mother's people were Irish, from Tipperary. I'd love if we could do something like that.'

Anna was pleased to keep this conversation going. 'What? You want our family to be on TV?' Peter didn't comment.

'No, silly, it would be great if we could create our family tree. You know Polish-Irish instead of Spanish-Irish.'

'What do you think, Dad?' Anna asked, hoping that he would dampen her mother's enthusiasm.

'Why not?' Peter said, but with an air of detachment.

'Could you take this on?'

Anna could see that her mother was not going to let go of this. She delayed her reply, trying to think of an excuse or a diversion, but then she decided to grin and bear it. 'Right! To get the ball rolling please let me have names, dates, addresses, so search your records, photos, certificates and your memories, and I'll take it from there.'

'Let me know when the TV cameras arrive,' Peter said.

'Oh, very funny, very funny,' Katherine said. 'Thanks Anna.' She then added in an emphatic way: 'Start with the Novaks.'

Anna was surprised that she wasn't more curious about her own family background but decided not to comment.

6

The town was slow to react at first, but about ten days before the county final, flags and bunting began to appear in the club's colours of blue and green, and in quick time every shop and public building was displaying its support. The elongated S-shaped main artery of the town, from Barrack Street, widening through O'Connell Street and narrowing again in Davitt Street, was full of colour. Many shops had window displays with the photo of the 1996 team very prominent. The team flag flew on the post-office flagpole; the door of the town library was decorated in the team's colours; and inside, a display prepared by local children held pride of place. In Davitt Street, Davy's Hotel displayed a large banner, and, not to be outdone, the advert for coming attractions in the Town Hall Theatre was replaced by 'Clondore County Champions'. Some thought this was tempting fate. Walsh's DIY and Hardware, on Barrack Street, at the northern approach to the town, had a large banner wishing success to the team.

In the side streets, residents contributed to the festive air by hanging bunting and flags from their windows or garden fences. On Friary Street, the railings of the primary school and St Michael's Roman Catholic Church were covered in banners, and on the Tullamore Road the community school and, as might be expected, Clondore GAA Park shouted their support. Farmers dyed sheep in the club colours, and on Saturday morning, much to the amusement of shoppers and coffee drinkers, Paddy 'Dettori' Dwyer (named after the jockey because he spent so much time and money in the bookmaker's) paraded his donkey through the town wearing a blanket of blue and green with his young daughter appropriately togged out as the jockey.

Overnight, a VW Beetle, hand-painted all over in the county colours, was placed in the public car-parking area outside the supermarket on O'Connell Street. From its appearance, everyone rightly assumed that it did not arrive there under its own steam, and great interest was shown in whether the town's only traffic warden would have the courage or the sense of humour to put parking fines on it. Clamping probably would have been welcomed by the owner to save the bother of dumping it.

Pupils of the primary and secondary school wore the team shirt every day, and young and old attended the team's training sessions in large numbers – another new experience for the squad. Local radio carried interviews with team members and mentors past and present, particularly those involved in 1996 when the championship was last won. The *Chronicle* published a special supplement on the event, no doubt expecting it to be purchased for former residents of the area.

On the day of the match, the parish priest, Father Warren, declared his good wishes at the 11 a.m. Mass. 'May the best team win, and, of course, we all know what team that is!' When people headed for their cars, they probably wished he had prayed for good weather as a heavy shower started. Some just opened an umbrella, others quickened their pace to varying degrees, and a small number continued as before as if they and their clothes were waterproof.

Coaches were parked on Barrack Street to take the team and supporters to the match with a convoy of cars lined up behind. Frank Walsh, Orla Maguire, Jimmy and Joan Walker travelled together. They were headed to O'Connor Park in Tullamore, the largest GAA ground in the county. The atmosphere was alive with the prospect of a third title.

On the team coach, many of the players sat in silence in their own thoughts. Some wore headphones, and their heads moved to the rhythm of their favourite music. Tommy sat with his eyes closed and for the first time felt the butterflies in his stomach. This subsided somewhat when he arrived in the ground and in the bustle of the dressing room but started again as he made his way to the pitch. He stared straight ahead, his jaw locked as if he was holding something in place. He felt sure his teammates were going through something similar. He tried, as he had been taught, to convert this nervous energy into a positive force.

The afternoon was bright and dry, suitable for fast, open football. The ground was full with a riot of team colours. As Tommy and the team ran onto the pitch, the reception by their supporters helped to settle their nerves with their chanting – Clon-Clon-Clon-Clondooore – with rising decibels on each syllable. The captain, Conor Ryan, called the team into a huddle for a last-minute pep talk.

Clondore got off to the worst possible start by conceding an early goal. Tommy shouted instructions at his teammates who were near enough to hear him on how to avoid a repetition. He kept trying the impossible, to recall the key instructions received while keeping an open mind and his concentration on his opponent all at the same time. It seemed to work for him and the team, and by half-time they had reduced the arrears to one point.

In the second half, the lead changed hands three times with the referee's decisions loudly contested by both sides. At the end of normal time, the scores were level 0–12 to 1–9.

Tommy thought, God I don't know whether to be relieved or

frustrated. Then the training on keeping a cool head kicked in, and he added his voice to those forcing the team's concentration on the job in hand.

In extra time, the decisive action of the entire match was Tommy's saving of a certain goal when the opponent's number nine bore down on Clondore's goal. Tommy somehow got his body in front of a bullet-like shot, and the ball rebounded off him to safety. He was mobbed by his teammates and the supporters went crazy. Sean Maher then brought on two subs, and this gave them the edge. Clondore managed to score four points to St John's three, making them champions by the narrowest of margins, for only the third time in their history and sixteen years since their last triumph.

Immediately after the final whistle, Tommy, his teammates and their supporters formed one great hugging, swinging and cheering mob. Then, at Tommy's suggestion, he and Dave McCarthy grabbed Sean Maher, lifted him on their shoulders and paraded him around the field, gathering supporters as they went.

Exhilaration from the victory and the sense of satisfaction he felt with his performance made Tommy forget how exhausted he was and for those few minutes he felt that Clondore was the best place in the world and any thoughts of leaving it were banished.

At 7 p.m., the local bagpipe band was playing in O'Connell Street beside a county-council truck decked out as a platform with a public-address system and with chairs for mentors and local dignitaries. It had obviously been decided in advance that, win or lose, a reception was going to be held to welcome the team home. By 7.30 p.m., a crowd had begun to gather, and children were amusing themselves and the crowd by climbing onto the platform only to be turned away by the master of ceremonies. 'For insurance reasons,' he said.

Mobile-phone calls suggested that the team would arrive at about 8 p.m., and by that time the street, for about fifty metres either side of the platform, was thronged and every vantage point overhead had heads and voices. When the coach and cavalcade of cars announced their arrival with honking horns, a huge roar went up, and the team's battle cry – Clon-Clon-Clon-Clondooore – was heard for the first of many times that evening.

The team had great difficulty in making their way to the platform despite the exhortations of the club chairman on the public address. With back-slapping and good-natured jostling, progress was difficult. As they broke through to the platform, Tommy, with a smile a mile wide, said, 'Lads, don't forget that there are only inches between a pat on the back and a kick in the arse!'

The squad, mentors, club committee and invited GAA officials and local dignitaries filled the stage. The drone of conversation was deafening as the crowd amused themselves with occasional shouts of 'Well done!' and 'Up Clondore!' and the slagging of individual players or 'Sixteen years, what took ye so long?' aimed jocosely at the team.

The master of ceremonies had difficulty in overcoming the noise when introducing the VIPs. The club chairman, Liam O'Brien, got the attention of the crowd by requesting 'three cheers' for the team, the manager and his assistants. He then continued, 'Where would we be without Sean Maher, captain in 1996 and now manager of this team?' He ignored the wisecracks from the crowd and went on. 'Only an outstanding team effort could have secured victory today.' Wild cheering and applause. 'You know the old saying that when the going gets tough, and it really got tough today, the tough get going, and nobody better than Tommy Walsh and his save of the century.' Loud sustained cheering. 'Any ideas the opposition were going to mount a comeback were quickly dealt with by Tommy. Nothing passed him.' More cheering. 'And what about the winning point by Conor Ryan, they'll be repeating the video of that score for years to come.' When the cheering stopped, he said, 'I expect that when the next team representing the county is chosen, those two and many of the other fantastic footballers we watched in admiration today will be included.'

Other speakers followed, lauding the team's victory, mentioning the pride of the town and the parish and quoting the value of hard work, skill, ambition and determination as necessary ingredients for success in sport and in all other walks of life. The proceedings were called to a close at about 9 p.m. A light shower encouraged a quick dispersal, most going to the local pubs. The team and the platform members adjourned on foot to Davy's Hotel on Davitt Street for a meal and liquid refreshments.

On their way, Tommy said, 'God, I could murder a pint.'

He was answered by a chorus of 'Only one?!'

When Tommy got home after midnight, he was surprised to find Orla with Frank in the kitchen for the first time. Before he could say anything, she immediately sprang to her feet, gave Tommy an enthusiastic hug and said, 'Well done. That was a terrific victory, and I'm glad I was there.'

'Oh, thanks. Winning is such a good feeling – what's rare is wonderful.' He noticed her appealing face, her dark hair and smart casual clothes. It was the first time they had spoken. He was impressed with her warmth and quiet confidence and could see clearly why his dad would find her very attractive.

Frank said, 'Tommy, I think your performance today was your best ever. It was extremely physical and fast-paced, but you dealt with everything thrown at you.'

'Thanks Dad. I felt good about it myself, but, of course, to win everybody had to be on top of their game.'

'You'll have a glass of wine?'

Orla chimed in, 'You've certainly earned it.'

'I've had a few drinks already, but go on then.'

The chat that followed added to Tommy's good impression of Orla. Tired and feeling that maybe right now three was a crowd, he excused himself and went to bed. As he climbed the stairs, he thought, What a clever move by Dad, to use the occasion to introduce Orla to the house. What about the age thing? He's sixty-three, but am I stupid to be even thinking about that?

A memorable ending to a memorable day.

Next morning, Tommy was appreciative but also embarrassed when all the pupils and teachers were assembled in front of the school to accord him a hero's welcome. Monica O'Rourke, the head teacher, gave a short speech highlighting Tommy's part in the victory and concluded with, 'You have brought honour to the school, to the parish and to the town, and to mark the occasion all homework for today is hereby cancelled.' That announcement guaranteed Tommy hero status. His reply was even shorter, thanking everybody for their support and saying how much the school meant to him both as a pupil and now as a teacher.

In accordance with custom and practice, a few of the team members took their turns to bring the cup to primary schools in the parish and to any pubs that issued an invitation, and there were many. It was all part of the promotion of the game and the recruitment of future generations of players.

Tommy enjoyed these events. It's nice being the centre of attention and being famous if only for a few days. Would I like to win another championship medal? Sure, but I won't stick around indefinitely just for that. Clondore is OK, I suppose, but I need to experience another place, another life.

7

Tommy read through the file given him by his father. Bishop Richard Walsh of Philadelphia, a first cousin of Tommy's great-grandfather, Michael Walsh, was the only notable name so he decided to start the family research with him. Everybody knows about him, he thought. He's the pride and joy of the family.

He read a full-page report in the *Clondore Chronicle*, dated 1910, on the bishop's silver jubilee, which gave his farming background in Gortroe outside Clondore, ordination in Maynooth in 1880, experience as a priest in the archdiocese of Philadelphia and elevation to bishop there in 1906. All of this, Tommy reckoned, would be well known to his father's generation but well worth recording for other current and future family members.

He sought further information on the archdiocese's website but found nothing, apart from Richard Walsh's name in the list of bishops. He sent an email to their archive, explaining that he was preparing his family tree and requesting information on his ancestor Bishop Richard Walsh (1855–1926).

Then he phoned Aunt Evelyn, who was a secondary-school teacher in Dublin.

'Hi, Aunt Evelyn. We haven't had a chat for a long time about teaching or anything else. I'm calling now because I asked Dad for the file on our family which you prepared.'

'Oh, he's decided to do something with it at last?'

'Well, no, I suggested it would be a good idea. I'd like to create our family tree.'

'I'm delighted about that. Can I help?'

'I've asked the archive in Philadelphia for more information on Bishop Walsh.'

'Good. We're very proud of him – our star pupil so to speak.'

'Have you any more information on the other people mentioned in the file?'

'Not really. You should check the National Archives website. I understand a lot of family information is now online. Come back to me with any questions.'

'Will do, thanks. Wish me luck.'

'Of course. I'm looking forward to having a family tree in my hand.'

He then phoned Aunt Jean, the wife of the postmaster in Longford, and went through the contents of the file with her. She was enthusiastic about the possibility of having a family tree and helped to fill out details on names, ages, addresses and occupations. Tommy enquired, 'Can you tell me anything about my paternal great-grandmother's family?'

'Yes. You should include their names, but I wouldn't enquire further if I were you.'

Tommy wondered what lay under that stone.

He recorded what he had learned and placed it in his file. He then made one of his regular phone calls to his sister Mary, using Skype. He wasn't a fan of social media but since Mary installed it to encourage Deirdre to keep in touch he thought he should use it now and then.

When Tommy saw Mary on screen, he said, 'Has your hair gone prematurely blond?'

'It's exactly as God gave me. It must be your monitor.'

Tommy decided there was no point in pursuing this. His hair

was sandy-red, but he didn't regard himself as a 'redser'. Deirdre was dark like their dad before the grey took over.

He told Mary about his work on a family tree. She indicated surprise and approval but did not elaborate. 'I suppose you heard we are county champions?'

'So you called looking for praise then?'

'Ah, very funny. No, I just wanted to update you on Dad's love life.'

'I'd be happier if you were reporting on your own, but, as they say, hope springs eternal. Go on then.'

Tommy described how he had been surprised and pleased to find Orla in their kitchen after the victory celebrations.

'Wow, that's interesting.'

'They were in Boyle's cafe the other night when I went there after training with a few of the lads. They had been at choir practice. We had a bit of a chat.'

'Could she be a gold-digger, after him for his money?'

'Aren't you the cynical one?'

'Could she?'

'No. No.'

'Maybe we should keep the possibility in mind. You never know.'

'You're barking up the wrong tree there. But where is the relationship going? Is it fair to Orla? What if anything is to be said or done?'

'Caution, brother, this is a sensitive subject. He – they – could say that this is none of our business. Maybe it's just a friendship, based on their interest in the choir.'

'Maybe I'm just being ageist. Anyway, don't worry. I won't rush in with two left feet.'

* * *

43

A few days later, as Tommy approached the kitchen door, he paused to listen to his father singing away as he moved about. He didn't recognise the song, probably from a musical or an opera, he reckoned. Frank was tidying the kitchen so Tommy lent a hand while talking about the start he had made on the family tree. 'Your sister Jean cautioned me about digging for information about your paternal grandmother's family. What's that all about?'

'Ah, pay no attention. Jean gets uptight about normal family discord over such things as inheriting land or making an "unsuitable" marriage, whatever that means. You won't find any scoundrels or scandals there.'

On a sudden impulse, Tommy decided to broach the subject of Orla, and, as he spoke, he already felt that he was making a mistake. 'Look, Dad, this may appear like a role reversal, and I don't want to interfere in your life, but in case it's important to you I want you to know that if you decided to formalise your relationship with Orla, it would be fine with me.'

God, he thought, that sounded like a political speech or a negotiating statement. Why did I open my big mouth? He may be too set in his ways. If he wanted to marry her he would have done it already. With my track record, what made me think that I could advise anybody about a relationship, especially my father?

An embarrassing and uncomfortable silence followed. Frank looked away. He coughed twice and then, turning to face Tommy, said, 'I know you have my best interests at heart, and I appreciate your concern.'

Tommy was glad his dad hadn't declared his intentions. At that point, Tommy didn't want to know.

Further silence followed, and, as Tommy wondered how he could extricate himself, his dad said, 'Let's reverse the roles again. What about your love life? I know Clare O'Connor is history.

Is there anyone special at the moment? You know the advice "Gather ye rosebuds" …'

Tommy laughed. 'No need to worry about me. I'm only a young fellow.'

He excused himself and left the kitchen, thinking that a reference to age was not the most diplomatic reply.

The response from the archive in the Philadelphia archdiocese had scanned attachments of a twenty-page pamphlet and newspaper clippings. The pamphlet had been issued to mark Bishop Walsh's silver jubilee as a priest in 1910. Most of the content had been included in the *Clondore Chronicle*, but with less laudatory language. Tommy was surprised to read two articles written by senior clerics in other Christian churches, praising Bishop Walsh's role in promoting inter-church relations. Good on you, Bishop Walsh, he thought.

When Tommy briefed Joe Dunphy on all the family material collected to date, he was advised to input everything in Ancestry. com which would create his family tree. Over the next week, he snatched time to do just that and decided to avail of the 'Member Connect' tool to cover the possibility that there might be someone out there researching a related branch of the Walsh family who would provide additional family history. Who knows, I might discover what Aunt Jean was reticent about.

Tommy left a print-out on the kitchen table for his dad and emailed a copy to his sisters and his aunts. He knew the content was very sparse and that there was a lot more information out there if only he knew where to look.

My ancestors were farming people so I need to find out more about the Land Registry and Griffith's Valuation, which I believe was a property-tax survey undertaken in the mid-1800s. A lot of valuable family information is in letters and documents stored away in sideboards and desks but rarely read. Could I persuade Dad to ask his relatives about this? Unlikely.

Tommy was conscious of Joe's advice not to get too bogged down in detail, but he was many miles away from that. In the following weeks he received enquiries from a few people named Walsh in America who were alerted by the online computer system. He couldn't establish any family connection but tried to explain the deficiencies in the Irish genealogical records and gave them information on online sources that they might usefully search.

8

Poland, 1891

Karol Nowak knew something was wrong from the moment he arrived at Irena Malinowska's house that Tuesday evening. He couldn't put his finger on it immediately. She had pulled back one side of the curtain in the parlour, their usual signal that the coast was clear, that her parents and older brothers were out of the house.

In response to Karol's soft whistle, Irena opened the kitchen door at the rear of the house to let him in. It was then, even in the darkened kitchen, as Irena rushed into his arms with tears flowing, that he knew he was right: something was wrong.

'Karol, I'm pregnant,' Irena wailed.

His first reaction was panic, which he tried to hide. His second thought was flight. 'Are you sure? How can you be sure?'

'I know, Karol, I know. We'll get married before my parents find out.'

'Of course I'll marry you,' he promised, wondering how she presumed so much.

His eager kisses stopped her tears. His thoughts were about ridding himself of this problem. The reaction from her father and brothers would be hostile and physical.

We made love only twice. Hopefully she is mistaken, but either way I should make a run for it. Her parents would never accept an eighteen-year-old coalminer as a suitor for their only daughter. Their sights are set much higher.

He stroked her hair. 'Please try not to worry. I'll be back next Tuesday with a plan, and I'm already thinking of friends who will help us find a church and a priest and everything else that we need.'

As was their usual practice, he left early to avoid meeting any of her family on the road home. He hurried away thinking, Tonight, of all nights, I don't want to be seen.

A plan was formulating in his mind as he walked, and it didn't include Irena. He needed to involve his brother, Leon, older by three years, without telling him Irena's shattering news. He tried to think of a convincing reason for them both to act decisively and urgently, and, before he reached home, the plan had taken shape. It was based on their location and the ever-present threat of conscription.

The small farm on which they lived with their older brother, Stefan, and their father, also named Stefan, was in Silesia in the Kedzierzyn region. Silesia, under Prussian rule, was like a finger poking into Russian Poland to the east and the Austro-Hungarian Empire to the south, south-east and west. Karol would use this to his advantage.

During lunch break in the mine on the following day, Karol beckoned Leon aside in a conspiratorial way. 'You need to keep this quiet, but I've just been tipped off that a conscription raiding party is due in our area in the next few days. I don't know which of the three armies is expected this time.'

'But we're miners,' Leon said.

'That won't save us this time. They're looking for younger men, and that includes us, I'm afraid.'

Karol saw that Leon was ashen-faced, as expected. He pressed home his advantage. 'I'm not staying around waiting for this to happen. I don't want to fight, or, God forbid, to die, for a foreign power.' He knew Leon would hate to be in the army, any army, and that he feared conscription more than most and would likely be shot for refusal to obey or as a deserter. He took Leon's silence as confirmation of a troubled mind.

Leon then said, 'I never expected to leave this place, but I have to think seriously about leaving with you. Where would we go?'

Karol was encouraged. He needed Leon to join him to help placate their father, and he needed Leon's money. 'I've been thinking for some time that we should go to America. I know they're looking for miners in Pennsylvania. We would have no problem getting work.'

'Could we not go somewhere nearer home?'

'Do you know any such place?' Karol already knew the answer.

'No, no, I don't, but we don't speak English.'

'Thousands of Polish men have gone to Pennsylvania.'

'I hate making such a drastic decision, and in such a hurry, but, as you say, we really have no choice.'

'We would need to leave the day after tomorrow, and we need to leave in secret because otherwise we could alert the authorities and we could be detained for questioning.'

'But how would we get away? How would we travel?'

'Leave it to me. I have a plan.' The younger brother was in charge.

9

Anna was getting more despondent about Josh, and it was breaking her heart. She had failed to get through to him, and she blamed herself. I should have kept my cool, lectured less, appealed more. I did show my love for him and that more than anything I wanted to fix things between us. He must have seen that, but no response, no reaching out.

Counselling, her last resort, now seemed a waste of time. When her parents were at work, she phoned her sister. 'Hi, Barbara, sorry to be calling you at work, but I need to talk to you. You know I'm concerned about Josh. Well, we had a fight about his drinking, and I said that I would get information for him on addiction counselling. He probably won't go, but it's all I can do.'

'You're hoping I can help, right?'

'Yep, I haven't a clue where to look, and you know I can't ask Mom.'

'It's not my area, but I'll ask around and get back to you. How are things at home?'

'Great. Mom has me working on our family tree. I could do without the hassle, but …'

'That's a great idea. Everyone's doing it, and I'm very curious about the Kelly side particularly. Mom never mentions them. Anyway, make sure you find a millionaire, alive but ailing!'

'Do my best. Send me the info as soon as you can. Bye.'

'Take care, sis.'

Over the next two weeks, her parents gave her documents and handwritten notes which she placed in a file. She consulted a number of genealogy websites, including 'Five Ways to Jumpstart Your Research' on Ancestry.com. She then assembled the information on her parents, her uncles Adam and Paul and her grandfather Andrew (Andrzej). The little she had on her great-grandfather Charles (Karol) and her great-grand-uncle Leo (Leon) she typed up as follows:

Charles (Karol) Novak (Nowak). Born 1870s. Father of Andrew. Emigrated from Poland to Reading, PA, in 1890s to work as a coalminer as he had done in Poland. Married Alice (Alicja?). No record of other children.

Leo (Leon) Novak (Nowak). Born 1870s (brother of Charles). Probably travelled from Poland with his brother and likely also worked in the mines.

I'd love to know more about them. Charles and Leo were two of the hundreds of thousands who came here from Europe, especially Poland and Ireland, in the nineteenth and early twentieth century, economic migrants as they would be called today. It must have been a great adventure, not hopping on a plane like now. They must have seen rough, tough, times as well.

Anna waited until her dad had finished dinner and then cornered him before he left again or got involved in some task in the garage or the garden. She sat across from him with pad and pen at the ready. 'Dad, can you add anything further for your family tree?'

'There's little to tell. You probably know my father changed careers relatively late in his life. He was fired from the steel mill. He was fifty-six, and why he chose to buy a guest house I'll never know. Surprisingly, without any experience, he was very successful. I suspect my mother was the driver behind the scenes.'

'She was Polish also?'

'Yeah, Regina Pawlak, known as Gina, could hardly be more Polish than that.'

'Did she have business experience?'

'Not sure. I think she may have worked in retail before she married.'

'Is that all you know?'

'Adam and I were still at high school and had to uproot and move from Philadelphia. Paul had started work in Philadelphia by that time and went through a succession of dead-end jobs before taking over the running of the guest house from Dad. He then met and married Valerie, so it all worked out. Too bad they had no children.'

'What about the next generation back?'

'Don't know if we are very different from other families, but we know very little about my grandfather Charles Novak or his brother Leo. They came to America as young men, with thousands of others, to work in the coalmines.'

'Is that all?'

'We think Charles was killed in World War I, probably in France.'

'Any details?'

'No, we have no record, no death certificate.'

'He must have been over forty when he was drafted. That's surprising. What age was your father when Charles was killed?'

'Probably five or six.'

'Did you ever think of asking your father about them or about your grandmother Alice?'

'I never met Alice. We think she died young as well. Dad never spoke about his parents. Maybe he had little memory of them.

He mentioned his maternal grandparents a few times – no great detail though.'

Anna put down her pen, gave a little sigh and said, 'Do you know what part of Poland Charles and Leo came from?'

'No idea, sorry.'

'Do you know when Leo died?'

'No, not even that. I think Leo was the older one.'

'Maybe he was killed in one of those mining tragedies?'

'That's possible. Wasn't there a terrible flu epidemic sometime around the 1920s that killed millions worldwide? Maybe Leo or Alice was a victim of that?'

Anna thought for a moment. 'I haven't a clue.' She wondered if this could be checked out.

'Strange the way people disappear from our memories, isn't it? Whole lives forgotten.'

'Yeah, very strange,' Anna replied and then added, 'Maybe this is all a waste of time.'

'Very likely,' Peter said without any indication of regret. He was silent for a moment and said, 'This isn't much, but the only other thing I can recall is that Leo was regarded as the black sheep of the family. I wasn't told this. I just picked it up from conversations overheard. Not a lot to go on, really.'

Anna glanced at the few notes she had made. 'Would Uncle Paul or Adam or their wives know any more about that generation?'

'Doubt it, but I'll ask.'

'Thanks. I hope they were more curious and better at eavesdropping than you.'

Peter smiled and nodded. 'Yeah, me too.'

Anna stood up and put her writing pad under her arm. 'I'm looking on the bright side Dad. Writing up the Novak family tree shouldn't take too long!'

A few days later, Anna asked Peter if her uncles had anything to say about their black-sheep grand-uncle.

'Very little. Paul didn't have any specific information but said he thought Leo was shunned by the family, that something major had happened.'

'And Uncle Adam?'

'He said that he had a vague recollection of hearing that Leo had a fight with a bishop and that this might have been the cause of the family rift.'

'Oh, that's interesting. Did he give you the bishop's name or know when it happened?'

'No date, I'm afraid, but the name he had heard was Bishop Walsh, based in Philadelphia and born in Ireland. That's all they know.'

'Well, it's more than we knew yesterday. So, a serious fight with a Bishop Walsh. Any suggestions?'

'A trivial fight with a bishop would be a contradiction in terms, especially back then when bishops were a law unto themselves.'

Katherine joined in. 'What could have been serious enough to cause a total breakdown within the family? In those days, a Catholic marrying a Protestant could have resulted in a split in a family, but that would hardly involve a fight with a bishop.'

Peter said, 'My father told me that when immigrants who were Polish or German or Italian first arrived in large numbers they wanted priests who spoke their language and that this caused disagreements between bishops and some of their parishioners but that was unlikely to have caused Leo's problem? It appears the rift may have been total. How sad would that have been?'

Anna replied, 'The diocesan records will tell us when Bishop Walsh served. I should be able to find out that much. We don't know if Leo got married. Maybe he returned to Poland – I think I would have.'

'Unfortunately,' Katherine said, 'we'll never know more.'

10

Tommy was still wrestling with his father's request to take over the management of the family business and with his embarrassment about asking his father what his intentions were about Orla Maguire. When he told Mary about this conversation, she replied, 'Tell me you didn't say that to Dad.'

'I wish I could.'

'Well, you know what they say about having a neck like a jockey's arse? I don't know whether to kick you or kiss you. What'd he say anyway?'

'Not much, but I think he said something about me having his and Orla's best interests at heart. He turned it round and asked me about my love life.'

'And so he should – you need stirring. Well done Dad. So what have you been doing about it?'

'You make it sound like a visit to a shopping centre, and, before you suggest it, I'm not internet dating or speed dating.'

They both laughed, but Mary persisted. 'You just make sure it doesn't come to that.'

Tommy was reading the arts section in the weekend supplement when a review of a movie set in the Prohibition era in America caught his eye. This set him thinking that Bishop Walsh experienced Prohibition and the 'Roaring Twenties' in Philadelphia, and he wondered if he could find any news reports from that time involving the bishop.

He decided to google the bishop's name. It produced a biographical note on Wikipedia, offers to sell him photos of the bishop and references in a Catholic Encyclopedia and genealogy websites. It didn't produce any information worth adding to his family tree. He then searched online for newspapers published in Philadelphia, and while some, including the Catholic Standard & Times, referred to their archives, none were available to search online. He knew that microfilmed information would likely be available in libraries there, but that was of no use to him. He decided, on a whim, to see if the New York Times or Washington Post, newspapers from cities he knew were about equidistant from Philadelphia, had archives online. He was delighted that both did. He gained access to the archives of the New York Times by paying a subscription and then completed the search template, including the bishop's name and title. Under 'period', he inserted '1906–1926', the year Walsh became a bishop and the year he died.

In the results, Tommy found a few items about the bishop's public statements and his attendance at important religious and civic events. And then the following:

AN INSANE MAN ESCAPES
February 22, 1913, New York Times
New York police warned that Leo Novak who had escaped from captivity was a dangerous insane man who had shot at Bishop Walsh in Philadelphia about six months previously. After his arrest he had been an inmate of the asylum in that city but had escaped and fled to New York.

Tommy hadn't expected to find anything so dramatic. He stared at the screen for some time. Then he resumed the search, hoping for a follow-up story, and found:

BISHOP WALSH'S ATTACKER
June 16, 1913, New York Times

Leo Novak, the man who last year tried to shoot Bishop Walsh
of Philadelphia, turned up at the insane pavilion of Bellevue
Hospital yesterday. After the assassination attempt he escaped
and fled to New York. He had been admitted to a hospital for the
insane but a few months ago he escaped again. Bishop Walsh is an
Irish born assistant bishop appointed in 1906.

Tommy continued the search up to the end of 1926 and found
some further reports on the normal public life of the bishop but
no further mention of the assassination attempt or the aftermath.
He then searched the archives of the Washington Post, finding
less routine coverage and no mention of the escape in February.
Then another headline caught his eye.

BISHOP WALSH'S ATTACKER FOUND
June 16, 1913, Washington Post
The physicians at Bellevue Hospital discovered that a patient
who had been brought to the hospital a few days earlier was
Leo Novak. He is the man who, almost a year ago, tried to
shoot Bishop Walsh in the cathedral in Philadelphia. Novak was
captured at that time, but escaped and fled to New York. It is
understood that the assassination attempt was made when the
fifty-eight-year-old bishop was leaving the cathedral after his usual
morning Mass.

Tommy went downstairs to the shop, and, in a break between
serving customers, he handed the newspaper clippings to his

father. 'I printed these for you.'

His father read quickly. 'My God, I never thought that being a bishop was such a dangerous occupation.' After a brief pause, he added, 'How come we never heard about this? You'd think an event like that would have been passed down to us.'

Tommy added, 'The reports say the bishop was shot at, but there is no mention of injury.'

'Yeah, it could have been so much worse. I know it says the man was insane, but was there another cause? Was he an anarchist?' He added, half in jest, 'It was fashionable at that time.'

'Well, with the name Novak it is unlikely he was Irish, but wouldn't you think all this would have been recorded in Aunt Evelyn's file?'

'I suggest you check the *Chronicle*. An assassination attempt on a bishop from Clondore would have been headline news at the time.'

'Thanks Dad, a good idea.' The shop became very busy again so Tommy left. He phoned Joe Dunphy, told him what he had found, said he would look for more information in the diocesan archive in Philadelphia and asked how to access the *Chronicle* for 1912. Joe kindly offered to check the archives, saying that if 1912 was not covered Tommy would have to check the microfilm records in the National Library in Dublin. Tommy gratefully accepted his assistance and delivered a copy of the clippings to Joe's office in Fitzpatrick's Garage. He sent the news reports to the archive of the Philadelphia archdiocese and requested the local reports, which, he felt, would give a fuller description of the event and the background story.

11

Poland, 1891

Leon Nowak was shaken awake thirty-six hours later by Karol and was immediately overcome with a feeling of despair at the inescapable journey facing him. They left under cover of darkness. Their brother and father believed Karol's invented story, and, while they were most upset at their departure, they felt that they had no alternative. The urgency helped to mask the sadness.

Going so far away was like a death. They would never see each other again, and they knew they would have a lifetime of painful absence. Stefan senior was somewhat consoled by the fact that his wife had not lived to see the day. Earlier, he had taken Karol aside to commend him for his unselfish act in taking his brother away from the danger that he himself might be prepared to face. Karol's embarrassment quickly faded.

Dawn broke as Leon and Karol left Kedzierzyn, travelling by a combination of walking and lifts on farmers' wagons and drays carrying heavy goods, until they arrived at their planned destination, the river port on the Oder, which they reached in the early afternoon. They laid low for the rest of the day, taking turns to emerge to check out what possibilities were open to them. They slept rough in a warehouse and rose early to avoid detection.

Then they went to the quay from where coal was being transported north, and Karol persuaded the captain of one of the barges to allow both of them to work their passage all the way to Szczecin on the Baltic coast. They knew this was a huge industrial town that served as a major port for Berlin.

In Szczecin, they took lodging in a cheap boarding house in the port area. Leon remained in the bedroom, his wonder as he travelled overpowered by his fear of the unknown. Karol went around the ale houses to enquire about sailings to America. On the third day of searching, he returned, all excited. 'We've two tickets for sailing tomorrow to Philadelphia.' Leon refrained from mentioning that it was his money that bought the tickets. Karol continued, 'I also met the agent for a coalmine in Reading, Pennsylvania, who gave me a written introduction to the mine boss, and he told me that half our passage money would be refunded if we signed on with the mine. So I did, for both of us.'

Leon's gloom lifted somewhat. Karol was very proud of his work.

On their passage to the United States of America, Leon remained in or near his bunk most of the time, only venturing out on deck for short periods, morning and evening. Karol must know everyone on board by now, he thought, even the ship's officers. He's been out and about all the time unless the weather kept him in the cabin. Leon took great satisfaction that when a severe storm hit he did not even feel queasy while Karol moaned in his bunk for the duration, grasping the vomit bucket for dear life.

In early June 1891, just a few weeks after leaving home, Leon and Karol Nowak were working in Reading and busy adding to the little English they had. They were now known as Leo and Charles Novak – one bewildered, the other elated.

12

Anna and her mother finished their coffees and cleared the dining area in the kitchen. 'When are you meeting Josh again?' Katherine asked. Anna could sense the concern in her mother's voice and was glad that she was not asking probing questions, like where is the relationship going and that sort of thing.

I wonder does she know about Josh's alcohol problem? If she does, I hope Josh will have seen sense before she raises it with me.

Anna reached for a stack of books and folders. 'I'll see him next week.'

On the following Friday night, Anna was with her friends and a few classmates in the crowded Crofton Inn, enjoying the music, the chat and the atmosphere. Martha gave Anna a nudge and gestured towards the far side of the room where Josh was arriving and looking for a spare seat. Anna wondered if she should join him but hesitated, worried about what state he might be in. She put her head down and tried to concentrate on her friends.

Less than half an hour later, and despite the noise levels around her, she heard raised voices. People nearby started to stand to see what was going on. Anna did the same. Without a word to her friends, she moved between the tables to check it out.

God, no. Josh is in the middle of it.

The customers around Josh grew silent, and Anna heard him shout at a waiter, 'How many fucking times do I have to order a drink around here?'

'I already served you twice.'

Josh grabbed the waiter by the arm. 'That was hours ago.'

When the waiter tried to free his arm, Josh pulled him roughly, and they collided with a table and dislodged bottles and glasses. Other waiters tried to help, which Josh resented, and he started throwing punches, most of them missing the target.

Customers were now fleeing, pushing tables out of their way, and more glasses and bottles went flying. Some went to the far end of the building, others fled to the car park. Anna was joined by Martha and Jane. Martha caught her by the shoulder and guided her away. 'C'mon, get away from here, it's gotten bad.'

Josh roared, 'Why are you attacking me? I'll have you sued for this.' He mouthed expletives as he lashed out at whatever head was closest. Four waiters arrived to overcome him, and they managed to get him flat on the floor and restrained him by sitting on his arms and legs. He continued a futile resistance until the police arrived, when he went berserk, haywire. He had a huge audience. He was cuffed, dragged outside, and taken to the station.

Anna couldn't hide her distress. When she and her friends got back to their table, a silence descended that no one appeared able to break. Anna then said, 'Sorry guys, I'm going home.'

Martha walked with her to the car park. On the way, Martha said, 'Anna, please. He's not your responsibility. Pity is not a good basis for a relationship.'

'Yeah, I know.'

Anna could sense that Martha was wondering if her advice was something Anna did not want to hear.

For the next few days, Anna stayed in her room most of the time. Her turmoil meant that there was no room in her thoughts for anything except Josh. Feelings of anger, regret, loss, and sorrow ran through her mind, each seeking solace. Nothing gave her comfort, no ideas, no tactic, no hope emerged. I gotta break free of this. I cannot let this drag me down.

13

As Anna was leaving the house, Katherine arrived home from her usual weekly visits, as a member of her school's outreach team, to families in the deprived areas of the city of Allentown. 'Meeting Josh?'

Anna sensed that her mother had questions which she was holding back.

'Yes. I'm meeting him in Jackson's Diner.' As Anna spoke, she reflected on Josh's apologetic phone call and hoped that the sober and attractive Josh would turn up.

'I'm worried for you, sweetie. That's what moms do.'

My God, does she think Josh is a physical threat? For a moment, Anna considered that possibility but forced herself to concentrate on the steps she was planning to take. 'No need to worry, Mom, all's well.'

As she was leaving, Peter was returning from the storeroom along the breezeway that linked the house to the two-car garage. In a loud voice he called out, as all dads do, 'Don't be late.'

'I won't.' The answer all dads get.

Anna was in the diner waiting for Josh to show up. His lateness she saw as a bad sign. That, and her lingering head cold, did not help her mood. 'Did you get the web addresses I sent you?' she said, as he arrived and sat opposite her in the booth.

'Well hello to you too,' Josh replied.

'Hello, Josh. Sorry for being so abrupt. You know how worried

I am.'

'Yes, thanks, I got them.'

'But have you read them?'

'Some of them.'

'And … ?'

The waitress interrupted with her pad at the ready. They ordered burgers, fries, and sodas.

'Well, what did you think?'

'I think they're not for me.'

Anna sat back, tried to make eye contact. 'How can you say that?'

'Because the advice is for people with a problem that I don't have,' Josh said with great conviction.

Anna decided she needed to try tough love. 'You've played only one football game this season. Why?'

'The coach … ah … I'm injured, OK?'

'I see. Have you missed lectures? I haven't seen you at school at all.'

'My dad had jobs for me to do. So you're checking up on me? What's with the interrogation? I don't like that.'

'I don't either.'

'How do I convince you I don't have a problem?'

'Even after last week's performance in the Crofton?'

'Oh, that. Who told you?'

'Yes, that. I was there.'

Josh was taken aback but without hesitation and in a defiant way said, 'Shit happens. It was a misunderstanding. Sure I had a few beers, but I didn't start the physical stuff.'

'I don't think many there would agree with you. Does your mother know about it?'

Conversation was interrupted when the food and drinks were served. Anna stared at Josh, determined to get an answer.

'Well, does she?'

'I told you already my parents don't give a damn about me or anything I do.'

'I find that impossible to believe,' Anna said, adding, 'Do you now have a criminal record?'

'My dad smoothed things out.'

'So your parents do know?'

Josh grunted.

Silence took over. Anna wondered whether she should change the subject and put pressure on him again when they had eaten. She certainly didn't expect him to say what came next.

'Why don't we go to my house and talk to my mom when we've finished here? Then you'll know what I'm talking about.'

This sudden change in his attitude was immediately seen by Anna as the possible breakthrough she had been hoping for. She reached across and held both his hands. 'Josh, I'd love to do that.'

Josh suggested travelling together in his new Honda Accord, but Anna decided that having to come back for her car would be a needless trip. Besides, she knew that heavy rain and strong winds were forecast for later that night. She had been to Josh's home once before, to a charity BBQ, and was again impressed as she followed his car up the winding driveway to a parking area in front of a very large house surrounded by beautiful trees and manicured lawns. Josh parked facing the house. Anna swung her car around beside his and facing the driveway. She was surprised to find that, apart from the security lights, the place was in total darkness.

When they were standing beside the cars, Anna said, 'There's nobody at home, is there? Your mother or anyone else?'

'Let's go in anyway. We'll have some privacy.'

'Sorry, Josh, no.'

'Get in my car then,' he said, as an instruction rather than a request, which put Anna on the alert. She reluctantly agreed. When they were in the car, she said, 'You tricked me into coming here, Josh.'

'I had to. I never get the chance to have you to myself.' He grabbed her around the shoulders, pulled her roughly. 'Come on, I want you in the house.'

She resisted and was pulling on the door lever when she saw his fist coming towards her face. She ducked, and his fist hit the window, causing a roar of expletives, forcing the door to burst open and propelling Anna out of the car and onto the driveway. The momentum rolled her over, and she scrambled to her feet and was in her car before Josh, who had been distracted by the pain in his hand, could reach her.

Through her tears and her shock she managed to start the engine and was moving forward when Josh got to her car, grabbed the mirror and tried to open her door. She accelerated. He was shouting, 'Sorry Anna, sorry, sorry,' as she sped away down the driveway. She feared that he would try to catch her, so, despite her panic, her shaking and her tears she didn't stop until she was near home. She pulled off the road to fix her face and to think of a story for her parents.

They were in the den, reading and watching TV as Anna put her head around the door and said, 'Night. Busy day tomorrow so I'm having an early night. Sleep well,' and she was gone. They exchanged quizzical looks and just shouted good night as she flew up the stairs.

Anna knew that her relationship with Josh was now over. She lay on her bed with her mind full of what-ifs and maybes. How did we get to this? Was I naive, did I miss earlier signals? How did things fall apart in a few months? Missing lectures, opting out of football, or more likely being dropped by the coach? How did attraction turn to concern, then pity and now fear? Was alcohol the cause or the result of his demons?

In one way, she was relieved that it was over, but in another she was seriously worried about his addiction and wondered was there anything more she might have done. What about his family? If they were helping him, it wasn't obvious. He clearly had no time for his parents, and his two older siblings weren't around. Was he the spoiled brat of rich parents or the neglected son?

On an impulse to do something to deal with her problems, she grabbed her phone, 'unfriended' Josh from Facebook and blocked his access. This gave her some degree of comfort, and, in an effort to blank all this trauma and trouble, she instinctively reached for the family-tree file on her desk and forced herself to read the content once more.

14

Reading, PA, 1898

Poles don't get much respect around here. There are hundreds of us, but we're all treated the same. We're just above the Irish in the pecking order, and that's saying something.

Charles Novak was weighing up his prospect for promotion, and he couldn't shift his pessimism. He wanted to move into a management or even a supervisory role in the mine, but the only foreigners considered for such jobs were the English or the Welsh. He'd heard the older men talking about the panic in the 1870s when wages were cut and many miners fired and about the violence by the miners' secret society, the Molly Maguires, against ruthless mine owners and their even more violent response. He reckoned this conditioned them to accept whatever was on offer, including the awful working conditions and the terrible impact on their health. He and Leo had been lucky to avoid accidents at work but for how much longer, he wondered.

He had now been a miner for seven years in Reading and almost three years before that in Silesia. It was time to move on. But where? This time he had no threat to use to persuade Leo to leave with him, so when his brother wouldn't listen to reason, as he saw it, Charles left on his own and headed for Philadelphia. He had enough money to pay for a lodging house for about two weeks.

He walked the streets of Philadelphia, amazed at the grandeur and the hustle and bustle. He couldn't see any sign of the depression of the 1890s which, he was relieved to hear, was coming to an end. He hoped to find a job in the city transport system, the docks or one of the many clothing factories.

Charles's first view of Wanamaker's 'Grand Depot' was a defining moment. This was Philadelphia's and perhaps America's first department store. He spent time at the circular counter at the centre of the huge building and at most of the more than one hundred counters that radiated out from it in concentric circles. He was dazzled by the array of electric lights and intrigued by the pneumatic tubes used to transport cash and documents. It was like all the circuses and travelling shows he had ever seen combined into one and then multiplied. For the rest of that day he could not get the place out of his mind. He returned the following day, found the administration office, completed a job application and waited there patiently to be interviewed. On the Monday morning of the next week he started work in the storeroom, very pleased with himself.

By 1906, eight years after arriving in Philadelphia, Charles Novak was one of three assistant managers of the men's department, and he had no intention of stopping there. He took full advantage of the store's policy that all employees were to be treated respectfully and that promotion was to be from within the workforce. He cultivated the right people and always aimed to please. His ambition was as unlimited as it was unrevealed. He also valued the free medical care, the recreational facilities, profit-sharing plans and pensions, particularly when he learned that they were unique to Wanamaker's.

Later that year, Alice Symanska walked into his life. She was beautiful in a willowy kind of way with fair curling hair. He loved the way her gold dress clung to her every curve, and, transfixed as he was, he managed to take in her large green hat which she wore at an acute angle, adorned by a white plume and a band of very fine lace.

Charles overheard her say to the sales assistant that she wished to purchase a present for her father. He immediately intervened, introduced himself as the assistant manager and said, 'Welcome to Wanamaker's. It is my pleasure to serve you today. How can I help you?'

Her delicate mouth widened into a radiant smile. 'You would know much better than I what my father would like so I'm in your hands.'

Charles showed her neckties, cravats, toiletries and anything else she hinted at or he could think of. He was thrilled with the impact he seemed to be making on this beautiful woman. Their laughter and flirtation were obvious to those around them, but they did not seem to mind.

When she had left, a senior colleague approached him and in a whisper said, 'I'd be careful there if I were you. She's the daughter of a valued customer, Mr Arnold Symanski. He's a wealthy man – he owns a building firm that carries out work here and elsewhere for Mr Wanamaker.'

Rather than being put off by this word of warning, Charles's interest increased. Alice's beauty was enhanced by her wealth, and he had now found a new opportunity and challenge. Before leaving work, he visited the accounts department and checked the significant amounts paid to Mr Symanski's firm and his level of spending in the store.

A few weeks later, Charles was one of a number of the management staff on duty to meet and greet suppliers of services at an evening reception in the store which Mr Wanamaker hosted annually. He was thrilled to see Alice arrive with her father. He did everything he could to impress her father and asked his department manager to put in a good word as to his character and abilities.

He watched for an opportunity, and when Alice became separated from her father, he approached her and said, 'How wonderful to meet you again, Miss Symanska. This is an unexpected pleasure.'

She looked around, waving her arm gently, and said, 'It's good to have the opportunity to see the store when it's not crowded.'

'Miss Symanska, I have thought about you every day since we first met.' Although Alice just smiled, he detected what he took to be an encouraging blush. 'Would you do me the honour of meeting for afternoon tea one day?'

'Yes, that would be nice, and please call me Alice.' She would never admit later that she had engineered the invitation to accompany her father in the hope of meeting Charles.

Alice's friend, Elizabeth, acted as chaperone for their meetings but left them on their own as much as convention would allow. They visited cafes, walked in parks, took journeys on the trolley, and Charles managed to steal kisses and to get an eager response to his embraces. His ardour increased when she happened to mention that she was the eldest of three daughters and that her father had always wanted a son. After the first few meetings, he made his affection and his intentions towards her very clear.

One day, they met at their favourite cafe in Fairmount Park. Alice wore a pink floor-length embroidered skirt, a broad belt with a silver buckle topped with a white blouse and a floral clasp at her throat. She carried a small straw bonnet. They had walked for half an hour admiring the spring blossoms. Charles suggested regular stops to rest so that he could hold her hand and place his arm around her shoulder. This time, she had come alone, which he interpreted as a significant development in their relationship so he decided to test her commitment. He asked about the well-being of her family and added, 'I expect your father would be very upset if he knew we were meeting.'

'Let me take care of that.'

This was precisely the answer he had planned and hoped for. It was music to his ears.

They were married in Alice's parish church in September 1908. Charles was thirty-five, Alice twenty-five. They spent their honeymoon on the coast in Cape May, a wedding present from her sisters. Charles couldn't think of a way to avoid inviting Leo to the wedding and was relieved when his brother could not get time off work – or at least that's what he had said. He felt Leo would not make a good impression.

In 1910, Mr Wanamaker replaced the old building with a new one on the same site, creating one of the biggest retail stores in the world. He included space for the John Wanamaker Commercial Institute for his staff which had special classrooms, a library and a reading room. The staff also enjoyed a gymnasium and a swimming pool. Charles was one of the first to apply for a degree course in business administration.

Charles and Alice's son, Andrew, their only child, was born in February 1912.

15

Anna decided to get rid of a major distraction by completing the Novak family tree. She watched extracts from the TV series Who Do You Think You Are? which led her back to the website Ancestry.com and to downloading its family-tree maker. She entered the information she had collected, disappointed that it was so sparse. She was attracted to the 'Member Connect' facility in the software and hoped that there was someone out there, in the USA or in Poland, who could provide additional information on her family history. Wouldn't it be just wonderful, particularly for Dad, if someone in Poland was trying to find the descendants of Karol and Leon Nowak who came to America in the 1890s?

On her family 'black sheep,' she created a profile page for Bishop Walsh and clicked on this icon. She knew it was a shot in the dark, just like buying a ticket in the 'Mega Millions' but with even less chance of success. She didn't know how else she could ever get an explanation about why her great-grand-uncle had been shunned by his family.

When she had checked her inputs and confirmed that she had clicked on all the required icons, she pressed 'send' and then printed the tree created by the system. She gave copies to her parents for them to distribute, feeling that this was a good job done and out of the way. That same evening, her assumption that her family research was completed took a bit of a setback when an email from Ancestry.com told her that someone else had included Bishop Walsh in their family tree.

Having started the process, Anna felt compelled to follow it through. By using the 'how to' guidelines on the system, she was given the name and email address of the connected party: Tommy Walsh. She knew from the address that he was located in Ireland, but nothing more.

Anna's dad was in the room beside the garage that housed tools and junk.

'I've discovered from the system that a man in Ireland is creating a family tree that includes Bishop Walsh. Maybe I'll contact him and hopefully he will give us some clue about the fight.'

'Isn't the Internet amazing? I doubt if anyone in Ireland would have heard of Leo's fight with the bishop, even a relation of the bishop. Still, you have to follow it up, don't you?'

Anna composed an email to Tommy Walsh, explaining the process through which she had been given his address, though she was aware that he had followed the same procedure. She then introduced herself and said that she was researching her family tree, focusing on the Novak/Polish side to be followed later with her mother's Irish family. She then stated,

My great-grand-uncle Leo Novak, who came to America from Poland in the 1890s, was ostracised by his family. Nothing of this has been documented, and the reason handed down by word of mouth is that he had a fight with Bishop Walsh. Nothing is known of the cause or the seriousness of the fight, if indeed a fight ever took place, or the action/reaction of either party. One of my uncles is under the impression that the cause of the fight was not trivial.

Bishop Walsh is not related to my family. However, I included his name in our tree in the hope that someone like you might have heard something about this fight. I know that if the information is not available in the US it is probably less likely to be known in Ireland. I live in hope. If you can throw any light on what was likely a minor event in a bishop's life, I would be very grateful.

Anna added her full name, her mailing address and telephone number and sent the message on its way.

Tommy Walsh's reaction when he saw that his inbox included an email from 'A. Novak' was that it was spam, offering him pharmaceutical products or services of a dubious kind or trying to extract his bank-account details. First he read Mary's email, one of her infrequent messages, usually sent with a humorous attachment. Then he read the notice on the training schedule from his Gaelic football club. Finally, he opened the message from A. Novak, anticipating that he would soon be hitting the 'delete' button.

'My God, this is a shot in the dark. What are the odds against this connection being made? What awful news for A. Novak?'

He drafted a reply explaining that Bishop Richard Walsh (1855–1926) was a first cousin and a contemporary of his great-grandfather, Michael Walsh, and went on to say,

Bishop Walsh was born in the townland of Gortroe near Clondore (where I live), a small town in County Offaly in the Irish midlands. He studied for the priesthood in Maynooth Seminary in County Kildare and was ordained for the Archdiocese of Philadelphia in 1880. He served as a priest there and was elevated to bishop in 1906. He died in 1926 aged seventy-one and is buried in Philadelphia.

In seeking further information for our family tree I recently found the attached news reports in the online archive of the New York Times and the Washington Post. If the Leo Novak mentioned in the articles is your relative, then I am sorry to be the bearer of bad news. The attached reports make shocking reading. I expect that this revelation will be upsetting for your family.

My dad and I cannot understand why this major event in the bishop's life had not been passed down to the current generation. I now intend to check the archive of our local paper, the *Clondore Chronicle*, and to seek more information from the archive of the archdiocese of Philadelphia. You may decide to delay telling your family until this information becomes available. In any event, I wish you and your family well in coming to terms with this news.

I am hoping to unravel this mystery. If you share this view, then we may need to be in contact again.

Best wishes,

Tommy Walsh

He included his address and telephone number, attached the newspaper clippings which he had filed in his computer system and sent the message.

The next day, he received a reply.

Dear Mr Walsh,

I was shocked to read the newspaper reports which you so kindly sent me. I feel sure that the man named is in fact my great-grand-uncle. My uncle was right. The fight certainly was not trivial.

I wish there was an easy way to tell my parents and my sister about this news. At least we know now what happened and when it happened. Like you, I would like to know why it happened, and I expect that my family's reaction will be the same.

Many thanks for unearthing this information and for your concern about the impact this will have on our family.

Best wishes,

Anna

16

The day Leo Novak suddenly refused to go down the mine, he was sure his job was gone. Going down the mine was like going to Hell. His days and nights had become full of terror. He had done it at home in Poland and for ten years in Reading, and he had had enough. He was sure his brother Stefan would welcome him if he decided to return to Poland, but that was not an option. Conscription, which would end his life one way or another, made Reading and mine work the lesser of two evils.

Leo wished he had someone to confide in, to help him, but he found his fellow workers coarse and intimidating. He thought of writing to Charles to seek his help but felt that he could not match his level of ambition. His loss of a weekly wage scared him, but he had no regrets.

He was amazed when the shift boss told him he was moving him to a surface job, sweeping and cleaning with a barrow, brush and shovel. Over a year later, he was told to report to the supervisor's office. He stood, cap in hand, in front of Mr Kilbride, who was seated behind a large desk. The company's charity is about to end, he thought. I'm surprised it lasted so long.

Mr Kilbride lifted his head and, without any pleasantries, said, 'You know of course, Mr Novak, that the mines here in Reading and the Philadelphia and Reading Railroad are all part of the same company.' Leo had no such knowledge but decided a comment wasn't expected. 'Well, we have no further use for you here, but I have arranged a job for you as a porter in the new Reading Terminal in Philadelphia. You start on the first of next month. I have written to them to expect you. You can collect your wages at the end of this week. Goodbye, Mr Novak.'

That was quick but hopeful. I could have been fired without notice today, never mind nearly two years ago.

When Leo arrived in Philadelphia for the first time and found the Reading Terminal at Market Street, he was delighted to learn that he would not be working in an underground railroad. In fact, the terminal was built one storey above street level and over the city market.

He was happy in his work. There was little pressure, other than the competition to earn tips, and that was regulated to a degree by the bosses in the same way they allocated rosters. Others worried about the effect on their health from smoke and soot, but having been a miner Leo paid little attention to this.

On most days, he travelled home on the electric trolley with his friend, Giuseppe Baudo. They had both started working at the terminus about the same time and were brought together by being a minority among a workforce of black men with whom they had little in common and who seemed to resent white men taking what they regarded as their jobs.

The work was physically demanding, pushing heavy loads to and from trains. One day, in 1910, when he was approaching forty, Leo began to reflect on this. I walk the platform at least thirty times each day, either bringing luggage to the train or hoping to secure a customer getting off the train. How much would that be? Let's see, at least seventy yards each way, thirty times, that would be 4,200 yards, that would be about two and a half miles. I'm surprised that I could calculate that without paper and pencil. My teacher, Mr Brogowski, would be very proud of me. So, six days a week, that's fifteen miles each week, by fifty weeks, that's 750 miles a year, and, how long am I here now in 1910? Must be six years, God doesn't time fly? – so I've walked over four thousand miles, nearer five, in that time. Pity I'm not younger, I could have used all this walking to train as an athlete. I was a good runner as a kid … I loved it but hated competitions.

The blast from the incoming train ended his calculations. He needed to be alert for this one, the 4.30 from Atlantic City and Cape May. It was on his work schedule today, and it was the best opportunity to earn tips from the wealthy returning from their holidays or from day trips. It was still early in the summer season so every customer counted. The wages for a railway porter were at the lowest end of the scale so the tips were very welcome. He knew that the city's population was exploding so he hoped that as the terminus got busier his earnings would increase.

17

Anna found her mother at the breakfast bar drinking a cup of coffee before they prepared dinner together. 'Mom, you know I emailed Mr Walsh in Ireland about Leo? I got more than I expected, and you and Dad are going to find it upsetting.'

'Oh, why?'

'He was researching American newspapers trying to find out more about Bishop Walsh when he came across reports naming Leo Novak. First, please read the email from Mr Walsh.'

Katherine's face darkened as she read the message. 'Mr Walsh seems to be a very considerate man,' she said, as she reached for the newspaper reports. 'Oh my God, what a shock. We were led to believe that this was just a fight with a bishop. Some fight!' She read on. 'Oh, the poor man,' she said. 'It's awful, but thank God he missed.'

'How am I going to tell Dad?'

'Did you forward Dad the email?'

'No, I thought I should discuss it with you first.'

'Good. When he gets home, I'll have a word with him. Then we can then talk about it.'

Later that evening, Anna joined her parents in the kitchen. 'I'm sorry, Dad, to have given you this news.'

'It's shocking, isn't it? Should the past have been left in the past?' A heavy silence followed, then Peter added, 'I'm glad my father isn't around to hear this news.'

Katherine tried to console her husband and her daughter. 'We don't know if your father was aware of all this and kept it a secret.'

'Well, that may be true, of course.'

In a further effort to help, Anna said, 'As Mom said, it could have been worse if he had seriously hurt the bishop. Or killed him.'

'Yes,' Peter replied, without conviction. 'Maybe we should just leave it at that.'

Katherine replied, 'I think we owe it to Leo to find out what happened to him. Did he spend the rest of his life in a mental institution, alone and unloved?'

Anna was relieved that the discussion had moved to the future. 'Mr Walsh is contacting the archdiocese looking for more information about it. Hopefully he will get some answers for us. Dad, will you tell Uncle Paul and Uncle Adam what we've learned?'

'I'd prefer if you did it Anna, please.' Peter hurried away, indicating to Anna that he wanted to distance himself from any further discussion or research.

It took a few days to get to talk to her uncles. Paul was somewhat detached from his brothers, partly by his choice and partly because he lived over two hundred miles away near Altoona in Blair County. Right now, he was too busy preparing for the winter holiday season in his B&B to take her calls. His exasperated wife, Valerie, eventually pinned him down.

'Uncle Paul, I've some sad news about the fight between Leo Novak and the bishop. First, let me tell you how I got it.' Anna detected impatience in her uncle so she read the email and the news clippings without stopping for comment. His silence demonstrated the same shock she had felt on hearing the news.

'He probably deserved it.'

Anna was aware that her uncle was, at best, a lukewarm

Catholic. 'What do you mean? Wasn't it the act of an insane man?'

'Yes, but did the fight we were told about play a part in this?'

'I assumed the story about a fight was invented by his family.'

'Possibly.'

'Mr Walsh is checking his local paper in Ireland and asking the archdiocese here for more information.'

'Good. It's better to know the truth even if we don't like it. Good detective work. Uncle Adam should recruit you.'

Anna was pleased to end the conversation on a happy note.

Uncle Adam was easier to contact. It was just a matter of finding out what shifts he was on and avoiding his work time or his sleep time. When he heard the story and how it was traced, he said, 'Great detective work. Contacting Mr Walsh was the key. Good job.'

'Gee, thanks. I feel very sorry for Leo. Insanity was bad enough, and I'm sure life in an institution was grim, to say the least.'

'Yeah, me too. I'm amazed that the family was able to keep this a secret. How did they do it? We know why: they were ashamed because he was insane. Did they also disown him?'

'So many questions. Uncle Paul suspects that there was more than insanity involved. As you detectives would say, did he have a motive?'

'Insanity doesn't need a motive, at least not in the way we would understand it.'

'Dad's response surprised me. It's as if he wished we hadn't even started on this. He doesn't seem to want to continue.'

'Oh, really? I'll have a chat with him.'

'Good.'

Anna then referred to the search Mr Walsh was continuing to make, which hopefully would provide answers or at least further clues.

Adam replied, 'Funny how things sometimes happen at the same time. You and Mr Walsh are researching information about a bishop, and my colleagues are reading old files about priests – paedophile priests.'

'I don't envy them. What an awful job.'

18

Philadelphia, 1912

Leo liked the word 'family', which he was still getting used to in 1912, two years after marrying Francesca Baudo, the widow of his friend Giuseppe and the mother of Gemma, now aged seven. He had been very happy to get married at the age of forty when he thought that the opportunity had slipped him by and happy to move from his single room to Francesca's four-room apartment.

Being alone after work hadn't bothered him a lot of the time. He was a regular visitor to the library, and reading filled his free time – novels mostly, nothing too demanding. Occasionally he read histories of Poland and America.

He liked to wander around the many quiet picturesque streets and quaint eighteenth-century and early nineteenth-century neighbourhoods. He liked to imagine that Warsaw would look similar though he had never visited it, nor any Polish city.

Leo missed company and was tempted to visit bars, but he had seen what alcohol had done to some of his workmates and stayed away. Loneliness was a regular visitor so marriage had presented a welcome prospect. He wasn't sure if Francesca now felt the same way. In fact, he didn't know what she felt about a lot of things. He had expected to be more valued, more appreciated as a husband. That worried him, and he knew that he shouldn't worry.

When he left work one evening, as usual by the rear entrance to the terminal, Charles was waiting for him. His brother's suit, starched collar and colourful tie seemed to create a barrier between them. They had met at irregular intervals over the years, and Leo would admit that his brother had taken the initiative on each occasion. As Charles rose to management status, Leo felt more estranged, less comfortable, in his brother's world.

Charles smiled and said, 'Let's have a drink. We haven't met in a long time.' Leo didn't show any enthusiasm. He anticipated more of his younger brother's well-intentioned but unwelcome advice. 'Just one, I promise. You won't be delayed. I promise.'

'Yes, just one.'

Charles suggested a bar frequented by the well-to-do, which made Leo uneasy. With beers in front of them, Charles lost no time in talking about Wanamaker's Department Store.

'Please don't try to lecture me again about looking for a job there. We never seem to talk about anything else.'

'Look, you left the mining job because you had to. I understand that. Working underground is not for everybody, and you stuck at it for as long as you could.'

'Which was far too long.' Leo shivered at the thought of it but decided not to comment further. He hated confrontation, and he knew that Charles would do enough talking for both of them.

Charles continued, 'I left because I wanted to try something new, to better myself, and I have no regrets.'

'Good luck to you. It worked out very well. Oh, how is baby Andrew?'

'He's very well, thank you. He's four months now and thriving. His grandfather dotes on him. Another thing I came to tell you: Alice and I are looking for a house to buy. We need more space. The loan is arranged.'

Leo was sure that Charles's father-in-law was the builder and that he was getting the house at a reduced price but didn't like to pry. 'Wonderful. Your house seems fine to me, but if you want a better one, well, that's OK. Don't lose touch when you move to the suburbs.'

'I won't. Leo, you could try your luck with Wanamaker's. It's never too late.'

Leo wondered why his brother kept on about this. He must know I don't belong there, but I appreciate his concern for me. He tried to dodge the issue. 'I've read all about his new swanky store and the evening classes he offers the staff.'

'I'm attending classes twice each week after a hot supper provided free. The Store School is what the staff call it, but the official name is the John Wanamaker Commercial Institute. I expect to get a degree in business administration, and the other good news is that I'm hopeful of getting promoted if I do well.'

Leo was happy that the focus had moved from him. 'Congratulations.'

Charles was not to be diverted. 'If I can do it, you can do it. You have at least as much brains. You could get a degree too.'

Leo knew that his brother was being kind. Charles and Stefan, his older brother, were much brighter than him as was Lydia, his younger sister, who had died very young. He didn't have to be told this. He had always known it. As a young man he wished his father would leave the small farm to him who was best suited to it, but tradition favoured Stefan.

Leo leaned back in his chair, as if to distance himself from the topic, and shook his head. 'Thanks Charles. It's not for me.' He hesitated and then added, 'Too much pressure.'

Charles kept on. 'Mr Wanamaker is an amazing man. I mean, he's obviously a very successful businessman, but he's unique in the benefits he offers staff. The newspapers love him. He was quoted the other day saying, "Half the money I spend on advertising is wasted; the trouble is, I don't know which half."'

Leo's face brightened as he replied, 'Make sure you work on that, it could be a question on your exam.'

'How right you are! I must remember that.'

Leo then attempted to get away from any talk of study, 'Did you shake the hand of President Taft? I heard he officially opened the new store.'

Charles laughed as he grabbed his drink. 'No such luck. The store was closed to the public, and for the staff it was a case of seeing but not touching. Still, it was a great event.' As an afterthought, he said, 'Why don't you come to listen to an organ recital at the store? They're held twice daily except Sunday.' He was about to mention the staff brass band when he remembered that it was a military band and that Leo would have none of that.

'I must just do that. Gemma would love it, and, oh, I wish you and Alice success in your search for a house.'

'Thanks. It's an exciting time for us.' Charles tried another pitch, hoping to entice Leo to some social event. 'Did you ever think of going to the vaudeville theatre? Our own W. C. Fields' latest joke is, "I never drink water because of the disgusting things that fish do in it."'

Leo smiled, but there was no flicker of interest.

'Do the other porters talk about baseball? I'm sure they discuss the Athletics, winners of the American League pennant for the past two years? You could come to one of their games with me.'

Leo was lost in thought for a moment and then said, 'I watch the young people play in the park, and I'm beginning to understand the rules of the game, but I would want to avoid the crowds that go to the professional game.' Charles was taken aback when Leo quickly added, 'Have you ever been to the Carpenters' Hall?'

'No, why would I? I'm not a carpenter.'

'Because the First Continental Congress was held there in 1774. You need to check up on your American history.'

'I never knew you were interested in all that.'

'I intend to bring Gemma there and to other historical buildings when she's older.'

Charles, feeling somewhat chastened by Leo's comeback to his exhortations, decided to switch his attention to Leo's marriage. He believed it had followed too brief a courtship and seemed to be dominated by Francesca. As they finished their drinks, he asked, 'How's married life? Are you being kind to Francesca and Gemma?'

'All's well, thanks.'

Charles had his back to the door so was surprised when he stood to leave and saw so many customers. For Leo's sake I'll suggest a quieter bar in future.

As Leo travelled home on the electric trolley, he had to stop himself thinking about his friend Giuseppe Baudo and the awful event that had ended his life: the bolting horses, the shouts of warning that came too late and the awful crunching sound which Leo now heard in his dreams. He preferred to dwell on the enjoyable evenings he had spent in Giuseppe's home with his wife Francesca and the evenings he had looked after their young daughter, Gemma, when Giuseppe and Francesca went to visit Francesca's mother. He became very fond of Gemma, which developed further when he became her 'Dada Leo' as she called him.

Leo had helped all he could during and after the funeral. He organised a collection among the workers to supplement the payment from the railroad company. When the mourning period came to an end, he received a note at work from Francesca.

Dear Leo,

Gemma misses her father terribly. She's very fond of you and if you could find time to call to see her I know it would take her mind off her sadness.

Francesca Baudo

Francesca also asked him to stay with Gemma a few times when she visited her mother. A few months later, they met at a company picnic in Fairmount Park. After that, they just drifted together. Leo was not aware that he had pursued or wooed Francesca or made a formal proposal of marriage, and yet they were married in Francesca's Italian parish church just over two years after Giuseppe was killed.

Leo had been keen on a neighbour's daughter back in his home village. I wonder if we would have married if I hadn't left for America, he thought, but that was twenty years ago. Maybe it was Reading and the rough life lived by miners, but I never met a woman there I was attracted to.

Now, two years later, as he neared his stop and a short walk to his home, he knew he could expect a warm welcome from Gemma – but from Francesca he couldn't be sure. He'd begun to wonder if he was now just a breadwinner and a stepfather.

19

On Sunday, Mary and her husband, Kevin Hayes, arrived on a day trip from Dublin. While Kevin was chatting to his father-in-law, Tommy beckoned Mary to follow him to the sitting room. 'Any ideas on who should take over the business from Dad? You know I don't want to do it.'

'Haven't given it any thought.'

'Well, I wish you would. You worked in the business here for long enough before Garda Hayes swept you off your feet and took you to Dublin.'

'Now hold on a minute.' Mary stared at Tommy and in a raised voice said, 'You don't want to do it, so you want to shift the responsibility to me?'

Tommy was surprised with this response. The last thing he expected was Mary on the defensive or any kind of clash. He knew he had screwed up and needed to retrieve the situation. 'Of course not! I'm just trying to get a solution for Dad.'

'And you've decided I'm it.'

'I haven't decided anything. It's not up to me, and I haven't said a word about this to Dad. Would you run the business if Kevin could get a transfer back to this part of the country?'

'It's difficult to turn back the clock, and, besides, we're happy in Dublin.'

'You haven't answered my question.'

'God, you'd make a great interrogator. You've sprung this on me and now you want instant answers?'

'Would Kevin be happier working in this business than being a garda?'

'There you go again.'

'Look at it this way. If you wanted to inherit the business but were not given the option, as the oldest of the family, would you be upset?'

'Tommy, stop pushing me. If you want a quick answer, it's no.'

'Look, Dad knows my view. Deirdre is unlikely to be interested so that leaves you. Dad probably thinks you and Kevin are settled in Dublin and therefore you haven't figured in his plans. Please think about this.'

'Why should I solve your problem?'

'Please.'

'God, you're bossy.'

I made a mess of that, too pushy. I should have just raised the issue and left answers to another day. But if Mary doesn't want it, what do I do then? Why am I getting scared? Maybe it's not so much the business I want to get away from but Clondore itself. If I had worked somewhere else, Dublin or London maybe, would I now be happy to come home for good? If I can get away, where do I go and would I continue to teach? I need to handle things a lot better.

Next day, when Tommy got to the shop, Jimmy Walker and his dad were chatting, seated behind the counter.

'Good timing, we were just talking about pilfering. It seems to be on the increase.'

'From the shop mainly, we think,' Jimmy added.

Tommy was not surprised by this since the yard held the bulkier items.

'It's probably because of the recession,' Frank suggested.

'I can only think of two possible solutions. Install CCTV,

which is costly, or keep the gate locked, which would mean all sales would pass through the shop or the gate would have to be unlocked by one of us on request.'

'That would suggest to our customers that we don't trust them … but maybe that can't be helped,' Frank said. 'We need to know how much loss we are suffering and what CCTV would cost. Then we can make a decision.'

They both looked at Tommy, and he knew he had another job to do.

'I'll leave it to you then,' Frank said as he was leaving the shop.

I'm beginning to feel trapped. The more I do, the more I'll be asked to do.

Tommy chatted with Jimmy for a while, but his mind was elsewhere. Jimmy was about to rise from the chair but changed his mind, saying, 'By the way, Frank told me about the deranged man trying to murder Bishop Walsh.'

Tommy, expecting that Jimmy would be eager for more information, said, 'There isn't much more to tell really, but I'm still searching.'

'I wouldn't want an awful event like that in my family, but then I don't have a family background to search.'

Tommy didn't want to pry but felt that Jimmy wanted to talk. He sat on the chair vacated by his dad. 'Just find a starting point and see where it leads you.'

'That's the problem. I don't have anything to go on.'

'What does your birth certificate say?'

'My mother's name, Bridget Walker, with an address of a nursing home. No address was given for my father, James Walker. My mother said he had been killed in the war when a bomb hit the factory in which he worked.'

Jimmy paused, apparently lost in thought, and then continued. 'She spoke with an Irish accent, but whenever I asked for more information about her family she fobbed me off, and when I persisted as a teenager she got very annoyed and I gave up after that.'

'Did your mother have any relations in this area?'

'No, it was like she arrived here by parachute, like a spy, and in a way she did.'

'Oh?'

'Your grandfather told me that he was approached by the local curate to rent the small house that used to stand at the end of what was your back garden, facing on to the side lane, near where the gate now stands. He said it was for a young woman and her child who had arrived in the town from England. This was in 1943 when the war was on.'

'No further details?'

'When I was in my late teens, your grandfather told me that an Irish priest in England made the arrangements with the curate he knew in Clondore.'

'So she just arrived unknown and possibly unwelcome.'

'Well, no. Your grandfather gave us a house, gave my mother work cleaning in your house and in the shop, and when I was fourteen gave me a job. Anytime I tried to thank him he would say sure that old house was falling down and hadn't been occupied for years.'

'How long did you live there?'

'Four or five years. I remember starting school and moving to our council house around the same time.'

Tommy worried about what he was going to say next but decided to press ahead. 'Did your neighbours or school friends make any comments?'

'There were some nasty remarks made in school and by one or two adults who should have known better. I just ignored them. Some hinted, not unkindly, that James Walker never existed or, if he did, my mother was not married to him. Either way, that would help explain why she never wanted to talk about him or about her family.' Jimmy's mind went back to his courting days when he dated several women, and one who was special, but he wondered then and now if his family background, or lack of it, meant he was not seen as a prospective husband.

'Do you think she may have been abandoned by her family or did she break the connection?'

'Don't know. You see, I have a lot of questions and very few, well, no answers.'

'I don't know what to say. The only thought that strikes me is that it's just as well you didn't express an interest in tracing your family before the ownership of the farm was sorted out. The possibility that you might have grasping relatives would have driven Sean bonkers.'

They both laughed at that.

'I wonder if the parish files contain information on your arrival here?'

Jimmy was silent for a moment and then said, 'Ah, look here, I'm a lucky man. Sure, I'd like to know where I came from, I'd like to have known my father and to have aunts, uncles and cousins, but of all the places in Ireland or England my mother could have fled to or be sent to, I'm so blessed she arrived in Clondore.'

'Glad to hear it.'

'There are always compensations, you know that too. Anyway, if someone gave me a piece of information on my mother's people I would follow it up. Otherwise … ' Jimmy stood up, shrugged his shoulders and went back to work.

Tommy tried to imagine what it was like to be alone in the world, no family, no relations, no roots, and what marriage must have done for Jimmy.

* * *

October was the month for the annual school debs dance, but the preparation, especially in the girls' homes, had been going on for months. The teachers were expected to participate on the night. Tommy reflected on his own debs when his date was Louise Donnelly, who, like many others in his class, emigrated shortly after. Would the recession force most of the current class to emigrate also?, he wondered.

The first time he attended as a teacher he felt closer to the pupils than to his colleagues. Now, his fifth year to attend the event, he again was amazed to see the transformation in the girls who looked several years older than five months before. Some of the boys looked like Junior James Bonds, while others didn't make the transition from casual to formal, wearing tuxedos that they couldn't fill.

The evening began with a reception in the school hall. Monica O'Rourke made a short speech welcoming the parents and the debs' partners. She complimented the former pupils on their appearance, requested them to maintain an ongoing interest in the progress of the school and exhorted them to carry into their adult life the ethos which the school had tried to instil in them.

The parents privately delivered the usual mixed messages of caution and enjoyment. Teachers and parents drove the debs and their partners to the nearby function room in Davy's Hotel, and then immediately repaired to the bar, much to the relief of all parties. They were well aware that they should not be seen around the hotel, and after a couple of drinks they departed for home or other pubs, happy that coaches would deliver their darlings home after the event.

The training regime set by Tommy's football club ensured that he was one of the first to leave.

20

This time the town did not make such a fuss. Much of the public display of support remained in place since the county final four weeks earlier, and the 'Good Luck Clondore' banners on the approach roads to the town now had a different aspiration.

The lack of buzz reflected lower expectations. Sean Maher was quoted in the *Chronicle* saying that to progress in the Leinster championship you needed to be county champions for a few years with the same team and that people should bear in mind that they were playing Glentomas, the County Meath champions and the team that reached the All-Ireland semi-finals last year. Supporters and townspeople wondered if this was more spin directed at the opposition or a genuine assessment of their chances.

The opposition was from another county and another diocese so at Sunday Mass Father Warren was more biased in his prayers for victory. Coaches and cars left in convoy for St Conleth's Park in Newbridge, County Kildare, a neutral ground less than a two-hour drive from Clondore.

Sean Maher's comments proved to be all too accurate. Clondore's back line was much busier than its forwards. In fact, the latter spent most of their time supporting their teammates. Glentomas were on top throughout and ran out easy winners in a score of 2–14 to 0–7. The next day, the headline read, 'Ruthless

Glentomas in Control.'

On return to Clondore, the supporters, those who had travelled and those who didn't, gravitated to O'Connell Street knowing that a formal reception was not planned. When the team bus arrived, the crowd cheered, and a lot of back-slapping took place as the team alighted, somewhat sheepishly given the result. Conor Ryan, the captain, said to Tommy, 'Getting support in bad times is a good start for next season.'

His dad complimented him on a fantastic display. 'They were coming at you in waves,' he said. 'Sean Maher was right: you have to win regularly at home before you can win away.'

Commendations and commiserations were voiced by Tommy's colleagues in the staffroom next day, and his first class that morning insisted on hearing his views on the match, which were followed by an enthusiastic round of applause.

Tommy got a call on his mobile from Joe Dunphy as he was about to leave the school.

'Sorry for taking so long, but when I found no mention of an assassination attempt or of Bishop Walsh I checked the microfiche a second time.'

'That's a surprise.'

'Yeah, I expected the story to be highlighted on a front page. We have to accept that the New York Times and the Washington Post didn't get it wrong, so why did the story not reach Ireland?'

'Why indeed?' Tommy replied.

Joe added another twist. 'If a Dublin paper covered this event, the *Chronicle* would certainly have majored on it.'

'Joe, I'm sorry about the workload. It's very strange, but let's wait and see what the archive in Philadelphia produces. Perhaps there has been some mix-up with the dates.'

'Let me know what they tell you. I don't like loose ends.'

Spoken like a true genealogist, Tommy thought.

That evening, when Frank was given this news, he said, 'I'm amazed. This event would have been the talk of the town and the county at that time, and the *Chronicle* should have been full of it. Looks like they missed the local story of the year.'

'Hard to believe, isn't it, especially when you think that the file your sister Evelyn created had a full page from the *Chronicle* on the bishop's silver jubilee in 1910? So how could they have missed a sensational story like an assassination attempt two years later?'

'I hope the archive in Philadelphia will resolve the mystery. Well, I'm off to choir practice. Christmas is coming and we have a lot of work to do. See you in the morning.'

'Say hi to Orla for me.'

'Yeah, sure.'

Tommy glanced at the newspaper open on the kitchen table while thinking about the number of hours his dad had devoted to the choir over the years. No doubt it's a great addition to church services, particularly at Christmas, but it must be great fun for its members, and clearly Dad gets a lot out of it. Would Orla be such a part of his life without it? Maybe I should take up singing ... I doubt they'd have me.

Tommy sent an email to Anna describing the mystery of the assassination attempt not being covered by the *Chronicle*. He then added, 'I hope that telling your family was not too much of an ordeal for you. I will contact you again when I get a reply from the archive of the Philadelphia archdiocese.'

Anna appreciated that Tommy had taken the trouble to keep her posted and replied directly.

My parents were upset. My dad said it should have been left in the past. He doesn't want us to continue. Mom has great sympathy for Leo and would like to find out what happened to

100

him and if he had been disowned to spend the rest of his life in a psychiatric hospital.

My Uncle Paul wondered what Bishop Walsh might have done to cause an assassination attempt but then he has little time for the clergy. Uncle Adam, a police officer in Philadelphia, complimented me on my detective work and also expressed great sympathy for Leo.

I look forward to receiving the information from the archive. Hopefully it will help explain the awful event and give us some information on what happened afterwards to Leo.

Best wishes,

Anna

21

The 2012 annual dinner dance and disco to be held as a fundraiser for Clondore Gaelic Football Club had the word 'Victory' in the title, making it easier to sell tickets. The *Chronicle* featured the event, majoring on the cup having pride of place and that the players would be presented with their winning medals. The club chairman, Liam O'Brien, had decided to overlook the fact that the medals had already been presented by the chairman of the county board immediately after the match and the speeches in Tullamore. 'We have to make hay while the sun shines,' he said, which received full support from the committee.

A 'Souvenir Victory Booklet' was prepared with the help of Tom Hickey, a part-time and volunteer sports columnist in the *Chronicle*, to be sold at the function and in local shops. Businesses of the town and district were expected to take advertising space. Frank Walsh subscribed because the club was close to his heart, and, besides, he felt it made good business sense.

Tommy arrived in the kitchen as his dad finished tidying after the evening meal. He was about to park himself on an easy chair when Frank said, 'I suggest that the shop should sponsor a family table at the dinner dance.'

'That's very decent of you, Dad.'

'Yeah, I thought that Jimmy and his missus, Mary and Kevin, Deirdre and yourself and partners, if you wish, should attend.'

Tommy did a quick count of eight – and ten if he and Deirdre brought a partner. He said, 'It would be nice to have the family together. Mary and Deirdre will be delighted with the idea. I hope they don't have other arrangements.'

Frank replied, 'Yeah, the notice is short so I'll contact them straight away. They'll stay overnight, I expect, so Mary and Kevin could stay here with us and Deirdre could sleep in Orla's house. We may have to rethink this if she brings a partner.'

'Thank God we have Mrs Duggan to prepare the spare room,' Tommy said. 'I'll have a word with her.'

'Thanks Tommy. It should be a great night with you and the team getting due recognition.'

Dad has been planning this for some time. Do I see Orla's hand in this?

Later that evening, when Tommy reflected on this conversation, he thought how much his mother would have enjoyed a family event like this, especially now that Mary and Deirdre had flown the nest.

When he checked his emails that night he saw that the list of five messages included the church archive in Philadelphia. He went straight to this message, anticipating it would contain an explanation that would be helpful to Anna Novak and her family.

The clippings from the New York Times and the Washington Post which you sent a few weeks ago were a total surprise to the staff here. We cannot be aware of the content of all the files in our archive but we felt that an assassination attempt on one of our bishops should have been common knowledge, especially among the more experienced staff here.

We did a thorough check in our files but found nothing. So, I checked the Catholic Standard from the end of June 1913, the month the later of the above reports was published, back to

January 1912 and found no mention of an attempt on Bishop Walsh's life. I also checked the News Digest for the same period. It records all of the daily major news stories in Philadelphia. It also includes reports on fire tragedies, major crimes, scandals and even damage or injury by adverse weather. There was no mention of the events reported in New York and Washington.

I am unable to offer you an explanation for this very surprising omission. I will contact you if I learn anything that might help with your research.

Jan Faber

Tommy stared at the screen, not quite believing what he had read over and over. At a minimum, he was expecting that the news reports from New York and Washington would be confirmed by a Philadelphia reporter. He had hoped for much more and got zilch. He tried to work out the implications, but his mind raced from one possibility to another. He needed to be able to think out loud, to discuss this with someone. He printed the message and went downstairs to his father who was in the kitchen watching the end of the Nine O'Clock News.

When the commercials came on, Tommy said, 'Dad, remember I told you that Joe Dunphy couldn't find any report in the *Chronicle*? I have now also drawn a blank in the archive in Philadelphia.' He passed the message over and sat in the chair opposite.

'Well, this beats Banagher' – his father's way of expressing total surprise – 'and I have to say that the first thought that enters my mind is cover-up.' Before Tommy could respond, he added, 'However, it would be wrong to jump to a conclusion. There may be other explanations.'

'Like what?' Tommy asked.

'Well, I suppose it's possible that the archive in Philadelphia just mislaid the file. It is also possible that the newspaper reports of the event were never included in the archive in the first place.'

'Yes, but if the event was reported in the Philadelphia press, particularly the secular press, surely it would have reached Ireland. On the other hand, we know it was reported in New York where many Irish lived, and it still did not make the Irish papers.'

They were both silent, contemplating the possibilities and probabilities. Tommy read the email again. 'Hold on a minute. Surely the critical information is that an attempt to kill the bishop did not appear in the News Digest, which contained daily reports on even relatively minor events. In other words, it was not reported in any Philadelphia newspaper?'

Frank countered, 'It's hard to argue with that. However, if we're saying that the story was deliberately kept out of the press, we have to ask who would have done this.' After a short silence, he answered his own question. 'It would have to be either the police or the church, wouldn't it?'

Tommy answered, 'Why would the police want to keep a lid on it? Maybe they were embarrassed. Maybe they failed to protect the bishop, and we know Leo escaped from custody. No, I can't see the police going to so much trouble to avoid publicity, can you?'

'Yeah, I think you're right. But could the church control the press? The Roman Catholic Church in Ireland at that time was all-powerful and influential, but the situation in America was very different. There were many people who would like nothing better than to publish a story that might embarrass the church.'

Tommy grappled with this for a moment and then said, 'It looks like it could only have been done if very few people, and only insiders, knew about it. One report said that the shot was fired at him when he was leaving the cathedral after his morning

Mass. The place could have been largely deserted at that time, but even a small number of people could have made a cover-up very difficult.'

'Difficult, but not impossible.'

They sat silent trying to tease out what had just been said. Tommy thought of another angle: 'If there was a cover-up, we have to ask why. What would they have been afraid of, embarrassed about? The church was hardly protecting Leo Novak.'

'We may never know, but that's something that could worry us,' Frank said. Tommy waited for him to expand. 'In the past few years we've had reports on sexual abuse by priests and the cover-up and failure to act by some bishops. We don't want to start a local whispering campaign about Bishop Walsh when we don't have the facts. In the current climate, the media would just love to publish what you have found.'

'But I told Joe Dunphy I'd let him know what I learned from the archive. I trust Joe. I also feel obliged to bring the Novak family up to date.'

'Of course you must. I'm suggesting that we keep control of the information as best we can until we learn more. Having said that, I've no idea how or where we can get an explanation. Have you?'

'Haven't a clue. It looks like a dead end. Let me think about it. Maybe the Novaks will have some suggestions.' Tommy took the email back to his bedroom for filing.

22

Tommy decided to wait until the next day before contacting Anna Novak. He rehearsed the points discussed with his dad and wished they could have arrived at a definite conclusion. Rather than include all of this in an email he took a different approach.

Dear Anna,

I expect you and your family will be as surprised as I was to read the message below which I received yesterday from the archive in the Philadelphia archdiocese.

My dad and I discussed the implications, and, while the evidence seems to point in a particular direction, we did not reach a conclusion. In summary, it seems that Leo Novak's escapes and his recapture in New York were reported only in the NY and Washington papers and the earlier attempted assassination in Philadelphia was not reported there or anywhere else.

I would like to continue trying to unravel this mystery. If you also want to do this, I suggest that it would be more productive to discuss the implications of what we now know by telephone rather than relying on email. Better still, it could be done for free if you are on Skype.

I look forward to hearing from you.

Best wishes,

Tommy

Tommy was at his desk in his bedroom correcting students' homework on market segmentation in the tourist industry in County Offaly when he received a text from Mary: 'Deirdre to sleep in Orla's house. What's going on?'

No point in texting an answer, she will want to know more, so he phoned back.

Mary was in her kitchen having just finished a long chat with a friend on her cordless phone. She was looking around appreciating how lucky they were to get such a nice house to rent while at the same time listing in her mind the changes and improvements she would make if she was the owner. When she heard Tommy's voice, she immediately said, 'Is Dad around?'

'No, he's at choir practice. Why do you ask?'

'I want to hear the low-down on the invitation.'

'Aren't you the sceptic?'

'Come on! Suddenly Orla's spare room is to be used by Deirdre? Tell me what's going on.'

'You know the expression "Never look a gift horse in the mouth." Just enjoy the occasion. Has Deirdre been in touch?'

'Yeah, and she's asking questions too.'

'Look, it's sixteen years since we were county champions, and I am the modest recipient of adulation. Isn't that worth a family celebration?'

'God, you're getting to be a real comedian. OK, you win. I'll control my curiosity.'

'So, you're coming then?'

'Wild horses or gift horses couldn't stop me.'

'Before you go, have you and Kevin had that chat?'

'Work in progress, brother. We had been chatting anyway about me returning to work locally after my break while Kevin was on night work. Funny though, he posed the same question as you: would I be annoyed if the transfer of the business was a done deal before I heard about it? You bet I would.'

Tommy was encouraged and decided to probe a little. 'I'm hoping you will be asking me to mention your interest to Dad.'

'Slow down, slow down.'

'Glad you're returning to work. I wondered why you were a lady of leisure for so long.'

'Did you now? Did you come up with any reason?'

Tommy racked his brain, thought about Kevin's night duty and then blurted out, 'I think I know, but I'd better not go there.'

Mary laughed, saying, I think you're right.'

Anxious to end the conversation, Tommy said, 'Looking forward to seeing you and Deirdre next week. Bye.'

* * *

Anna made a cup of coffee when she got home from her classes and sat at the kitchen table beside the patio door and the glass panels that took up the entire wall. She checked her emails on her laptop, enjoying the evening sunshine and the view across the front of the house that dipped and rose again before reaching the road about seventy yards away.

Her immediate reaction when she read the message from the archive was that she had reached the end of the line and that what happened to Leo would remain a mystery. She read the note from Tommy Walsh again and wondered why he would want to persist with the research, but she had no idea what to do next and appreciated any help she could get.

Later that evening, Peter was preparing vegetables at the kitchen island that doubled as a breakfast bar and Katherine was standing in front of the oven set in the floor-to-ceiling cabinets when Anna entered, declaring, 'You've read the email from the church archive on your phone? It's amazing isn't it?'

That got their attention, work stopped, and they both grabbed their phones. Their reading was punctuated by 'Oh, Good Lord, my God.'

Katherine was the first to speak. 'Isn't Mr Walsh helpful? You'd think he'd want to quit at this point.'

After nods and words of assent, Peter said, 'This has to be a cover-up. If this was important enough to be covered by the New York and Washington papers, it was much more so for the Philadelphia press. A cover-up wouldn't have been done for Leo's sake.' This conclusion led him to see Leo less as an assassin and more as a possible victim. After a brief hesitation, he added, 'We have to search for more information. I know I've been less than enthusiastic, but this changes things.'

A relieved Anna replied, 'Are you assuming the church covered it up?'

'Who else?'

Anna said, 'But for a cover-up to work, the police, the doctors, and anybody who saw it would have to be in on the act.'

Her mother added, 'Yes, but look at the child-abuse scandals and the amount of covering up the church has managed to do in recent years particularly here in Philadelphia and in Boston. Other people must have been complicit in that as well.'

'Fair point, Mom.'

Peter said, 'People kept silent for their own reasons. But assuming this was a cover-up, why would they do it?'

Anna said, 'Mr Walsh is anxious to solve the mystery as well, which surprises me. Should I accept his offer of help?'

'Everything we've learned to date is thanks to him,' her dad said, 'and, besides, I've no idea who else to turn to.'

'Yes, of course you should accept his help,' Katherine added. 'Now that we have got this far, we owe it to Leo to keep going.'

The next day, between lectures, Anna escaped to the diner to send an email to Tommy.

Dear Tommy,

Yes, we were very surprised by your news that the archive contained no reference to what must have been a major news story in Philadelphia in 1912 and 1913. We're beginning to think there was a cover-up.

My dad now thinks we should keep searching.

Both my parents appreciate your offer to help find out what happened to Leo, especially since the evidence doesn't look good for Bishop Walsh.

I agree we should talk about it on the phone. Yes, I am on Skype, and I will send you contact info by separate email.

* * *

'Hi, Tommy. Why are you contacting me on Skype?' Deirdre was curious and a little suspicious about the change in routine.

'Well, that's rich coming from you. You forget that Mary set it up so that you would keep in touch. Remember when you started in college you promised to contact Dad on Skype every week? Besides, I have nearly forgotten what you look like.'

The real reason was that Tommy wanted more practice on the system before he used it to contact Anna.

'Trust you to remind me. Why are you contacting me at all? Is Dad unwell?'

'He's in great form. How about you? How are things in Limerick? How are your studies going?'

'Could be better, I suppose.'

'Are you still planning to be a music teacher?'

'I'd like to talk to you about that.'

'I'll help all I can, but you should talk to a music teacher. I'll introduce you to Alan Manahan. He teaches music privately to individual pupils here, and he also teaches in a school in Tullamore. You are coming to our Victory Dinner Dance, aren't you?'

'Of course, and I'm just as curious as Mary as to what it's all about.'

'As I said to her, it's just a family celebration of a great sporting achievement, particularly by me.'

'Goodbye, Big Head.'

* * *

When Anna returned from the shopping mall on Saturday morning, Peter Novak was sweeping leaves in the garden. He said, 'I contacted Paul and Adam about your news from the archive. You won't be surprised to hear that Paul is convinced that it wasn't covered in the news but he didn't know how they managed it. Adam seems to agree but wondered why the archive admitted it, given the implications.'

'Oh, I'm sure they're happy that any potential embarrassment could be explained by the passage of time. Anyway, they didn't admit to any wrongdoing, just that they couldn't explain the absence of any record of the event.'

Peter replied, jokingly, 'I suppose it's unlikely that a record of a cover-up would be included in the files. That would give it away, wouldn't it?'

'You mean like Inspector Clouseau in one of those old movies?'

23

Philadelphia, 1912

A knock on the door late at night is always frightening. Charles jumped out of bed and rushed to the door before he heard a second knock. He did not want Baby Andrew to wake up. He was surprised to find his brother Leo on the doorstep, out of breath and agitated. Charles brought him into the kitchen cum living room. When he asked him to sit down, Leo refused, moving from one foot to the other, repeating over and over again, 'Francesca has thrown me out of the house.'

'Why? What happened?'

'I did nothing wrong. I did nothing wrong.'

Alice heard some of their conversation and emerged from the bedroom carrying blankets and a pillow. Charles arranged a bed for Leo on their couch.

Leo again said, 'I did nothing wrong.' He refused to say more.

'Try to have a good night's sleep, and we'll talk in the morning.'

When Charles woke early for work, Leo was gone. He returned that night and each following night looking progressively worse and refusing to talk. He just stared with eyes that were dead and distant.

Charles and Alice were very worried about what the neighbours might think or say to each other. This became a total embarrassment when late one evening, about ten days later, the police took Leo away for questioning. They informed Charles that a parish priest had made a complaint about Leo's insulting and threatening behaviour, which Charles knew to be totally out of character, especially towards a priest.

Leo returned the next evening but did not speak.

That night, in a whispered conversation, Alice said, 'He now looks and acts like a vagrant.'

'I know. I asked him to return to his home to get a change of clothes. He just shouted no.'

'Maybe you should go. Francesca would explain what's going on.'

'No, she would only dump the problem on me. Remember: she must have given our address to the police.'

'He hasn't washed or shaved for days.'

For the next two weeks, Leo returned most nights to sleep. Charles reckoned that on the other nights he was sleeping rough in the parks. Thank God it's summertime.

Alice, very pale, and with a tremble in her hands, said, 'Love, I'm now frightened by Leo and worried what might he do to our baby.'

Charles was worried too but not to the extent that he wanted to make enquiries or get involved in any way. 'At least he has washed and is wearing my clothes.'

'You need to get him away from here.'

'How am I to do that? You've seen that he won't listen to reason, and Francesca seems to have washed her hands of him.'

Charles jumped from his chair when he heard a knock on the door. Alice recognised the voice of the police officer who had called previously, and she strained to hear the conversation.

'Mr Novak, is your brother here?'

'No, he's—'

'He's wanted for questioning about an attempted assassination of Bishop Walsh in the cathedral this morning. If he returns here, treat him with caution and contact the police immediately.'

Charles was stunned, speechless.

'Can you offer any explanation why your brother has acted in this way?'

'No. I can't believe this. It's totally out of character. He's a very loyal Catholic.'

'Where do you work Mr Novak?'

'I do not wish to be contacted at work.'

Charles returned to the living room, white as a ghost. He fell into his chair, saying, 'Did you hear that? God, he's tried to kill a bishop. Oh God Almighty, what now? What next?'

'Yes, I heard, and I should bring Andrew immediately to my parents' house.'

As Alice turned to look for a bag to pack, Charles said, 'No, let's discuss what's best for us. It's better not to make rash decisions.' He went on, 'What could possibly have happened to make Leo do this awful thing? After I spoke to him a few months ago I told you I was worried about his marriage. If we had been told that he had assaulted Francesca I would be horrified, but at least we could make sense of that. Maybe—'

'Do you have insanity in your family?' Alice blurted out, fearful that the question would annoy Charles.

'No. God, no,' he replied as if the question should never have been asked.

'Would it give you comfort to know what might have triggered this awful act?'

'No, well, maybe, but I have no intention of trying to find out.'

In his mind, Charles had to admit that Alice might be right about insanity, adding further damage to his reputation and to his career prospects. Knowing the cause wouldn't be any help to me. His mind raced on possible evasions. About one-third of the workers in Wanamaker's are Catholic – Polish and Irish mainly – and this awful news would be on everyone's lips the next morning. What will I tell them? What will I say to my boss, to Alice's parents? Charles found his world, so carefully built, tumbling all around him.

They decided that at work next day he would deny any connection with Leo. They also agreed that when the time came to move to their new home they should consider reverting to the Nowak form of their name – anything to distance themselves from Leo's infamy.

In his state of panic, Charles recalled a previous threat to his reputation and to his ambition. What if Irena Malinkowska tracked me down and revealed to the world how I abandoned her and our son or daughter?

He had decided at that time that he would rely on the same pretence that persuaded Leo to leave for America with him: the fear of conscription. How he might buy Irena's silence continued to occupy his mind for some time during his early years in America but until this moment of consternation her name had not crossed his mind for several years.

At work next day, nobody mentioned the attempt to assassinate the bishop, an omission that Charles found incredible and very strange. He expected that every newsvendor would be shouting out the headline and that word would filter through by mid-morning or lunchtime at latest.

A tiny seed of optimism began to grow.

When, by mid-afternoon, no mention was made, it was like waking from a bad dream, happy that his night's terror was all a mistake. He bought a newspaper on the way home and read every article. He then folded the newspaper very tightly as if he was putting an end to his troubles.

When he got home that evening, he said, 'No news is certainly good news for us. Maybe the police had blundered about the event or about the suspect. Maybe our worries are over.' Before Alice could comment, he added, 'Do not say a word to your parents, at least not yet.'

For the next two days, he scoured the newspaper each morning before work. Not finding any mention of an attempted assassination convinced him again that Leo would never do such an awful thing. He hoped that by now the police had admitted their mistake and that Leo had returned home. He again decided not to make contact and left it to Francesca to sort out.

That evening, the police called again to say that Leo had been arrested, charged with an attempt to assassinate Bishop Walsh and detained in a psychiatric hospital but that he had escaped. He was currently at large and considered dangerous. They instructed that they be contacted urgently if he should return to Charles's house or if he or Alice learned of his whereabouts.

When leaving the house, the police officer added, 'The doctors will likely want to talk to you when your brother is recaptured.'

'I've no idea why he committed such a terrible crime. I don't ever want to see him again or to talk to doctors or anyone else about him.'

The terror returned. Charles relied on the absence of publicity to resist any suggestions from Alice about informing her parents or moving even temporarily to their home.

'Charles, we have been told that Leo is deranged. He's not responsible for his actions. I'm scared for myself and even more for Andrew. We have to do something.'

'Everything you have suggested would reveal all to the world, and we have been very lucky to avoid that so far.'

'But Charles—'

'No. That's the end of it.'

That night, Alice knew that Charles also had difficulty sleeping, and when she sensed that he too was awake she decided to resume the conversation that had ended earlier in acrimony. 'Darling, please don't get cross with me, but he's your brother, your only family in America.'

'Enough.'

'Leo needs your help. The doctors need your help to try to find out what caused his insanity. I don't want him near this house but—'

'No.'

'Well, at least talk to his wife.'

'Enough, I said.'

Sleep would not come to Alice, troubled by the thought that if she lost her mind would she be disowned too and troubled by the conviction that if Leo was her brother she would of course visit him.

24

Brendan Farrell was curious. A nose for a story, it came with the territory. As a newspaper man, it was automatic, like breathing or eating, and it had served him well over the years, as a reporter in Dublin where he learned his trade and in the quieter surroundings of Clondore.

When he purchased the paper in 2002, he set about reducing costs. He cancelled arrangements with part-time reporters and in their place recruited voluntary contributions from clubs, associations and interest groups. He outsourced the printing and distribution. His aim then was to build the circulation to a level that would attract one of the newspaper barons to buy him out. He still had hopes, but the recession had scared potential purchasers and he felt he had to keep plugging away.

His curiosity was aroused by the hours Joe Dunphy had spent viewing the microfiche of the 1912 editions of the paper. Sheila Brady, his general assistant and right hand, had picked up 'Bishop Walsh' and 'assassination attempt' in her conversation with Joe whenever he removed his head from the fiche viewer. Sheila also told him that Joe had found nothing. She knew this because he did not take notes or use the printer.

He was long enough in Clondore to know about the connection with Frank and Tommy Walsh. He could have phoned Joe to get the low-down but decided to do a little searching himself. No point in second guessing Joe, he thought. If the *Chronicle* had covered it, Joe would have found it. And if the *Chronicle* didn't have it, then it was very unlikely that another Irish paper, local or national, had the story.

So he switched to America and used his spare time at intervals to search the web. He failed to find online records of newspapers in Philadelphia or Baltimore. He then tried New York, which led him to the New York Times. He entered 'Bishop Walsh Philadelphia' and '1911–1913' and found the same February 1913 article which Tommy Walsh had found earlier.

Brendan decided that self-congratulations were in order. Fantastic. Now I have a front-page story. I wonder if Joe found this as well. I'll write it first and mention my article to Joe before the paper appears in the shops. That way I can expect to get a follow-up story when I phone Frank Walsh for his comments.

He wrote the headline 'REVELATION: ASSASSINATION ATTEMPT ON CLONDORE'S BISHOP WALSH' and followed with a short piece describing the result of his research, outlining the background and declaring his surprise that this event had not been covered in the *Chronicle* when it happened. He finished with an invitation to 'watch this space'. He wasn't sure of the last point but decided he hadn't much to lose.

* * *

'Hi, Tommy, Joe Dunphy here. Has Brendan Farrell been in touch with you or your dad?'

'No. Why would he be?'

'You'll be disappointed to hear that he has just phoned me to say that he followed up on my research and found an interesting item which will appear in tomorrow's *Chronicle*. He didn't elaborate. He thanked me for bringing this story to his attention. That surprised me because I don't recall saying anything specific about why I was searching the archive, and while I was there he didn't ask me any questions, but I must have said something that got him thinking and searching.'

'I wonder what he turned up.'

'I can only guess he found what you already had found or something similar. Mind you, if you saw the state of his office you'd wonder how he ever finds anything.'

'So, what next?'

'He may phone your dad this evening, but it's more likely he'll phone tomorrow when the paper has gone on sale. You need to think about that because whatever you tell him will probably be quoted in next week's edition.'

'Thanks for the heads-up Joe. Forewarned, etc.'

'Sorry for any trouble.'

'No problem. I certainly wouldn't have sought publicity, but if Brendan had asked me what I was researching I'd have given him the same information I gave you.'

Tommy was anxious to talk to his dad before Brendan Farrell got to him so he went straight to the shop. 'The cat's out of the bag, Dad. Joe Dunphy has tipped me off that Brendan Farrell will be phoning to get your response to an article which will appear in tomorrow's paper.'

'How did that happen? How much does he know?'

Tommy repeated Joe's explanation and added that Brendan hadn't disclosed what the paper will say.

'Well, we're now in an interesting situation, aren't we? We'll learn the difference between discussing confidentiality and secrecy in theory as it applies to everyone else and what to do when it lands at our own door.'

They discussed every possible angle. How much did Brendan Farrell know and would he disclose all he knew in the first article? How much disclosure would satisfy and how much would demand more? Would the national papers take up the story? What would full disclosure achieve, especially for Leo Novak? What answer would they give if asked to speculate on the reasons for Leo's actions? They decided that the way to disarm Brendan Farrell and to avoid further conversations with him would be to disclose all they knew and to answer questions as frankly as possible.

* * *

Frank and Brendan Farrell were sitting at the kitchen table. Frank couldn't help noticing the dark nicotine stains on Brendan's fingers. He's a 'hail fellow, well met' type of man, known to everyone in town and the surrounding area. He trades stories and gossip on a 'give some to get some' basis, so what I tell him will probably become widely known even if he doesn't publish a follow-up story.

After some general chat, Brendan said, 'You've read the article then?'

Frank recalled the catchy headline and the implication that more was to come. 'Yes, Brendan, I have. Your source appears to be the same as ours.'

'Oh, you knew about it already?'

Frank detected disappointment in his voice. 'Yes, but only by a month or so. Tommy came across the information when he searched the web. He was gathering information about Bishop Walsh for our family tree.'

'Were you surprised?'

'Totally. Nobody in our family had ever heard about it. That's why Tommy asked Joe Dunphy to search your archives, and, as you know, your paper didn't have the story, which was another surprise.'

'So were you able to source any other reports in American newspapers?'

'The one you quoted was in the *New York Times*, I think. The *Washington Post* also had a similar report.'

'Could I have a copy please?'

'Sure. I'll ask Tommy to email it to you. We sent those reports to the archive in the archdiocese of Philadelphia hoping they could give us cuttings from local papers or magazines. They had never heard of it.'

Brendan stared wide-eyed. 'What? How come?'

'They had no explanation. They did a thorough check but couldn't find any reference to an assassination attempt on Bishop Walsh.'

'Curious, to say the least. Any ideas why?'

'You could speculate for ever. Maybe the file was lost or not returned by some researcher.'

'Did the possibility of a cover-up cross your mind?'

'Yes. With the recent disclosures in the Irish and American church it was bound to, but, as I said, speculation is a kind of dead end, particularly for an event that happened a hundred years ago.'

'Why did Mr Novak try to kill the bishop? What reason do you think?'

'He was insane, so the reason could have been a figment of a deranged mind. He may have seen himself as a victim of some kind.'

'Could he have been sexually abused by a priest?'

'Yes, possibly, but his actions could have been for any number of reasons. For example, he could have been anti-Catholic or anti-Irish, and, as you know, both were widespread in America at that time.'

Brendan replied with disappointment in his voice, 'Yes, that's true, I suppose.' He hesitated and then added, 'Would it be true to say that you find this whole thing embarrassing?'

Frank wondered if Brendan was fishing for a headline. 'No, not at all. There is no known motive for the attempted assassination, and, besides, it all happened a very long time ago.'

'Frank, thanks for your help on this. I'll probably run another story next week based on what you have told me. If I hear from anyone else, I'll let you know.'

'Glad to oblige.'

Leaving Walsh's shop, Brendan was pleased with the material for a follow-up story, scandal being a reporter's dream. Now how far could I go with this? I could publish a sensational story which might be taken up by the Dublin papers and perhaps even the Philadelphia media, but the bulk of my readers might not like that. They like the truth so long as it's somebody else's truth. Anyway, this story is a welcome change from the usual everyday stuff.

When he arrived at his office, he immediately drafted a headline 'ASSASSINATION ATTEMPT COVERED UP?' He then did the first of a few drafts of the article. He made no reference to his conversation with Frank Walsh.

When Brendan Farrell had left, Tommy joined his dad in the kitchen. Frank gave him a rundown on his conversation. 'Well done, Dad. You handled that like an experienced PR man. Do you think next week's article will create problems?'

'I expect it will be OK, but I suppose it pays to be careful. Please send the American newspaper reports to Brendan, and will you copy his article to Anna and explain the stance we have taken and tell her we will forward any other reports that appear.'

'Yes, of course. I'd better send a copy to Mary and Deirdre as well. They wouldn't be pleased to hear it from someone else.'

25

Philadelphia, 1912

Francesca sat by the window in her easy chair, watching the world go by on the busy street below. She reflected on the terrible events of the previous weeks and tried to figure out what she should say to her sick mother and to Gemma, who was sleeping peacefully in her bed.

I was hasty, she thought, but what was I to do? I got such a shock, and he tried to blame the poor priest. I did what any mother would have done. But then he got the police involved all by himself. I had nothing to do with that.

When the police called to her door, she had been relieved to send them to Charles's house. That would have taken him down a peg or two. But when they returned to tell her that Leo had been charged with attempting to kill Bishop Walsh, she was stunned. She couldn't believe he was capable of such a thing. All she wanted to do was hide and keep Gemma away from all that.

It was a mistake to marry him, she thought. It was all my doing. I pursued him. God, I was shameless. But I missed my Giuseppe so much. Gemma missed her father too.

Francesca had never wanted to hear the details of the accident.

It was enough to know that Giuseppe went to work one day and never came home. Now she realised she had been in shock and shouldn't have tried to get a father for Gemma and a husband for herself. It all happened in the wrong order. But then she had money troubles as well.

Leo and Gemma were very fond of each other. But he could never compare with Giuseppe. It was wrong of me to expect that he would. I should have kept him as a friend instead of trying to make him the husband he could never be. I can't bear to hear Gemma asking when her Dada Leo will be coming home.

Francesca told her it could be a long time because he was living with his brother now. She was determined that her daughter would never know the truth, but she knew Gemma was too bright to be easily deceived. Neither did her mother know anything about the assassination attempt.

Thank God it didn't appear in the newspapers, Francesca thought, but Mama will wonder why Leo is not visiting her. I'll have to think up some story that he's gone to California or maybe back to Poland. Yeah, Poland. She might believe that. Maybe they both will.

When the police officer called to say that the doctors in the hospital wished to speak to her, she told him she had nothing to say that would console Leo. She felt terrible about that, but Gemma came first. That's what she told herself.

26

Philadelphia, 1913

Leo tried to fix his mind on what had happened to him, or what he'd done, but try as he might he could not put the pieces together. He felt surrounded by a dense fog that refused to lift. He didn't know where he was or how he got there, or even how long he'd been there. He seemed to remember escaping, but from what? He wondered if that was something he'd dreamed about or had hoped or planned to do.

There were narrow slit windows in his room but too high on the wall to allow him a view of the outside. He figured he was in some kind of hospital, but he was not allowed to leave his room. He couldn't recall anyone he could turn to who could help him relive the recent past, which added to his despair. He could recall growing up in Poland, his father's name and the names of his brothers and sister. Like chanting his spelling and multiplication tables at school, he repeated over and over, 'Stefan, Stefan, Karol, Lydia … Stefan, Stefan, Karol, Lydia,' in the hope that other memories would return. He continued to chase elusive thoughts that kept skipping away from him like dry leaves in the wind.

He did not see other patients, but he heard noises. Some were painful and disturbing, but at least he knew he was not alone. He had no interest in food but ate whatever he was given in silence, even when a doctor was present.

The man wore a white coat so Leo assumed he was a doctor. He encouraged Leo to talk about himself and his life. He tried to talk about Poland, about how his country had been split up by occupying forces – Russians, Prussians, Austro-Hungarians, about conscription and how his sister Lydia died from scarlet fever when she was only seven. The doctor showed no interest and kept pressing him about last month, this year. The more he pressed, the less Leo could remember.

From the beginning, he experienced the all-pervasive smell of urine, human waste and strong antiseptic and wondered how this could be allowed to persist. He tried to get a glimpse of what passed outside his room every time the door was opened. He saw patients dressed in dirty clothes, some near naked as they shuffled along a corridor that was filthy and squalid with peeling paint on the wall and ceiling. From the numbers that passed his door and the non-stop and loud exchanges between patients and staff, he reckoned the place was crowded. He began to feel that being stuck in his room had its merits.

By remaining silent, staff tended to ignore him, and he took advantage of this by listening to their conversations. In this way, he learned that the transfer of patients from other hospitals was the main cause of overcrowding. He also heard complaints that the deplorable conditions in the hospital were caused by corrupt government starving the hospital of much needed funds.

Mr Bradshaw, a senior psychiatric nurse, entered the room, locked the door behind him and sat on Leo's bed. 'Now, Mr Novak, I hope you will be able to remember more for us today.'

Questions, questions, questions, more bloody questions.

'Did you ever have any association with anarchists?'

Leo remained silent.

'Are you friendly with any Roman Catholic priests?'

'Bastards!'

'Do you pray, Mr Novak?'

'Not now, but I used to.' He thought that maybe prayer was his only hope.

'Do you like music?'

'Chopin.'

'Do you like Christmas?'

What a stupid question. Everybody loves Christmas. He shrugged his shoulders and said, 'I want to go home.'

'Oh? Please tell me your address.'

Silence.

'You have done very well today. You're making good progress.'

When Bradshaw unlocked the door to leave, Leo tried to force his way out of the room. Help was summoned. He was given a bitter brown liquid to drink and placed in a long-sleeved canvas garment that wrapped his arms tightly around his waist and was fastened behind him.

After many sessions of verbal confrontation with Nurse Bradshaw, Leo began to remember a most upsetting row with someone named Francesca. He said she was known to him, but he couldn't remember anything about her. All he could recall was that she had yelled at him to leave the house they were in and that if he didn't she would call the police. He burst into tears, loud and despairing like a child. And then someone gave him more of the bitter drink.

In the weeks that followed, the failure of memory was replaced at intervals with glimpses of the recent past, replacing one source of distress with many. The more he remembered, the greater the pain. Self-doubt leading to self-loathing overcame any thoughts of criticism or blame of others. He wished he could lose himself in work and imagined himself as a hospital porter.

Dr Rydell genuinely believed that mental illness could be cured. He tried to control his frustration at the overcrowding in his hospital. He was proud of his staff who did the best they could in the circumstances, but he was ashamed of the conditions in which his patients were kept. He knew visitors, the few who came, were appalled by what they saw. He realised that only a government inquiry would bring about an end to the scandal, but public acceptance or denial of the situation meant that there was no political pressure to find a solution. A change to private ownership, he felt, was the only hope.

Dr Rydell was reviewing Leo's case with Nurse Bradshaw. 'I would dearly love to have more time to deal with the new patient, Mr Novak. He seems to be a man of limited intellectual ability, docile, fearful but with flashes of determination.'

'And enough courage and guile to have escaped twice from captivity,' Nurse Bradshaw added.

'You're well aware that Mr Novak's wife and brother don't want anything to do with him. It's most distressing. He presents a very interesting case, which requires a lot more attention if he is to make progress, and this, as you know, is just not possible.'

27

On Saturday evening, the group of eight was assembled in the sitting room, the largest gathering there had been in the room for many years. Tommy had driven that afternoon to Roscrea to collect Deirdre from the Limerick train. Mary and Kevin arrived an hour earlier and had a sandwich and a cup of tea in the kitchen. Jimmy, dressed in his Sunday best, and Joan, elegant in a plum-coloured lace dress, were trying not to look like intruders. Joan took great pride in her appearance, had always been a beauty and, despite the passage of time, was still striking with clear green eyes and auburn hair perfectly groomed. Orla wore an azure-blue wool dress. Mary was in a cream silk belted dress which suited her sandy-light-brown hair, and Deirdre wore a blue and pink floral number.

Earlier, Mrs Duggan had lit the fire and prepared food and drinks using the best china and glasses, treasured by Tommy's mother. The room looked and felt cosy, warm and welcoming, though it would hardly qualify for inclusion in any glossy magazine or Sunday supplement.

The topics of conversation were the weather, the recession, politics local and national, goings-on in Dublin and Deirdre's student life in Limerick. The Dinner Dance and Disco and who would be wearing the most daring or the most dazzling outfit got a mention. Mary quizzed Deirdre on the quality of the men in college without getting any incriminating answers or even telegraphed clues. When she grilled Tommy on the same subject he said, 'Do you ever give up?'

'I'm only doing my duty to promote the best interests of my younger brother and sister. Well, come on, answer me.' Tommy just smiled. 'That smile says more than a thousand words. Who is she?'

'That would be telling,' Tommy said, thinking he had at last found a way of pacifying Mary, and went off to replenish drinks.

On his return, his dad stood up and said that he wanted to propose a toast now because there wouldn't be an opportunity to do so later in the hotel.

'Winning a county championship is never easy. If it was, we wouldn't have to wait sixteen years for another celebration. So, this is an important day for our Gaelic football club, for our town and most of all for Tommy, who played such a vital part in bringing back the cup. So raise your glasses and join me in congratulating Tommy and wishing him continued success on the football field and in all aspects of his life. To Tommy!'

'To Tommy,' the group echoed and managed to clap while holding their drinks. Each one then complimented him with a 'well done' or a hug or an arm around the shoulder.

The buzz of conversation took over briefly. Then Frank spoke again. 'I have something else to say before we head to the hotel.' This got their immediate attention. 'I'm delighted to tell you that I asked Orla to marry me and that I'm relieved and honoured that she said "Yes."'

A moment's sharp silence was followed by a simultaneous whoop by Kevin and Tommy and a rush by Mary and Deirdre to embrace their father. Amidst their tears and their laughter they did the same with Orla, who was in a daze.

Despite the excitement, her thoughts went back to a time when she had hopes that her relationship with Frank would develop and deepen but had learned to settle for just friendship as the best on offer. So when Tommy threw his arms around her, she whispered, 'I know the part you played in all of this, and I will be forever grateful.'

Tommy was taken aback and for a moment was speechless. 'I'm … I'm really delighted for you both.'

It was apparent to everybody that Jimmy Walker was visibly overcome, and this spoke eloquently for him. Joan had a quiet word with Frank and Orla in turn.

Mary said, for all to hear, 'Now, Dad, look what you've done. Look at the state of me. I'll have to do my make-up all over again because of you.'

The women concurred, and everybody laughed. Just as thoughts were developing on moving to the hotel, Frank intervened again. 'One more thing.' Looking at Tommy, he said, 'I want you to be my best man,' and before anyone could react, he turned to Jimmy Walker and said, 'I want you to be my groomsman.'

The surprise was more than doubled when Orla, taking a step forward, said, 'I don't have a sister, so I am hoping that you, Mary, will be my matron of honour and you, Deirdre, my bridesmaid.'

Words of joyful acceptance and more hugs, kisses and tears followed. Kevin embraced his wife and said, 'Now you can fix your make-up.'

They were all relieved that the weather made it possible to walk to the hotel, and, as they were leaving, Mary caught Tommy by the arm. 'I told you so, didn't I? I knew something was stirring and you didn't believe me. Now, learn the lesson: never ignore a woman's intuition.'

'Alright, you win.'

Deirdre asked her dad if he had fixed a date.

'No, not yet, but hopefully around Easter or early summer.'

As Tommy went to lock up before leaving, he thought, Dad, you're some operator the way you arranged and choreographed all this, especially the announcements.

The function room was filling up as they arrived at their reserved table, and they took a while to survey the very familiar surroundings now transformed by flags and bunting in the club colours of blue and green. The enlarged photos of the 1996 and 2012 teams, measuring about five feet by four, were erected behind the top table at eye level and were getting a lot of attention.

After the usual effort to extract people from the bar, a four-course meal with wine was served. The usual buzz of conversation accompanied the meal, and you could see Frank and Orla's announcement spreading around the tables like a disjointed Mexican wave. As it spread, there were glances and gestures towards the couple, and a number left their seats to congratulate and wish them well with handshakes and hugs.

The formal parts of the evening were expertly dealt with. Liam O'Brien, the club chairman, and Denis Murphy, the chairman of the county board, made mercifully short speeches in which the words 'glory', 'honour', 'pride', 'effort', 'skill', 'determination' and 'team spirit' featured. They received a very polite applause, and then the team chant, 'Clon-Clon-Clon-Clondooore' brought a party atmosphere to the room.

The presentation of medals must have given some amusement to Denis Murphy since he had already done the honours immediately after the victory in Tullamore some weeks previously. If it did, he didn't show it. With emigration again having a serious negative impact on clubs all over the county, he must have wondered how many of the medal winners would be around for the championship the following year.

To speed up the process, the squad came to the top table in groups of three – the full-back line, the full forward line, etc. – with the goalkeeper joining the two centre-field players. It all happened so quickly that the onlookers seemed to be cheering non-stop. Of course, the Walsh table reserved their loudest and most prolonged applause and cheering when Tommy and the other members of the half-back line received their medals. The final special presentation, to the captain, Conor Ryan, and the team manager, Sean Maher, received the loudest cheer of the evening. At the Walsh table, all eyes and smiles were for Joan, Sean's mother.

Liam O'Brien called for attention before the crowd dispersed. 'Now, I want you all to remain in the room while the tables are pushed back, the dance floor cleared, and the musicians prepare to play. As you know, it is our tradition to start the dance with a "Siege of Ennis" in which everyone, young and old, and I mean everyone, is expected to take part. So please cooperate and we'll be ready to start in no time.'

As people moved to the edge of the room, Frank said, 'The dance needs groups of eight. We number eight so let's have a go.'

Groans and varying expressions of reluctance followed, but when the music started they were in the middle of the floor. Two groups of four stood facing another line of eight and so on until the entire dance floor was covered. Jimmy and Joan, Frank and Orla, and Tommy, to a lesser extent, knew what to do, and the others followed their lead.

The facing eights advanced and retired twice then each group of four moved laterally over and back, one group to the right, the other to the left and then resumed their starting position. Then each facing pair swung each other in a circle and then resumed their position. Each eight advanced and retired again twice as at the outset. On the second advance, the line facing the musicians raised their arms to allow the opposite line pass under, and the sequence started all over again. This continued until the eight that started at the back of the room reached the front.

The tempo and the duration tested stamina. Many of the younger dancers were all arms and legs and little finesse while the older people danced in a much more stylish and controlled way and were less ruffled and out of puff as they returned to their seats.

Bart Clancy, the band leader and piano accordion player, complimented the dancers. 'Well done everybody, and I'd like to commend the Gaelic Athletic Association and your club for fostering and promoting Irish dancing. It's wonderful to see. Mind you, watching some of you dance reminded me of the Percy French song "Phil the Fluter's Ball". You know the line, "Begorra Mrs Cafferty, yer leppin' like a hare".' The dancers laughed and clapped, and as they settled in their seats, Bart added, 'Ye're so good at the Irish dancing we'll now have "The Walls of Limerick".'

This was met with groans and shouts of 'Oh No!' to which he responded, 'OK, OK, I suppose ye deserve a rest so the next dance will be an old-time waltz.'

The band played a selection of Irish ballads in waltz time. Tommy watched Frank and Orla and Jimmy and Joan as they moved effortlessly around the floor and thought how wonderful it was that love had come late into their lives. His friend and team-mate, Dave McCarthy and Clare O'Connor, Tommy's ex, then passed by, hand in hand, and he wondered how long he would have to wait for love.

It's no wonder Mary feels the need to stay on my case.

Bart and his band then showed their versatility with numbers such as the Paul Simon song 'You Can Call Me Al', Glen Miller's 'In the Mood' and current pop tunes. When they stopped playing and the disco was being set up, Tommy and Deirdre joined the other team members and their friends. Mary and Kevin hooked up with her friends, and the older four moved to the bar for a nightcap.

As the night drew to a close, a heated argument developed which Tommy, fortified with wine and beer, decided to join even though he had not contributed to the earlier discussion. When his opinions were challenged, he adopted the same defiant pose that he displayed on the football field as if a physical response was called for. This drew a similar posture from others. When Deirdre realised the danger of escalation, she feigned illness and drew on Tommy's better nature to escort her home.

On leaving the hotel, she had the good sense to say that his defence of his friends was fully justified, and she complimented him on his loyalty. Once they reached the fresh air, Tommy needed physical support so she decided to reverse roles and saw him safely to his door. As she made her way to Orla's house, she relished the prospect of teasing Tommy, whenever he got too uppity, about the evening she had to rescue him.

As Tommy climbed the stairs, his determination not to make any noise had the opposite effect. His last thought was, Who will live where? I'll move out. And then sleep grabbed him.

28

Having suggested contact by Skype to Anna, Tommy needed something constructive to say. Looking for inspiration, he scribbled a note of the facts so far.

1. Leo Novak was ostracised by his family, and Anna Novak's father and uncles believe that the reason was a row with Bishop Walsh and that this row was understood to be 'not trivial'.

2. The New York and Washington papers reported that Leo Novak 'shot at' and 'tried to shoot' Bishop Walsh and had twice escaped from captivity. The Novak brothers believe that this man is their grand-uncle.

3. The assassination attempt and the escapes were not reported in the religious or secular papers in Philadelphia. The Novaks believe that this points to a cover-up by the Catholic Church. Dad would likely concur.

4. The church would not be worried about the assassination attempt being publicised per se, but they would be worried about revealing why Leo Novak was driven to make the attempt, hence the cover-up.

5. So why did he do it? The psychiatric hospital and the police must have records which would provide answers.

This led Tommy to wonder if a psychiatric hospital, assuming it could be identified, would reveal information on a former patient even to a relative. The file would obviously contain information on diagnosis, treatment and progress or lack of it, but Tommy doubted it would have detailed information on what provoked the criminal act. The most likely place to find this information, if it existed at all, would be in the police records, but he had no idea if police records went back to 1912 and, even if they did, how could he possibly find them.

He spent the next two hours correcting the Leaving Certificate students' work on a project he had set on a brochure to attract foreign investment to the Clondore area and the wider County Offaly. So far, he was quite impressed with their efforts, and it prompted him to contact the Industrial Development Authority to see if they would send a representative to make a presentation to the class.

It was now past 10 p.m., and though he had not arranged any time schedule, he decided to Skype Anna, hoping she would be at home. He was very surprised at the vision that greeted him on screen. Her age, her short blonde hair and her blue eyes. God, she's stunning.

'Hello, Anna, I'm Tommy Walsh.'

'Oh, ah … hello.'

'I hope I'm not calling at a bad time?'

'No, it's just that I was expecting someone older.'

'Well, that makes two of us.' They laughed, and it broke the ice. Tommy continued, 'I expect we both thought that people involved in tracing family relations are usually older.'

'I got involved because my mother likes the TV show *Who Do You Think You Are?*'

'I've seen that programme on the BBC. In my case, a conversation with my dad got me interested.'

'Can I first clear up something that's on my mind?' Anna asked.

'Sure, fire ahead.'

'Given what we now know, I'm surprised that you are continuing the research when it's likely to show Bishop Walsh in a bad light.'

'Good point. I suppose I don't like unfinished business. I also want to see justice done for Leo, and if that unearths bad news for the bishop, well, we can discuss the implications of that if and when it happens. OK?'

'Thanks. Sorry to be so direct. So, I should introduce myself. I live in rural Pennsylvania near Center Valley, where I am in my final year of a sports-management degree in DeSales University.'

'We've something in common then. I teach business management in our local community school, the equivalent of your high school. I'm also involved in sport. I'm a member of the Clondore Gaelic football team.'

'I play soccer. I did a tryout for an intramural team, but I didn't make the cut.'

'You must be good though. That's a high standard.'

'Gee, thanks. By the way, what is Gaelic football? I've never heard of it.'

Tommy laughed and said, 'I'm not surprised. It's not well known internationally. Best thing to do is to check the website on the Gaelic Athletic Association – very easy to remember, gaa. ie – and follow the link to GAA TV. You should also check out the videos on the game of hurling. Your lecturers and fellow students will be impressed. When you've had a look, I will try to answer any questions you have.'

'Will do. Is your team any good?'

'Brilliant, even though I say so myself. We won the county championship for the first time in sixteen years.'

'Congratulations.'

'We've just had a victory dance and disco. You'd have enjoyed that; we did a Siege of Ennis dance.'

'What's that?'

'The GAA promotes Irish culture as well as Irish games. A Siege of Ennis is like your square-dancing – very energetic and great fun.'

'You had a blast then?'

'Sure did. Before I brag too much about our team, I should tell you that we didn't get past the first round in the provincial championship, so I haven't got a swelled head just yet.'

'You won't be turning pro then?'

'Impossible. It's a totally amateur sport.'

'Really? Our interest in sport will give us plenty to talk about.'

'I'll look forward to that.' After a short silence, he added, 'Would you like to start on where we go from here with the research?'

'Yes, please.'

'Well, at least we now know that there would be no point in searching the archives of the Catholic Standard and Times in Philadelphia. I had thought that we should engage someone to do just that which would have been a waste of money.'

'Yeah, just as well we didn't go down that route.'

'There are two places, I believe, where the information we need might be found: the files of a psychiatric hospital and police records.'

'Yes, but how do we locate either one?'

'Haven't a clue.'

'Maybe Uncle Adam could point us in the right direction.'

'I wondered if we should seek professional help. Leave it with me for now. I'll concentrate on the psychiatric hospital. We also need to find out if Leo had a family and hopefully to identify living relatives.'

'I'm very happy to leave it to you then.'

'I'm delighted to meet you, Anna, even if only over the Internet. Oh, I almost forgot to tell you, the editor of our local newspaper, the *Clondore Chronicle*, has twigged what our research is all about. Anyway, he did his own research and published an article in the recent edition and contacted Dad for a reaction.'

'Was that embarrassing?'

'Not really. I had been tipped off in advance. Dad disclosed all we know as the best way of avoiding further publicity. I will copy the article to you and any follow-up article that appears. Sorry that this happened, but I don't think any harm has been done.'

'Good. Thanks for telling me. Bye, or should I say "good night"?'

'Either will do fine. Bye.'

When the screen went dead, Anna was surprised by her reaction to the on-screen encounter and how much she enjoyed talking to Tommy. *He's very different to Josh. I wonder what Martha would think.*

* * *

'Tommy contacted me on Skype.'

'So it's "Tommy" now, is it?' her mother joked.

'Yes, and he's much younger than I expected, and he said the same about me. It seems like he's only about three years older than me, and guess what? He teaches business studies and plays Gaelic football. I wonder if any of our professors know about that game?'

'Did he have any suggestions about the research?'

'Yeah, he said he'll try to identify the psychiatric hospital where Leo was held. He admits, like me, that he has no idea how this could be done. He mentioned police records also, but that's a real long shot.'

29

Tommy didn't have any reason to Skype Anna. He just wanted to see her again. 'Hi, Anna. I've been racking my brain about psychiatric hospitals and police files without any progress.'

'I wish I could help, but I'm clueless.'

'I have the time to do the research, but I know nothing about the US Census or about Philadelphia or places in Pennsylvania. You told me you lived near Center Valley. Please tell me more.'

Anna was amused by this and said, 'Gee, I wish all the questions were as easy. We live in the country in a three-bedroom house which my dad built about twenty years ago. Center Valley, a town of about 11,000 people, where I attend DeSales University, is close by. Coopersburg, about a mile south of us, has a population of over 2,000. I work part-time in a bookstore close to the college. My parents work in Allentown, a city about six miles away. So, now it's your turn.'

'I got a business degree in the university in Galway on the west coast about forty-five miles from here, and, as you know, I teach business studies in Clondore Community School.'

'Tell me about Clondore.'

'It's a midland town of 2,000 people – about the same as Coopersburg. It's in the western side of County Offaly and close to the River Shannon. Tullamore, our county town, has about 12,000 people, and is about thirty minutes from here, and Dublin is about ninety miles away.'

Anna, taking notes, said, 'I'll have to study the map. My dad is a bank manager in Allentown, and Mom teaches in an elementary school there. What do your parents do?'

'Dad owns a DIY and hardware store in the town. I help out, unpaid, I'm afraid. We live over the shop.' After a brief silence, he added, 'Mum died in 2004.'

'I'm sorry to hear that. That must have been tough.'

'Yes it was. I was about seventeen at the time.' Anna was touched by the emotion in his voice. After a brief pause, Tommy continued, 'We had a very pleasant surprise a couple of weeks ago when my father announced his engagement to be married.'

'How wonderful! Isn't it great to be having a normal conversation that doesn't involve research and digging up the past?'

'It would be even better if we could do it over a cup of coffee or a beer.'

Anna was a bit taken aback, but in a pleasant way. 'Ah … Ah … Yeah, I'd sure like that. Technology is all very fine but … '

'I suppose we had better get back to next steps?'

'Yeah, I guess so.'

'I'll have a go at trying to find Leo in online records, how long he spent in hospital, did he marry, did he remain in America or go back to Poland?'

'Wow, that's a lot of questions. I'd be lost without you. Sorry Tommy, it's study time, so I've got to go now, OK?'

'OK. But, sorry, one more quick point: hopefully when you include the answers we're seeking on your family tree, a relative will contact you through the "Member Connect" facility – you know, in the same way you contacted me.'

'Yeah, thanks for reminding me. Bye.'

'Bye, Anna.'

* * *

Joe Dunphy spent an hour with Tommy introducing him to the workings of the US Census. Next evening, Tommy decided to make a start. The only clue he had was that Leo had spent time in a psychiatric hospital, and, since the assassination was attempted in Philadelphia, he assumed that the hospital was in that city or surrounding area. The Census was taken every ten years and was available online up to the year 1940.

Leo was admitted after the assassination attempt in 1912, so not knowing when he was discharged, Tommy began by clicking on 'Search All Records' and then selecting the 1920 census. He input Leo's first name and surname, gave his address as 'Pennsylvania', his year of birth, as supplied by Anna, as '1870 +/– 2 years', and Poland as his place of birth. On Joe's suggestion, he typed 'Inmate' in the section headed 'Keyword'.

He was worried about the number of blank spaces on the screen showing how little he knew about Leo. He clicked 'Search' and was surprised when a list of Novaks appeared. He narrowed it down to the three most likely, and clicked on 'View Image' for each one, which brought up the original handwritten census form. The one that was the closest match to the details he had input showed a Leo Novak residing in Webster House in West Philadelphia.

How lucky is that? I expected to spend hours on this and possibly find nothing. 'Wonderful, wonderful, wonderful,' he said out loud. His elation was dimmed when he realised that by 1920 Leo would have spent at least seven years in hospital.

He googled 'Webster House' and found their website, a possible source of more information about Leo. It could have been closed years ago, but hopefully their files will tell us what we want to know. Elated and anxious to share the good news with Anna, he sent her an email.

Good news, Anna, good news. Leo is listed in the 1920 Census as a resident of Webster House, a psychiatric hospital in Philadelphia. It didn't say how long he was there. The details on Webster House can be found on websterhouse.org. To save you time, I have extracted the description of this facility:

Driving through the gates of Webster House Behavioral Health Facility in West Philadelphia, the first impression is that it could be a hotel or a retirement home. The main building dominates. It houses the reception area, administrative functions, dining rooms, treatment facilities and a secure area, with smaller residential buildings set in the surrounding attractive parkland.

Webster House was established in 1915 as a private hospital to which many of the patients of the state-owned South West Philadelphia Psychiatric Hospital were transferred. At that time it was located in what was rural Pennsylvania.

From the beginning, it catered for adults with psychiatric and behavioural problems, and today the facility specialises in alcohol and drug rehab programmes.

I wonder what it was like when Leo was there. Grim and depressing, I expect. At least we now know where he spent many years.

I suggest that, when you get a minute, you should email the manager of Webster House. Again, to save you time, here is a draft which you could copy and paste and amend as necessary.

Dear Mr Fielding,
    According to the 1920 Census, my great-grand-uncle, Leo

Novak, was a patient in your hospital. I am preparing my family tree, and I should be grateful if you would tell me when he was admitted, when he was discharged and any information from his file which you can divulge. I will telephone you next week to answer any questions you may have.

Yours etc.

Your contact details.

I could contact the hospital, but it would be better coming from a Novak relative, don't you think? Talk to you soon.

He didn't expect it to be quite so soon. He was about to shut down his computer when he heard the Skype ringing tone. He answered, expecting the call was from Mary, and was thrilled to see Anna's face appear on screen.

'What a genius you are.'

Tommy laughed and said, 'Beginner's luck, beginner's luck.'

This got Anna to laugh in turn. She went on, 'So at least seven years in the hospital, and that's depressing. But it's better to know than not know.'

Tommy said, 'Hopefully I'll find out that Leo had some happy times before 1912, before the attempted assassination.'

'Oh, I hope so, I really do.'

'I hope my beginner's luck doesn't run out.'

'So far, so good. I'll email the hospital now.'

'Bye, Anna.'

'Bye, genius.'

30

Tommy opened an email from Anna.

This is the reply received today from Mr John Fielding. It's not encouraging, but hopefully the archivist will find what we are looking for.

Thank you for your enquiry re Leo Novak.

Our records here are not as good as they should be. I understand that on at least one occasion records were handed over to a university for research purposes. Also, it is likely that files were destroyed or mislaid during one of the many building renovations over the years. However, Donna Hurst, an archivist, is currently on site preparing a history of the hospital to mark our centenary as a private hospital in 2015. I will pass your request to her and ask her to reply directly to you.

A few days later Anna was back.

Hi Tommy,

I received this message from the archivist yesterday morning.

Dear Anna,

You sent a request to the hospital for information about Leo Novak. As Mr Fielding said, the records are very poor. The only record I found is that he arrived here in April 1915 and was discharged in March 1931. The record of his arrival here has the word 'transferred' opposite his name. If he had been sent here by a doctor or by order of the court, I think his record would have said 'referred'.

I think it is safe to assume that he was transferred here from the South West Philadelphia Psychiatric Hospital with most of the other patients when that institution was closed down.

Sorry I don't have more to tell you. If I come across anything of interest I will contact you.

Best wishes,

Donna Hurst

I phoned her before going to class yesterday. She confirmed that being discharged meant that Leo was not sent to another institution. She also confirmed that there was no record of where he went to, no forwarding address.

The dates fit. From the time of the assassination attempt in 1912 and certainly from June 1913 when he turned up at Bellevue Hospital in New York, until April 1915, when he was sent to Webster House, he was probably in a secure psychiatric hospital. The poor man was probably regarded as criminally insane.

Now, how do we find out where he went in March 1931, and what happened to him thereafter? If he returned to Poland, and I think I would have if I was in his shoes, we may never know the rest of his story.

I suggest we wait a few weeks to see if you can find Leo in the Census either pre or post his time in hospital. If not, we may have to close the research.

No need to reply unless you have another bright idea.

* * *

When Katherine turned on her phone on arriving home from work on Friday evening, she found a copy of Anna's email to Tommy. She received the news with mixed feelings, glad to have another piece of Leo's life story but sad that he had spent so much time in a psychiatric hospital only to disappear again.

She tried to imagine what it must have been like having been committed to the hospital for eighteen or nineteen years, probably institutionalised, and then, as far as anyone knew, having nobody to turn to for support. God forbid, but if I was in that situation my heart and my spirit would be broken.

She figured that Peter had already read the message.

When Anna returned from class, the three discussed the email and exchanged expressions of concern for Leo.

On the following Tuesday, during her coffee break, Anna listened to a recorded message from Donna Hurst requesting to phone her. She detected an excitement in her voice so she phoned immediately. 'Hello, Donna. This is Anna Novak. I got your message.'

'Leo Novak never left the hospital.'

'What? But you said he was discharged in 1931.'

'Yes, that's correct. I knew that his name rang a bell with me, that I had come across it somewhere else in the files. My hunch was correct. I did more digging and found that, yes, he was discharged in 1931, but the very next day he became an employee of the hospital.'

'Oh, doing what?'

'His employment record says that he was a groundsman and gardener and lived in the gate lodge of the hospital, long since demolished.'

'Does the record say when he retired?'

'He didn't. He died in January 1940 and was buried in the

150

local Roman Catholic cemetery which I believe closed many years ago.'

'So it appears that he worked right up to the time of his death.'

'Yes. He was still on the employee register in January 1940.'

'This is amazing news, and I know that my father and his brothers will be relieved. It was really nice of you to take the time to uncover this, and I really appreciate it.'

'Thanks, glad to do it. It's the more satisfying part of my job. Maybe he will feature in the history of the hospital.'

'That would be just wonderful. Bye, and thanks again.'

'You're welcome. Glad to bring some good news.'

Anna typed a file note on the telephone conversation which she sent to her parents' phones and to Tommy.

Later, when her parents were discussing Anna's note, Peter said, 'I don't know whether this is good news or not. I wonder if Leo felt unable to leave the hospital, unable to deal with the outside world or if he had no person or place to go to.'

Katherine, saddened by the news, replied, 'He may have had both reasons. Charles was long dead by then, and maybe Alice as well.

31

Philadelphia, 1915

'It's not our war. I keep saying it. It's not our war.' Charles's show of anxiety was not based on a conviction about what he had said but rather on a fear of the opposite. He was having yet another conversation with his colleague and friend, Alfredo 'Alf' Manin about the war in Europe which had started in August of the previous year. They were having a hot supper at the company's expense in the dining room of Wanamaker's Department Store.

'Yeah, I hear you, but for how much longer?'

'For ever, I hope.'

Classes had finished until the autumn. Only those preparing for their final exams were present. Voices carried loudly in the high-ceilinged almost empty room so it was difficult to have a private conversation. They didn't want pro-German students or teachers to join in. That could become heated.

Alf replied, 'Surely you agree that the sinking of the Lusitania is going to make a difference?'

'Not really.'

'Come on, an American liner torpedoed by the Germans with a loss of 1,100 lives, including 128 Americans and twenty-seven of those from this city? That cannot be tolerated.'

'I know all of Europe as well as Russia and Turkey are at war, but that is no reason for us to add to the death and destruction. If we joined, the number of American dead would be in the thousands. Think about that.'

Study class was about to start, so they had to finish their supper and go.

Charles read whatever he could find on the development of the war, particularly any developments that threatened Poland. His concentration, however, was very much on his studies. He was determined to top the class, confident because of company policy that this would advance his career.

A few evenings later, back in the dining room, a colleague, Albert Bauer, who Charles did not know well, sat down beside him. 'I couldn't help overhearing your conversation the other evening with Alf Manin so I thought you would be interested in this article from this morning's newspaper.' He placed the folded page in front of Charles, who, without a word, immediately started to read.

PRESIDENT WILSON ADDRESSES 4,000 NEWLY
NATURALISED CITIZENS

In his address in the Old Convention Hall, the President referred to the recent sinking of the Lusitania by German U-boats. He said, 'There is such a thing as a man being too proud to fight. There is such a thing as a nation being so right that it does not need to convince others by force that it is right.' The rousing ovation given his remarks seemed to indicate that Philadelphians agreed with his views.

Charles made eye contact, but, before he could say anything, Albert Bauer said, 'I expect you are as relieved to read that as I was.'

'I wish he'd put it in plain English, but yes, I'm relieved. Hopefully that will dampen the enthusiasm for war.'

A few weeks later, Alf Manin caught up with him as they arrived for work. Charles wasn't sure if he detected a level of excitement or foreboding in his friend. 'We've joined the war on the Allied side.'

The look on Charles's face made his feelings clear. 'Well, I don't see that as anything to be pleased about.'

'Me neither. My brother and my cousins will be fighting the Austrians before long. Imagine the might of the Austro-Hungarian Empire? And what if we are being defeated? Could I sit here and watch from a distance? I don't think so.'

Charles decided that Alf might have a different view if he had a wife and child to consider but kept that to himself. Instead he said, 'At least your country decided at last to join the right side, but anyway, even if you wanted to enlist you couldn't get to Italy with German U-boats on the prowl.'

The time-clock meant that further discussion had to be postponed.

Charles continued to follow the news coverage of the war with avid interest but without any fear of personal impact or involvement. He kept telling himself that it was on the other side of the Atlantic and had nothing to do with him.

The exams were held on four evenings in the first and second week of June 1915. Alice asked each evening about how he fared. She knew how much work he had done, the many hours of study each evening and at weekends, so she was confident of his success. Her enquiries were merely to show support and encouragement.

In early August 1915, Charles was dismayed to read that Warsaw, part of Russian Poland, had been captured by the Germans. He regarded both, as well as the Austrian Empire, as unwelcome occupying forces in his country. He knew that Poles were being conscripted by all three powers as well as by Poland, or what was left of it. Soon after, he read that the Russian army, after initial successes, had suffered heavy casualties in Galicia and in other parts of Poland and was now in retreat. Although Silesia had not been specifically mentioned, he feared it soon could be, because the war was now immediately across the border to the south and south-east.

Charles worried that his brother Stefan and his father, Stefan senior, if he was still alive, could soon be in a war zone and the devastation that would cause. He assumed his brother would be beyond the age of active service in any army, but he could be forced to abandon his small farm and flee. And to where? Charles hadn't been in touch since he and Leo left Poland in 1891, twenty-four years earlier. He couldn't risk being found by Irena Malinowska or by her family who would be seeking retribution. His resolve was now tested by the plight his brother, and possibly his father, could be facing.

He said nothing to Alice because he knew she would argue he should first look after his brother nearer home. For three years he had resisted any contact with Leo for fear of jeopardising his carefully built career and place in society. Now, he thought, if I try to help Stefan, will I have to relent and also contact Leo? He really wanted to help but wondered if the postal system would still function and if maybe he would be wasting his time and effort. How do I avoid stirring up my troublesome past? How can I not disclose my address or my family details and what do I say about Leo? What can I say to Stefan that would help and how do I explain my silence for so long?

He wrestled with this for the next few days and decided to draft a letter to Stefan which he hoped would help clarify his mind on the best way forward. He composed several drafts in his head and a few on paper and finally decided on the following:

Return Address: Mr Charles Novak, General Delivery, Philadelphia, United States of America.

Dear brother,

I am embarrassed that it has taken a war to make me write to you after all this time. First, I hope this letter finds you well and in good spirits, and dare I ask about our dear father? Hopefully he has reached and enjoyed his seventy-second birthday.

Leo and I continued to work as miners when we got to America. I changed my job completely and thankfully have never been out of work. Leo has not done as well and is currently ill in hospital.

When I read that Warsaw had been captured by the Germans I worried that your area could become a war zone or be overrun by attacking or retreating armies. So I want you to know that if you want to come to America when the situation allows, I will do everything in my power to help you, our father, and your family, if you now have a family.

I expect to move to new accommodation soon, so in the meantime please use the above temporary address.

Again I apologise and ask your forgiveness for my neglect, but I hope my offer of help, however late, will be some consolation for you in this most difficult time.

Your loving brother,

Karol (Charles)

His difficulty in translating the letter into Polish surprised him. My God, I've nearly lost my native tongue. He posted the letter on his way to work.

In late August, word spread around the staff in Wanamaker's that examination results were contained in pay packets. Charles was delighted to read 'Graduated with Distinction'. He wanted

Alice to share in the good news so he resealed the envelope and when he got home made a great show of tearing it open with words of confident speculation. He handed her the letter, and she jumped into his arms, covered his face with kisses as she said, 'Charles, I'm so proud of you, my love.'

He then produced a bottle of wine and a bottle of soda which he had purchased on the way home. Andrew, still only three, shared the excitement without knowing or caring about the reason. Soda was always welcome and maybe ice cream might follow.

When Andrew had gone to bed, they talked about their good fortune and what the future might hold. Charles expressed optimism about his career prospects, and they spoke about a choice of school for Andrew. Being practising Catholics, they would want him educated in their parish school. They knew from their friends that the Catholic school was of a much higher quality than the public school, and, while they weren't happy to pay school fees as well as state taxes, they decided it was worth the sacrifice.

Alice then widened her eyes, smiled and said, 'Could we go back to Cape May for a second honeymoon? It's been seven years, can you believe it?'

'Sure, why not?'

'In the meantime' – Alice whispered to hide her boldness – 'let's have an early night to continue the celebrations.'

32

On a very wet Sunday afternoon, Tommy resumed his search of the Census, hoping it would tell him more about Leo and his family, if he had one. He assumed he had lived in Philadelphia, though Reading was also a possibility. He opened the results from the 1910 Census, two years before Leo's attempt to shoot the bishop, and input the information used previously on name, age, location and country of birth and clicked 'Search'.

A list of possible matches emerged and by referring to 'View Image' for each one he was satisfied he had found his man. The handwritten details showed that Leo, aged forty, was the head of the household and married to Francesca. The designation M2 after her name indicated that this was her second marriage. Under 'years married', a zero was written, indicating that they had been married for less than one year. Francesca's surname was not stated. Her birthplace was given as Philadelphia and her parents' as Italy. Poland was the birthplace listed for Leo and for his parents. The only other occupant of their rented apartment was Gemma, aged five, described as a stepdaughter to the head of the household, and her surname was stated as 'Baudo'.

'Wow, this is amazing. So Leo married Francesca Baudo, either a widow or a divorcee, with a young daughter.' Tommy noted that the Census described Leo as a railway porter. I wonder when he quit being a miner. He drafted an email to Anna on what he had found and added,

Leo married a little more than two years before he attempted to shoot the bishop and likely only two or three years after Francesca had become a widow or a divorcee (a very eventful and traumatic few years).

When Leo was discharged from Webster House, did Francesca or Gemma offer him a home to go to? Since he remained on as an employee, it seems unlikely. Unwanted, unloved?

Critically we now have information to be included in your online family tree. We have to hope that one of the current Baudo generation will contact you and that, unlike your uncles, he or she will have information on Leo to give you.

Amazing what can be found out when you know where to look, isn't it?

Anna replied the next day.

Yes, it's truly amazing. My parents now regard you as a hero. Before you get too conceited, what about the police files? You see, I'm a real slave-driver! It seems that everything we learn about Leo is sad and depressing. I would like to think that it was his preference to remain in Webster House, in his own little world, and not because he had no place else to go.

I've already updated our family tree, so hopefully somebody out there will see it and contact me.

You're my hero too!

Talk soon.

Tommy answered straight away.

I see it's a case of much wanting more. All I know is that police files won't be found in the Census. Anyway, so far, so good. I'll do my best.'

33

When Anna entered the kitchen at around eight, her dad immediately glanced in her direction, saying, 'Tommy has worked wonders. We would never have found the information on Leo and Francesca and her daughter. You know, I still find it difficult to understand why he wants to continue helping with the research. He has to be aware of the potential damage to the bishop's reputation.'

'I asked him that very question when we started.'

'And?'

'He said he wanted to get justice for Leo and if information was found that would be embarrassing for the bishop he would discuss how to deal with it at that time.'

'Remarkable. You're lucky to have found him on the web.'

'Yes, I am.' Anna reflected on another reason for enjoying the contact that her father would not have expected. She added, 'Let's hope he can find something positive, something pleasant in Leo's life, even if it is bad for the bishop.'

* * *

Anna met Martha on Saturday morning at the Promenade Shops at Saucon Valley on Center Valley Parkway. Martha couldn't wait to get the low-down on Tommy Walsh, so coffee first, shopping later. 'OK, so tell me. What's he like?'

'Who?'

'Ah, come on, you know who, your mystery man in Ireland of course.'

'Well, he's a fantastic researcher.'

'I'm more interested in the physical than the historical.'

'Well, he's much younger than I expected – about twenty-five or so.'

'Perfect.'

'You must remember that this is all about research on my family.'

'Yeah, yeah, but who knows what else might happen. What else did you find out about him?'

'He's a high-school business teacher, and he plays Gaelic football.'

'There you go. You have plenty of shared interests. Next time ask him about the football. Now describe him as if he was a missing person.'

Anna laughed and said, 'He was sitting at his desk so I can't tell his height, but he has broad shoulders, thick sandy hair and piercing blue eyes.'

'So what's his most attractive feature?'

'He has a beautiful smile. It kinda lights up his face.'

'This sounds very promising. It's the kind of research I like doing. So, when am I going to meet this smiling, sandy-haired Irishman?'

'Maybe never. This research could be over soon.'

'Anna, you don't convince me.'

'Look, he's someone on a computer screen. You might as well be asking me about Damian Lewis, you know, the guy in Homeland.'

'So he looks like him, does he?'

Anna took a last sip of coffee as she thought about the question. 'Well, I suppose, a bit.'

'But Damian Lewis is not contacting you one on one.'

Anna had to concede, and they laughed as the subject changed to shopping.

'Come on,' Martha said. 'Help me to get something nice to wear for Thanksgiving. I hope I haven't waited too long.'

* * *

Barbara arrived from Philly at about seven and immediately set to work with her mother and Anna in the kitchen. A sort of Thanksgiving routine had been established over the years with Katherine doing the cooking, Barbara helping to prepare the food, Anna setting the table and assembling the pre-dinner drinks and the wines. Dad set up beds for the guests, cut logs for the fire to last at least a week and pitched in when requested.

Mid-morning on Thanksgiving Day, Uncle Adam, his wife Karen and Christopher, the youngest of their three children, arrived and were brought immediately to the den. They all sat around the fire to catch up on family news and the latest gossip. Their two older children had flown the nest and were celebrating with their own families: Emma in New York and Andrew in Chicago. Over coffee, Anna updated the visitors on the latest developments in the family research.

Christopher, who was hearing much of this for the first time, asked, 'How did you manage to piece together all this information which has been hidden for so many years?' Anna explained how she had made contact with Tommy Walsh in Ireland whose family tree included Bishop Walsh. 'So, have I got this right? The research shows the bishop in a bad light, and if further research is good for Leo it will likely be bad for the bishop?'

Peter replied, 'Yes, that's about it, and only for the help Anna received from Tommy we would never have got this far.'

The conversation then returned to general topics. Anna and Christopher shared experiences about college life. Barbara and Adam talked about living in rough neighbourhoods in Philly and being required at work to achieve more with fewer resources. When Karen offered to help with the chores, Katherine took the opportunity to tell her guests, 'The turkey is ready to go in the oven for dinner about seven. Lunch will be buffet, and Karen will help anyone who needs it. Adam and Karen are in the guest room as usual, Barbara will share Anna's room – I'll let them fight about who gets the cot – and Christopher, I'm sorry, but you are here on a cot tonight. Now please everyone relax and make yourselves at home.'

Dinner was served in the living room with the formal dining table at one end and a blazing log fire at the other. Katherine was pleased with the festive feeling of the room, enhanced by the smell of burning wood and cooked turkey. Karen was so impressed with Anna's work in setting the table that she insisted on taking a photograph.

In offering grace before the meal, Peter gave thanks for the health and many blessings enjoyed by those around the table and by all other family members, and he asked that they remember those less fortunate, those helping others on that day and those serving the country in foreign parts especially in Afghanistan.

Adam then said, 'I would just like to give thanks that Anna and Tommy Walsh have been inspired to find out so much about Leo.'

Karen proposed a toast to the host family. Plates and dishes were passed to and fro across the table in a marvel of avoided accidents and wine, and conversation flowed.

When the table was being cleared for the serving of the pumpkin pie, Adam suggested that the men should volunteer to do the dishes and all that went with it. The women expressed their approval by a loud cheer. Coffee and other drinks were served by the fire. There was unanimous approval to have a TV-free evening, and the chat went on until an unusually late hour.

34

Philadelphia, 1915

Leo had become adept at picking up bits of information from overheard conversations among the male nurses or the hospital attendants. Because I don't talk, they think I don't hear. Still confined for most of each day, he had very little contact with other patients. Even when he had his twice-daily chaperoned fifteen minutes in the exercise yard, he was isolated from others. He knew he was not the most sociable, but he missed the company of others. One or two people to talk to would be nice.

The rumour machine was well oiled, and each story seemed more far-fetched than the one before. The latest was that the hospital was closing and everybody was to move to a new location. He gave this little thought.

When Nurse Bradshaw came to his room, he surprised Leo by confirming what had been rumoured. 'I have good news. In a few months you'll be moving to a new facility with most of the other patients. I'm glad for you. I think you will be much happier there.'

At last a rumour has turned out to be true, Leo thought, but he was wary about what it would mean for him.

'It's in the country, away from the city – much healthier for everyone.' The nurse allowed time for Leo's usual silence and then added, 'This new place, Webster House, it's named after its original owner, Joshua Webster. He and other wealthy men are financing this new hospital. It will be what is called a "not for profit foundation".'

Leo liked what he heard, but it was too full of the unknown to allow him to comment. He just said, 'Are you going there too?'

'Yes, I am.'

'Good. That's good.'

As the everyday sounds of distress reduced, Leo knew that the move to the new location had commenced. When he was the only one using the exercise yard, he reckoned he would soon be leaving. He wondered why he was one of the last to go.

In early April 1915, he was brought through the length of the building to get to the departure point. He had known from the sounds, the smells and the rare sight of other patients that he had been fortunate to have remained separated. Though the place was now empty, what he witnessed on his way frightened him to the core. The filth, the stinking rooms, raw sewage, rags of clothes and threadbare blankets. It was so much worse than he ever could have imagined. To live like this would be like the worst nightmare ever, and, God knows, I've had many to choose from.

Frightening images from his childhood floated in and out of his mind: the epidemics, the stories about witches and devils and, later, the periodic threats of conscription that eventually forced him to flee and the crippling terror of the mines. All competed with the present as if to remind him that he had been frightened before and got over it, giving him some solace.

My God, I'm glad I was too sick to have experienced this hell hole. How could people be made to suffer for years?

He hurried to get away as fast as he could, hoping he would never witness anything like that again. Then he began to worry about what he faced in his new location. He relaxed when he was seated in the horse-drawn carriage with two other patients and an attendant. He had missed seeing the sky and only recently had snatches of time in the open air so he hugely enjoyed the journey through the countryside.

Oh, how beautiful, he thought, as he went through the gates of Webster House and along the tree-lined avenue to a very large house with some new buildings attached and others located nearby. It's like I've been invited by the landlord to be his house guest.

As 1915 progressed, Leo was allowed out of his room to move around the hospital, but only with an attendant. He continued to participate in irregular sessions with Mr Bradshaw or with other staff. He no longer relied on silence as his comfort. Little by little he got used to conversations with other patients at mealtimes and during group activities.

Near the year end, he was being escorted to the dining room for lunch when suddenly he became very agitated, gulping air, with words stuck in his mouth. He then roared, 'It's him! It's him! Jesus, yes, it's him!'

He jumped forward away from the attendant and ran towards a young priest who had just come from the dining room and was walking towards him. When the attendant grabbed Leo, he struggled in a bad-tempered way and shouted, 'It's him I tell you. He ruined my life! Let me go, let me go.'

The priest for a moment just stared, seemingly frozen on the spot, then abruptly quickened his pace and, looking straight ahead, went past Leo, headed for the reception area and left the building.

The next day, at an emergency case conference, Leo's attendant was asked to report on what he had witnessed and heard.

'Had you ever seen the priest in the hospital previously?' Dr Rydell asked.

'No, and as far as I know, neither had Mr Novak. I questioned him, but he wouldn't answer so I have no idea why he became so agitated and so aggressive.'

Nurse Bradshaw, who probably knew Leo better than anyone, expressed surprise. 'Leo never had any difficulty with the Roman Catholic priest who visited regularly in the state hospital. He was always polite and deferential in his own quiet way. Why the change?'

The doctor asked the attendant, 'Do you know anything about the priest?'

'His name is Father Bruno Favaloro. I understand he accompanied one of his parishioners who visited a relative.'

'Do you know the name of his parish?'

'No, but I believe it is located on the far side of the city.'

Dr Rydell wrote to the archbishop's secretary, describing the reaction of his patient, Leo Novak, on seeing Father Favaloro when he recently visited the hospital with one of his parishioners. He then added, 'It could be of great assistance, in treating Mr Novak, to know what could have happened in the past between him and Father Favaloro, to now cause such a reaction. Any light you can throw on this would be most appreciated.'

A reply arrived three weeks later. 'I regret I am unable to offer any assistance in this matter. I have questioned Father Favaloro, and he is not aware of the incident reported by you and has no recollection of ever meeting a Mr Novak in the past.'

Since Leo was now free to move around the hospital, his next counselling session with Nurse Bradshaw was held in the administrative area and not in his room as usual. They sat around a circular table in the centre of a small conference room. After initial pleasantries to which Leo did not reply, Nurse Bradshaw outlined the letter to the archbishop's secretary regarding Father Favaloro and then quoted the reply.

'So that's his name then. I'd be surprised if the letter had said anything else,' was Leo's grumpy reply.

'Tell me why you feel that way?'

Leo's silence was what the nurse had come to expect. He was surprised when Leo asked, 'Are there any children as patients in this hospital?'

When the reply was in the negative, he added, 'Well, no more need be said then.'

The nurse tried to get Leo to elaborate on his answer or to open up on the cause or even the background to his illness. 'As I've said to you before, it's very difficult for us to help you if you don't confide in us.'

Silence.

He could have told Leo that inquiries about him with the police were fruitless. All he had learned was that Leo had been arrested after his escape from detention. He decided that disclosing this would not be helpful. After waiting in vain for Leo to respond, he said, 'I understand you are very perturbed about the war in Europe. Is that the case?'

'Yes, my brother lives there. I've lost touch with him, and I don't know if my father is alive or dead.'

'Tell me about your brother.'

'He owns a small farm in Silesia, now part of Germany, so he could be in great danger.'

'So you grew up on a farm?'

'Yes, a very small holding. We had two cows, and we sold the milk we didn't need.'

'How many in the family?'

'I hardly remember my mother. She died when I was very

young, and my sister died when she was seven, so it was just men in the house: my father, my two brothers and me.'

Nurse Bradshaw then raised what he knew to be a difficult subject. 'Your brother who lives here in Philadelphia, he has not been in contact?'

'No.'

He could see that Leo was visibly upset but felt he had to ask, 'Should you write to him asking him to visit you?'

'He and my wife must know where I am, but neither has bothered to come here.'

'Why do you think that is?'

Leo tensed, sat upright in the chair, as if he was about to flee. Then his shoulders sagged, he looked towards the floor and said, 'They're ashamed of me.'

Touched by Leo's response and determined to do everything possible to help him, Nurse Bradshaw said, 'Will I write to your brother asking him to visit you?'

'A waste of your time.'

'Well that's unfortunate. Current best practice now requires family members to take an active role in the treatment of patients. Anyway, back to farming. Did you work on the farm?'

Leo was relieved by the change of topic. 'Of course, everybody had to lend a hand, even when I worked in the mine.'

'Would you have liked to have been a farmer?'

'Yes. But Stefan was the eldest so that settled that.'

'Well, we don't have a farm here but we have several acres of lawns, trees and shrubs, and we have a large kitchen garden. Would you like to help out with that, just as you did in Silesia?'

Leo's face brightened at the thought of the freedom to move around the beautiful grounds and the opportunity to earn his keep. 'Yes, please, yes. Oh, thank you.' He was close to tears.

Leo was one of three patients selected to work in the hospital grounds. He had the advantage of having a farming background. He also had a hunger to learn everything there was to know about trees, shrubs and plants and was fortunate to have an able teacher. John Lee had been head gardener for fifteen years and had remained in that role at the request of Mr Webster when he donated the property.

Leo imagined himself back on the family farm, and his recovery gained momentum. For the first time in many years he had begun to think about the future rather than the past.

35

Tommy arrived home for lunch. As he entered the hall, he could tell that bacon and cabbage was on the menu. Mrs Duggan varied the menu, but he could tell each time by smell what she had cooked that day. How come, he thought, that the smell of cabbage and fish always lingers longer?

As he sat at the kitchen table, his dad said, 'That Skype system is a wonderful invention. I've never seen your bedroom so tidy, and I notice that you brush your hair and spruce yourself up before Anna appears on screen.'

'Well, one has to keep up appearances, doesn't one?' Tommy replied in an exaggerated English accent. 'The real value is that it costs nothing.'

'I think there's more to it than that,' Frank said jokingly. 'By the way, when am I going to be introduced to Anna?'

This took Tommy by surprise. 'This is just boring research stuff,' he said, but he knew his father was not convinced. As Tommy reached across to the worktop for the butter dish, Frank referred to previous conversations about taking over the running of the business.

Tommy tried to evade the issue. 'I found out what's going on with the missing stock, Dad. I had a lot of digging to do.'

'So, what's the story?'

'Remember when we put in the computer system we did a total stocktaking? So I went back to that as a starting point and then examined the stock purchases and sales up to last month. This suggests to me that the problem is not stock leaving the shop without payment, it's stock not being delivered to the shop in the first place.'

'So you think one of our wholesalers is cheating us?'

'It looks that way, and the culprit seems to be one of the suppliers of gardening equipment – spades, rakes, hedge clippers, tie-backs, gardening gloves and that sort of thing.'

'My God, I wonder which one?'

'How many are there?'

'Three, I think. Yes, three.'

'You'll have to wait until you check the next delivery from each one. If I'm proved right, I'll calculate the estimated loss over time.'

'Thanks for that, Tommy. That work demonstrates how well qualified you are to run this business.'

Tommy decided that he would have to face the music. 'Well, I have given that more thought, but I haven't changed my mind. I tried to find another solution, and I have a suggestion to make.'

'Oh, I'm not sure I'm going to like this, but fire ahead.'

'I have discussed the problem with Mary, and she has shown some interest. It was not a detailed conversation, and we didn't arrive at any conclusion.'

Frank frowned and said, 'What do you mean, shown some interest?'

'Before you think I have jumped the gun or made suggestions I had no authority to make, I emphasised that I had no idea what other options, if any, you might be pursuing. I didn't know of your marriage plans at that time. Anyway, I made it clear that I couldn't speak for you.'

'Good. So how did she react?'

'It was obvious she had never seen herself taking over from you and apparently had assumed that I would relent. As you know, she's not tied to Dublin job-wise, and I posed the possibility that Kevin could get a transfer back to these parts.'

'I have to confess that I never thought about this either. I assumed her life was now in Dublin or wherever Kevin's job took them.'

'Anyway, she said she would have a chat with Kevin, and we left it at that.'

'So, where do I go from here?'

'Well, if you think the idea has merit, maybe you should take the initiative.'

'Yes, I will, and if we make progress I'll talk to my solicitor and accountant.'

Tommy, feeling relieved, started to say something when Frank added, 'And if we don't, it will be back to you, and I will want to hear a positive response.' He then rose from the chair and headed down to the shop.

* * *

Anna and Martha arrived together in a crowded Crofton Inn. As they searched for seats, Martha said, 'It's high time you had a night out and got away from the studies and all that research about dead people. It's time to live a little.'

'Thanks Martha. I need cheering up a bit.'

'More than a bit, Anna, more than a bit. That story you told me about events all those years ago would depress a saint. Anyway, to more positive things: how's Tommy?'

'You make it sound like we're dating or something.'

'Well, you are seeing a lot of each other.'

'Technically yes,' Anna said, 'but only technically,' and they both laughed at the distinction.

'It's still early,' Martha said, not willing to give up. 'What about that video clip on Gaelic football? Now there's a game for real men. Here's an idea. Invite Tommy over to give a demonstration on the game to one of our classes. Better still, invite the whole team over – why should you have all the fun?'

Their laughter turned heads of customers close by. Behind the fun, Anna warmed to the possibility of actually meeting Tommy but calculated the chance at zero.

The piano player was encouraging the customers to come to the microphone to entertain the crowd before the band arrived on stage. Martha saw an opportunity to get Anna to let her hair down, and, when she resisted, Martha went to the stage, introduced Anna and called for an encouraging round of applause.

Now that she had been ambushed, Anna felt she couldn't back out so she forced herself to quickly think of a song that the crowd would sing along with and decided on 'Stand by Your Man'. She sang of how difficult romantic relationships can be but how love conquers all. When she got to the chorus exhorting 'stand by your man', a few began to join in. When it was repeated, and encouraged by Martha, the entire crowd were on their feet, singing as if it was an anthem.

She finished to loud drumming on tabletops and shouts of 'More! More!' Anna waved her arms in the air, gave an exaggerated bow and returned to her seat. When the noise died down, Martha heard a guy behind her say, 'I know it's an oldie, but I heard an amazing version of it recently by the Dixie Chicks. Anna should audition for them.'

'You were awesome, Anna!' Martha said, and before Anna could reply, she added, 'Did you think of Josh while you sang?'

'No way. I tried standing by him, remember?'

'What about Tommy, then?'

'Don't be silly. Well, maybe a bit. And now from the romantic to the tragic: have you seen Josh around lately?'

'No, though Jane said she saw a couple of photos on Facebook.'

Martha was reluctant to give details, but when Anna pressed her, she added, 'Well, he seemed to be enjoying himself. In one photo he was with his drinking buddies, and in the other with a group of women who Jane described as "not our type".'

'Wherever he is, I hope he is getting his life in order. Why is Jane not here?'

Martha, lifting her eyes upwards, said, 'Oh, she's probably studying as usual,' but Anna knew that Martha was putting in the hours as well, and she worried about paying a price for the time she was spending on family research.

36

Philadelphia, 1915

In late August, Alice opened an envelope.

INVITATION

The Faculty of the John Wanamaker Commercial Institute
invites:

Alice Novak and her parents to a Graduation Ceremony

In the Wanamaker Department Store

On September 15, 1915

At 7.30 p.m.

Mr John Wanamaker will preside at this event.

Please show this invitation on arrival.

Traffic was confined to a single lane outside Wanamaker's Department Store to make room for the staff military band of seventy-five pieces and the number of automobiles and carriages dropping guests for the graduation ceremony. Alice and her parents presented their invitation at the door and were escorted through the building by a member of staff. The sound of the military band was replaced by the giant organ located on a mezzanine floor above the arches that stretched across in front of them and under which they passed with all the other invitees.

Alice's mother glanced upwards at the ceiling five floors above them. 'It's like a cathedral of commerce, isn't it?'

When they passed the large statue of an eagle, Arnold Symanski turned to his wife, saying, 'Darling, how many times have we said over the years, "Meet you at the eagle?"' Just before they reached the gymnasium where the ceremony was to be held, they stopped at the large glass doors to the staff swimming pool which they had heard about but had never seen and marvelled at the size and grandeur of such a facility for staff.

Eva put her arm around her daughter's shoulder and said, 'Oh my, do you think Charles could get me a job here?'

'Why don't you ask him, mother?'

All three laughed as they walked on.

The gymnasium was transformed into a festival hall with red, white and blue decorating the podium and the walls. When all the guests were shown to their reserved seats, they were welcomed by the master of ceremonies who then outlined the programme for the evening. He introduced Mr Wanamaker who walked to the centre of the podium. Dressed in black, he was tall, erect and sprightly for his seventy-seven years. He saluted his guests and then sat centre stage in an ornate chair among the faculty members.

When the applause died down, the graduates, some seventy in number, entered from the main doors and walked in single file on each side of the room to the seats in the front rows. Charles smiled and gave a low-key wave as he passed.

Most of the graduates were conferred with business degrees. A few were awarded a degree in French or German, some with an ambition to represent the company purchasing goods in Europe, others merely for the love of the language or perhaps to honour their parents. After each student was awarded and applauded and other formalities concluded, the MC invited everybody to an evening supper in the staff dining room. There the guests took their places while the graduates circulated around the room congratulating each other loudly in a wide range of accents, creating a wonderful aura of celebration.

When the meal was over, Alice excused herself and went to the ladies room. When returning, she noticed that her seat had been taken by a young attractive dark-haired woman. The position of her chair relative to Charles drew her attention. The chairs were side by side but facing in opposite directions. Just like a love seat, she felt. When the woman spotted Alice, she left abruptly.

'Who was that?' Alice asked as she moved her chair around.

'She's the sister of my Italian friend who also graduated tonight,' Charles replied in a matter-of-fact sort of way. 'Look, there he is.' He pointed to a group of colleagues at the far side of the dining room.

'She left in a great hurry, didn't she? Who is she?'

'Anetta Manin.'

'Manin? That doesn't sound Italian.'

'Well, it is, from near the Austrian border, I think.'

Alice wondered and worried but was afraid to pursue the matter because of what she might learn.

Her father, who was standing nearby talking to one of the faculty who was also a senior manager in the store, tried to interpret what he had just witnessed. With previous worrying signs running through his mind, he decided he would make discreet inquiries.

The year 1916 started very well for the Novak family with the announcement that Charles had been promoted to manager of the men's department to replace his retiring colleague. Alice and Charles discussed the improvements in their lifestyle that the additional income would provide. Alice recited a long list of labour-saving devices they should purchase.

'Hold on,' Charles said. 'I haven't earned one cent more yet. Let's save first, OK?'

'Don't spoil my fun, darling.'

He decided not to mention the possibility of moving to a larger house which had been on his mind assuming the promotion came through.

Andrew ran towards his dad who scooped him up in his arms and twirled him around the kitchen. 'How is my little man today?'

'Good, Dada, good, good.'

This was the established routine for the evenings he arrived home from work before Andrew's bedtime.

Alice, happy for both of them, said, 'Dinner will be ready in a few minutes.' Pointing towards the table, she added, 'Have a look at that article in today's paper.'

The report described the closure of the South West Philadelphia Psychiatric Hospital in the previous year and the transfer of patients to a new privately funded facility. Just as Charles finished reading, Alice said, 'It shows how awful the place must have been for Leo. We can only hope that the new place will be very different.'

'I'm happy for him and all the other patients. He deserves the best.'

'As you've read, it's now called Webster House and has new, hopefully more enlightened management.' Charles knew what was coming next. 'Isn't it a good time to contact the new doctors there? It would mean a double boost for Leo.'

Charles wondered if he should mention his letter to Stefan but decided it would only increase the pressure on him.

'You don't seem to realise the implications of what you're

suggesting. I love my brother and have always looked out for him, encouraged him. Insanity is bad enough, but attempting to shoot a bishop?' He folded the newspaper, tossed it to the far end of the table and then added, 'Just think of the damage he could do to my career, to our family. I'll not take that risk. Please don't raise it again.' The silence that followed was broken by Andrew's plea for attention.

Charles continued to read about the war and to discuss the major events with his work colleagues. Most of the news was about the Western Front, but he knew that though his homeland and neighbouring areas did not regularly make the headlines they continued to suffer. It couldn't be otherwise, he thought, with Germany, Russian Poland and the Austro-Hungarian Empire all sharing borders.

Despite the escalation of the war and the awful casualties reported, he became more confident that America would continue to remain neutral. He saw time being on his side. The longer America stayed out of the war, the nearer he would get to the upper age limit for conscription. At forty-two, I may have reached that point already, he thought. Having avoided conscription in Poland, he was confident he could do the same again.

When President Wilson was re-elected, Charles suggested to Alice that it was because he had kept America out of the war. He added, 'That fellow, former President Roosevelt, made my blood boil. Imagine suggesting that he would raise a volunteer division to join the war? You may be sure that men like him would not be on the front line. He should mind his own business and not be stirring up trouble.'

'I think he was just looking for notice,' Alice replied. 'If you get accustomed to being in the limelight, it must be difficult to remain in the shadow. Anyway, that's what politicians do: they make life difficult for their political opponents.'

In 1917, when the war entered its fourth year, the British decoded a telegram in which Germany invited Mexico to join the war against the United States, a war that Germany would finance with a promise to return Texas, New Mexico and Arizona to Mexico. The content of the telegram was made public to the American people, changing public opinion which had strongly favoured neutrality.

Albert Bauer sought out Charles at work. 'The last time I spoke to you was to agree with your view that the sinking of the Lusitania did not justify America going to war. I had hoped then that by avoiding further escalation Germany might come to its senses and reverse its policies. Well, my view has certainly now changed. Inviting Mexico to enter the war cannot be tolerated.'

Charles reflected briefly and then said, 'Thanks for speaking your mind on this. Yeah, it looks like a major turning point. I regret that it has come to this, though I have to admit that if America enters the war it will likely be good for Poland.'

Albert replied, 'I'm sure you know the expression, "Never poke a bear with a stick in the ass." Well, that's what Germany has now done.'

Charles couldn't hide a smile. 'Yeah, it certainly looks like that,' he said, not wanting to be too critical.

'As a German American I am sad for both countries, especially Germany, because this will inevitably lead to its destruction. It's only a matter of time.'

'Have you family in Germany?'

'I was born here, but yeah, my uncle, two aunts and several cousins are there. I don't know if the cousins are directly involved. How about you?'

'My brother is a farmer in Silesia, probably too old to be conscripted.'

Albert replied, 'We have something in common then, even if our families in Europe support opposing sides.'

They then shook hands as an expression of mutual understanding.

Shortly after this, seven US merchant ships were sunk by German submarines. Charles knew what to expect. In late March, Germany sank four more US merchant ships, and on 2 April President Wilson appeared before Congress and called for a declaration of war on Germany. This was endorsed by the Senate and the House of Representatives, and on 6 April America formally entered the war.

The Selective Service Act 1917, which introduced conscription, was passed in June. Charles was relieved that the draft established a liability for military service of all male citizens between twenty-one and thirty-one years of age. However, when the upper age limit was later changed to forty-five, he wished he could claim conscientious objection just like members of the Amish, Mennonites, Quakers or the Church of the Brethren. Charles identified with Class Two of five draft categories. It stated: 'Temporarily deferred, but available for military service: Married registrants with dependent spouse and/or dependent children under sixteen with sufficient family income if drafted.'

Still, he thought, at the end of this year I'll be forty-four so with a bit of luck I could be forty-five by the time they catch up with us old guys. Even if that did not happen, he was confident that age and business experience would divert him to a non-combatant role.

All the talk at work was about the preparation for war. 'Did you read about the plans for the shipyards?' Alf Manin asked. When nobody replied, he added, 'It's planned to be the largest in the world, and it is estimated that, at its peak, a new ship will be launched every four working days. How about that?'

Charles said, 'I heard that the Ford Motor Company here in

Philadelphia is to switch to making steel helmets for the entire US army. Could that be true?'

John O'Brien, who had recently started to work as a porter, as Charles had done almost twenty years previously, answered, 'Yes, I heard that too. Amazing isn't it?'

Albert Bauer said, without any degree of enthusiasm, 'Well, nobody will be out of work, and that's a fact.' All his colleagues knew that Albert would be feeling the brunt of the anti-German hysteria and intolerance that was sweeping the city.

What was left unsaid was that with all this emergency employment at home, they, and men like them in regular jobs, were more likely to be drafted.

37

Jimmy Walker was pleased with the Clondore Christmas lights. They were his doing really. It was his suggestion, made at a meeting of the Clondore Business Association in late summer, that three different designs and colours be used to match the town's streetscape. He had often wondered how Clondore managed to avoid the one long street that was a feature of small Irish towns. Now he was delighted that the S-shaped main artery of the town, comprising Barrack Street, O'Connell Street and Davitt Street, was full of colour, with each street having a different but complementary display. The whole effect was enhanced, he felt, by the cold crispy air.

I didn't make many suggestions over the years, but I'm proud of this one.

Many shops had window displays and a mesh of tiny white lights above or around their fascia boards. Walsh's DIY and Hardware sported Christmas decorations in and around the shop and yard. Christmas trees, real and artificial, Christmas lights and decorations, poinsettias and potted arrangements of other shrubs, and seasonally packaged glass and tableware were on sale. Frank had thought of asking Orla to help on her days off but felt that might be rushing things and decided to wait until the following year.

Jimmy stopped at Emma's Hair and Beauty Salon and thought of the Christmas window display in what had been O'Rourke's Stationery and Fancy Goods when he was a boy. He reflected on the time he spent there on his way to and from school trying to select what he would put in his letter to Santa. He recalled not wanting to be greedy but at the same time taking advantage of what he felt Santa could afford, which would be much more than he could ever ask of his mother. Oh, he thought, the innocence of it all.

Jimmy felt good about the way things turned out for Frank. He had the fondest memories of Liz and the way she treated him when she started working in the business as a new bride in 1981.

I learned a lot from her too, the way she dealt with problems. How clever she was when a customer asked for her help to transport a Christmas cake that had very intricate icing, like a spider's web. She got me to cut a piece of timber larger than the base of the cake and to drive a six-inch nail up through its centre. She just lowered the cake on the nail – problem solved.

He also remembered the sad time around her illness and death and the impact that had on Frank, how long it had taken him to come to terms with his loss, when the bottle had become his secret friend. He recalled the number of times he had decided that he should intervene to make Frank confront his problems and his demons and the relief he had felt when he realised that this was no longer necessary, that Frank was recovering unaided and was all the stronger for it.

Amazing, he thought, how Tommy had taken on his mother's role of fixer of other people's problems. Observing their relationship, Tommy and Frank seemed to alternate the father's role without embarrassment to either. It's been a good year, thank God. Now if only Tommy would agree to take over the business when Frank decides to retire. Speaking of which, I'll be seventy within two years and need to make plans also.

* * *

Tommy assumed that Mary would cook Christmas dinner as usual but decided he should phone. 'Just wondering will the usual Christmas arrangements apply?'

Mary had a busy morning in the kitchen and had just finished talking to her friend, Jennifer Burke, one of her fellow members of the Garda Social Club. 'I hope so, or else I'm going to have a monster turkey for just Kevin and myself.'

'Good. I'll buy the ham then. Will Kevin have time off? When will you arrive?'

'He got lucky again, and we plan to be there on the 23rd. You just make sure the tree and the decorations are in place.'

'When will Deirdre arrive?'

'Dunno. I'd hoped you could tell me. I need her all day on Christmas Eve to help out. Will you ask her to call me?'

'I will, but why don't you text her as well so there's no room for doubt. Mary, one more thing, just be aware that Dad may, and I stress may, talk to you about the business.'

'You prompted him then?'

Tommy was relieved to hear a query and not a complaint. 'Well, when he raised the subject I repeated my answer and suggested that you just might be interested.'

'How did he react?'

'Surprised. As I told you, he'd assumed your life was in Dublin or wherever Kevin was stationed.'

'Well, at least I know what to expect. We're finding it very difficult to get to grips with this, but I suppose having a chat with Dad can only help.'

'I don't know if Dad will raise it or what he might suggest. Remember, when we spoke I knew nothing of his intention to marry Orla, and that may change things.'

'You're right. Don't forget to set an extra place at the table.'

'That would be embarrassing. Bye.'

* * *

Frank and Orla were at lunch in a hotel near Birr, a possible venue for their wedding reception.

'So, it's settled then. You'll join the family on Christmas Day?'

'I don't want to rush things. I should give your children time to get used to our marriage plans, but, yes, I would love to be there. Friends and relatives have been very kind to me at Christmas, but it has been a lonely time for me.'

Frank took her hands in his and said, 'Well, not any more.'

'I don't want to be too pushy, but shouldn't I be helping out on the day or on Christmas Eve?'

'Mary's in charge, so I suggest you give her a call. I'm sure she would welcome help. Tommy will be involved as well, which reminds me I need to talk to you about where we'll live. I know he'll be thinking about that as well and will have suggestions to make. I told you he doesn't want to take on the business, but in most things he thinks of others before himself.'

'You've major decisions to make, and you know I want to keep on my job in O'Donnell's. I just love legal work. I'd love to have been a solicitor. You mentioned that Tommy had got Mary thinking if she might take over the business, so the decision on where we will live depends on that, don't you think?'

'Yes, of course. One step at a time. I'll have a chat with Mary over the Christmas.'

Orla gave him a playful nudge, saying, 'Maybe we could live in my house, but that would be a huge comedown in the world for you.'

Frank in his happiness wondered again why he had delayed so long in asking Orla to marry him. Their relationship had evolved slowly from their shared interest in the church choir and, prior to that, the town's musical society, and they just moved from there to meeting for coffee on a Sunday morning, to occasional dinners and trips to shows in Limerick and Dublin. Why the hesitation? Since Tommy's intervention spurred him into action, he reckoned it must have been a subconscious worry that his children might be upset, might have felt betrayed in some way. And how stupid did that turn out to be?

* * *

Tommy followed up on his promise to phone Deirdre. 'Mary needs to talk to you about the usual hassle at Christmas. Will you call her? Orla will be there, so an extra effort is needed.'

'I expected to be roped in. OK, I'll call her.'

'Why is it that Mary or I always phone you, never the other way around, and why don't you phone Dad more often?'

'I know, I know, I'll make up for it. I was about to say "I promise," but that wouldn't convince you, would it?'

'No. I suspect not being in contact is down to college problems or man problems.' More likely the latter, he thought. 'But I suppose I shouldn't pry?'

'No, you shouldn't.'

'Don't talk about phoning – just do it, OK?'

'You probably won't believe this, but I was about to phone you just now. I want you to arrange for me to meet Mr Manahan.'

'He won't have time to see you before Christmas. When do you go back to Limerick?'

'Could I meet him between Christmas and New Year?'

'I'll talk to him. Any progress on your career plans?'

'I'm hoping he will point the way. See you on Christmas Eve or on the 23rd if Mary has her way.'

'Right Deirdre, see you soon then.'

38

Anna was catching up on overdue phone calls. Her sister was next on the list. 'Hi, Barbara. All your Christmas shopping done?'

'Yeah, at last. Why do we have so much hassle? I know, I know, I enjoy the end result more than anyone, but I just wish it could be less frenetic.'

'Thank God for Secret Santa. I don't have the time or the dollars to do anything else.'

'So, how's school?'

'Semester exams begin on Monday, and, as usual, I have a tonne to do. Working on the family tree has been amazing but a huge demand on my time, despite all the help I've gotten from Tommy Walsh.'

'Mom tells me that he has become a great attraction in your life.'

'Don't you start too! Martha has been giving me a hard time about him.'

'Mom brought me up to date on the fantastic research you've done. The thought struck me the other day that if Leo hadn't escaped twice from custody we might never have heard what happened to him.'

'That's interesting, and you're the only one who's said that.'

'It's too bad that our grandfather was an only child, that there are no other Novaks who could provide family information or do some of the research.'

'Yeah, I wish, and I'll bet Tommy would welcome it too.'

* * *

Tommy and Anna were chatting on Skype when Anna heard a strange voice off camera.

'I've been hearing a female voice in my son's bedroom so I thought I should check up on him.'

When Frank was in front of the computer monitor, he said, 'Hello, Anna, I'm Frank, and I have been asking Tommy to introduce me, but I've had to take the initiative.'

Anna laughed at his approach. 'Hello, Mr Walsh. I'm very pleased to meet you.'

'Call me Frank, please.'

'Oh, congratulations on your engagement – Tommy has told me all about it. I'm very happy for you.'

'Thank you, Anna, I'm on cloud nine myself. I'm also very impressed with the results from the research you've both been doing. Well done.'

'Thanks. We've just been talking about where we go from here. We Novaks really need to know if Leo was the subject of a police report.'

'Tommy and I share that objective, so I had better leave you two to progress the work. Delighted to have met you at last, Anna, and hopefully we can chat again soon – that's if Tommy doesn't now lock his door.'

Anna laughed and said, 'Bye, Mr Walsh – sorry, Frank.' Anna enjoyed the interlude and thought it a neat way to meet Tommy's dad. She could see from Tommy's smile that he enjoyed it too.

'Back to business,' Tommy said. 'I expect to be busy in the shop between now and Christmas, but then I should have time to work on the police report. In Ireland, we seem to close down for a week or more after Christmas.'

'Not so here. At most it's a one-day shutdown. Tell me more about your Christmas.'

'It'll be different this year because Orla Maguire, Dad's fiancée, will be with us for Christmas Day.'

'That's cool. Tell me about Orla. Is she a widow?'

'Oh, no. Orla never married. She is about four years younger than my dad but looks much younger than that. She works as a solicitor's clerk here in the town. They've known each other for years as members of the church choir. My two sisters and I are thrilled about their decision to marry.'

'What do your sisters do?'

'Mary, my older sister, lives in Dublin. She's married to Kevin Hayes, a policeman – or a garda, as we call them. She worked with my dad before she married and is not working right now. Deirdre is studying at a teacher-training college in Limerick. She's thinking about a career as a music teacher.'

Each answer created a further question with Tommy describing the allocation of tasks for the preparation of the Christmas dinner and the church ceremonies to mark the day. 'Now it's your turn, Anna, tell me about Christmas in Center Valley.'

Anna was enjoying the 'getting to know you' conversation, but she said, 'Love to, but not now, gotta get back to the books.'

Tommy, reluctant to end the conversation, said, 'Bye for now, Anna.'

'Talk to you soon, bye.'

When Tommy went to the kitchen, his dad said, 'Well, you kept that a secret, didn't you?'

'What do you mean?'

'You never told me how beautiful she was. Now I know why you spend so much time on Skype – and don't tell me it's all about research.'

'Yes, she's lovely, isn't she?'

'I'm trying to recall who she reminds me of, a TV or movie star. You told me she's of Polish and Irish extraction, but with her blond hair and blue eyes she could be Scandinavian.'

Tommy laughed and said, 'You don't miss much, do you?'

'You can't but be impressed by beauty, whatever your age. What will you do when the research is finished? It can't go on much longer.'

Tommy was silent for a moment. 'You could be reading my mind.'

'If you feel about her the way I suspect you do, find a reason or an excuse to visit her.'

'You're moving way too fast. For all I know she may be in a serious relationship.'

'I'm sure you'll find a way to check that out. Be bold, Tommy, be bold, just as you encouraged me to be.'

39

Philadelphia, 1917

The draft commenced in July 1917 and gathered pace when the age of eligibility was increased to forty-five. Philadelphians would serve in all branches of the armed forces with by far the largest proportion going to the army's 79th Division. This division was based in the newly created Fort Meade, situated halfway between Baltimore and Washington, DC.

Charles was surprised to see Mr Symanski striding towards him in Wanamaker's. By the look on his face he knew his father-in-law was unlikely to be intent on a purchase. Before Charles could welcome him, Mr Symanski said in a quiet but gruff manner, 'We need to talk privately.'

Taken aback, Charles said, 'Is Alice OK, and Andrew?'

'This is not about them, it's about you.'

Charles led him immediately to his small office, anxious that his colleagues would not hear whatever was to be said. When they were both seated, Mr Symanski said, 'I have been hearing disturbing tales about your relationship with a young woman, Anetta Manin, a relationship I have been told is deep and dangerous.'

'I know her. She's a sister of a colleague and friend, but I can assure you there is no question of anything improper going on.'

Mr Symanski retorted, 'I didn't come here to debate with you but to warn you. You know that any scandal of this type could put your job in jeopardy.'

Charles, knowing his father-in-law's friendship with Mr Wanamaker, knew the danger posed by this remark. 'Yes, of course, but please be assured that nothing of that kind is going on.'

Mr Symanski ignored his denial. 'I do not intend to disclose what I know to my daughter, but in the event of her finding out, do not expect any support from me. Get your house in order, or face the consequences.' With that, he stood up and left the room.

Charles hurried back to his usual position behind the counter, hoping to convey that such a brief discussion could not have been of any great importance. Who is the busybody who exposed me, and how do I get out of this one? He had been confident that the precautions he had taken had worked. He met Anetta in secluded places, and when they went to cheap hotels he had always given a false name. He was sure Anetta's friend and decoy would not have informed on her. That led him to wonder if Anetta had betrayed him, but he quickly dismissed that possibility. Experience had shown him that it was much too early in their relationship for that to happen.

The impact the rumours would have on Anetta's reputation never crossed his mind. Only now did it strike him that his work colleagues might have been reproachful about an illicit relationship with a woman more than twenty years younger than him. Alf, her brother, had introduced them, but Charles was at pains not to show any interest in his sister so as to keep him in the dark. If someone told Alf, he would certainly have blown the whistle.

Then the frightening thought struck him. Had Alice become

suspicious? He had taken care to avoid telltale marks on his shirt collars or lingering perfume odours. Each time he and Anetta met he went to a bar on his way home to explain the time delay and to have the benefit of the pervasive smell of alcohol. Could a colleague, likely a female, have warned Alice, maybe anonymously? Would she believe it? Would she act on it? Oh my God, what if I lost her? The realisation that he could pay such a price for his pleasure was a new and shattering experience.

A few days later, a possible solution came in the form of an event he had hoped to avoid. Waiting for him when he returned from work was a letter with an official look about it. Alice, anticipating bad news, stood beside him as he opened the letter and then looked over his shoulder to read.

NOTICE OF CALL AND TO APPEAR FOR PHYSICAL EXAMINATION

You are hereby notified that pursuant to the act of Congress approved May 18, 1917, you are called for military service of the United States by the Local Board from among those persons whose registration cards are within the jurisdiction of this Local Board.

The letter gave his serial number and described how any claim for exemption or discharge should be made. It instructed, 'You will report to the office of this Local Board for physical examination on August 10, 1917, at 2.00 P.M.' It then warned: 'Your attention is called to the penalties for violation or evasion of the Selective Service law, approved May 18, 1917, and of the Rules and Regulation made pursuant therein, which penalties are printed on the back hereof.'

At one point, Charles had given serious thought to the possibility of an exemption without having any fixed idea how this could be achieved. What he had previously feared he now saw as an opportunity to escape from Philadelphia for a period, away from Anetta Manin and whoever was informing on him. Anyway, he thought, I expect to be allocated some sort of desk job.

Alice, as if she was reading his mind, said, 'Darling, it's one time in my life that I would wish an illness on you – nothing too serious mind.'

'That's a possibility, but even if I'm drafted, at my age I won't be put in harm's way.'

'Let's hope so,' she answered, holding back the tears. They kissed and held each other, neither one wishing to end the moment.

Two weeks later, Charles received notification that he had passed the physical examination and that he was to report for training in Fort Meade, Maryland, on Monday of the following week. Charles felt that Maryland provided the distance and the space he needed. He gave Alice the opposite message.

* * *

On a warm evening in late September when Andrew was in bed, Alice answered a knock on her front door. An attractive young woman stood there. 'Hello, my name is Anetta Manin …'

'I know who you are. You'd better come in.'

They sat on facing easy chairs in the parlour, and an awkward silence was broken by the visitor. 'This is very difficult and embarrassing for me, but I felt I had to talk to you.'

Alice did not make any attempt to put her at ease but just stared at her with a quizzical look.

'With Charles heading for war, I felt I had to remove one worry from your mind.' Alice remained silent. 'The relationship that developed with Charles should never have happened – was not intended to happen.' When Alice did not respond, Anetta added, 'You were aware of the relationship, weren't you?'

'No, but I guessed as much.'

'Oh, perhaps then it was a mistake for me to come here, but my brother said it was common knowledge in Wanamaker's so I assumed you knew.'

Alice did not immediately respond but then said, 'You cannot expect me to be pleased that you are here.'

'No, of course not, I just want you to know that my relationship with Charles ended many weeks ago and will not be resumed when he returns.' Anetta then stood up to leave.

As Alice opened the front door, she said, 'I appreciate that you came here with the best of intentions.'

Anetta started to cry as she said, 'I envy you, Mrs Novak.' She hurried away and did not look back.

Alice stood in her hallway, then leaned against her front door as if to prevent Anetta returning. She shrieked her pain and then, worried she would wake Andrew, rushed to her parlour, fell into a chair and the tears started to flow. She cried because of what she had just been told but also for all the times she had suspected infidelity but was too scared to do anything about it. She spent many minutes just giving vent to her desolation. Then she tried to compose herself and to figure out what she should do.

Should I write to Charles? No, at least not until I know what I want to do, to say. I love him, and I know he loves me, but obviously that hasn't been enough, has it? Can our marriage be saved? I have lived with the fear that he was unfaithful. I now have to try to live with the reality.

My parents! Oh, my poor parents. They are going to be so shocked and so hurt. Maybe I should not tell them. Could they have heard the rumours? My sisters … thank God they have no experience of this, but maybe they could help me?

The fact that Charles was now in Camp Meade and heading to Europe gave her some comfort. At least now he would be removed from the temptation of female company.

His first letter home confirmed his assignment to an administrative role as he had confidently expected. 'I am now in the Quartermaster Corps thanks to my experience and managerial position in Wanamaker's. Not only will I avoid combat, but I will have the opportunity of learning new skills, new techniques, which will help me advance my career when I'm home again. Better to be born lucky than rich, as they say.'

His later letters referred to all the repetitive and boring marching, the hated drill sergeants and the non-stop rumour machine that had them about to ship out to a variety of unfamiliar European destinations.

Alice did her best to explain to Andrew why his dada would not be coming home for a while. She tried to relate to his concept of time and, above all, to prevent him from fretting. Now that Andrew had started school and she had free time to herself, she made enquiries about helping with the war effort as a volunteer – perhaps in the Red Cross, in liberty-bond drives or even a local group knitting socks, headbands and sweaters.

It would also be good for me to get out of the house. I'll talk to some of the mothers at the school.

In his letter dated February 1918, Charles said that now that their six months' training was coming to an end, their departure to Europe could happen any time soon. He wrote again two weeks later.

The Quartermaster Corps and other support services are leaving in the next few days to begin the preparatory work for a large number of troops to follow later. We have been given very little information, and all I am at liberty to tell you is that we are headed for Europe. As I said several times, I'm going as a manager and not as a soldier so there is no need to worry about me.

I am already counting the days when I will be home to hold you and to love you. Please kiss Andrew for me. I will write as often as I am allowed.

His first letter from abroad confirmed he was in France. Either he did not know exactly where he was or he was not allowed to disclose it. His description of his work gave Alice an understanding of the scale of the operation, and she was proud of his ability to make a real contribution. I wouldn't know where to begin, she thought.

Later letters were less frequent and did not enlighten her about the war. She didn't know whether this was a good sign or whether Charles was sparing her the gruesome details.

Alice had thought many times about Anetta's parting words that fateful September evening. 'I envy you, Mrs Novak.' They reinforced her growing belief that Charles was worth fighting for. Men at the front must also be worried about their wives or sweethearts back home, not only about their well-being and safety but about their fidelity as well. So, I'm not the only one with heartache.

She read the newspaper reports, discussed the war with her parents and listened intently to the views of the other mothers at the school and at the knitting circle which she attended on two mornings each week. She was reticent to pass on news from Charles, conscious of her good fortune when she learned that most husbands were front-line troops. I would be worried sick. At least I can be sure he's coming back – but to what?

On a June morning at the knitting circle one of the wives said, 'In a letter I received a few days ago, my husband said that a flu epidemic had hit the troops with hundreds taken to hospital and many soldiers and nursing staff dying. Could this be true, do you think?'

'No, no,' Mrs Caldwell answered. 'If it was true, the letter would have been censored. No bad news is allowed.'

'Well, if it's true, I hope the soldiers don't bring it home with them,' Alice said.

'Haven't we enough to worry us?' another member added.

In August, she heard about the troop movements to reinforce the newly organised US First Army and a month later read about the 1.2 million US troops who had commenced the Meuse-Argonne offensive that stretched along the entire Western Front. A lot of work for caterers and suppliers, she thought. I'm so glad he's among them.

In early October, she received a telegram from Western Union. She knew all about the fear that this struck in people's hearts but opened it thinking it must be from her father or one of her sisters. She read,

WASHINGTON, DC. 7.18 p.m. OCT 4th, 1918

MRS ALICE NOVAK

PHILADELPHIA, PENN

THE SECRETARY OF WAR DESIRES ME TO EXPRESS HIS DEEPEST REGRET THAT YOUR HUSBAND PRIVATE CHARLES NOVAK IS OFFICIALLY REPORTED AS KILLED IN ACTION SEPTEMBER NINETEENTH IN FRANCE.

THE ADJUTANT GENERAL

This has to be a mistake. He's in catering and supplies, for God's sake. Then the doubt started. She asked her neighbour to look after Andrew and left immediately to talk to her father who she felt confident would be able to sort out this confusion.

Fruitless efforts were made over the next three weeks to establish the facts. Then a handwritten letter arrived.

Dear Mrs Novak,

I expect you will have received a telegram by now informing you of the unfortunate death of your husband Charles. I want to express my great sadness at your tragic loss.

He spoke about you often and very fondly.

We were in the same section of the Quartermaster Corps and became great friends from our time in Fort Meade and during the months we spent here in France.

We were moving supplies to nearer the front line. Though we were still several miles from danger, or so we thought, a stray bombardment struck our area of the convoy, killing about twenty men and wounding many more. I witnessed the awful event and I hope it is some consolation to you to know that Charles did not suffer.

Our job was to prepare hot food and to arrange its distribution to the troops. Where hostilities made this impossible we supplied trench rations, mainly in cans.

Our officers here valued his knowledge and experience as a manager in Wanamaker's. Senior officers frequently ordered Charles to accompany them when inspecting other functions such as general material distribution or the field bakeries and to prepare reports on what he found wanting. I have no doubt that but for his untimely death he would have been promoted or even offered a commission.

You won't be surprised to hear that he was one of the most popular men in our squad.

I have been authorised to tell you that Charles is buried near a village beside our supply stores and that the exact location will be forwarded to you when this awful war has ended. Please God, this will be very soon.

I have lost a good friend but I know your loss is so much greater.

Mike Dean (Private)

PS If I can help you in any way please contact me C/O 79th Division, US Army, Fort Meade, Maryland.

Alice's grief was compounded by not having a body to bury and by the thought of Charles lying in a temporary grave somewhere in France. She did not have the distraction of arranging a funeral or contacting Novak relatives. She didn't have an address for Charles's brother in Poland. She couldn't bring herself to write to Francesca. And poor Leo? I don't want such devastating news to be the only contact with him. The poor man has suffered enough. Should I inform the hospital? Do they need to know?

She asked her father to inform Wanamaker's, and when he suggested a Requiem Mass, she welcomed the spiritual support it would offer her, her family and her friends.

In January 1919, a letter was received in the main post office in Philadelphia addressed to Charles Novak, General Delivery, Philadelphia, United States of America. There it remained until the time limit for holding such letters came and went.

40

Philadelphia, 1922

The vegetable and fruit garden in Webster House measured one hundred and thirty feet by seventy-five feet and was enclosed by a cut stone wall seven feet in height. The entrance, wide enough to take a horse and cart, was situated at the furthest point from the original house. At first, Leo found the enclosure restrictive and intimidating, but now, six years on, he valued the seclusion and privacy it gave him. He had been told that the high walls aided growth by creating heat and protection from high winds. He wondered if such a space existed in country estates in Poland.

There was no part of the job that Leo did not enjoy. Each task in each season gave him great satisfaction, from the physical turning of the soil, the spreading of manure and the back-breaking weeding to the more skilful pruning and grafting. He was inclined to keep working after normal quitting time – so much so that John Lee, the head gardener, often had to usher him out, saying, 'Come on, Leo, leave. I have to lock up.'

Leo was proud of the knowledge he had accumulated and applied – 'a time to sow and a time to reap,' as he recalled from the Bible. The harvesting of seeds and the planting of bulbs that had been lifted and separated after flowering endeared him to the cyclical wonders of his job. In the growing season, to maximise the use of space, when something came out of the ground something else went in. In the winter months, the work hours reduced but continued to fascinate – even such tasks as the preparation of weedkiller for the following spring.

He welcomed working on his own but also enjoyed the exchange of information and gossip with his colleagues. He was now more relaxed with other inmates. At mealtimes, he would happily describe, for those who would listen, the work that went into the vegetables or fruit on their plates or the flowers and shrubs visible through the window.

One day, while working in the greenhouse, he heard his name called by an attendant who was somewhere outside the high walls. He rushed outside, shouting, 'Here, in the garden.' The attendant, knowing Leo's background, approached with a smile on his face, excited about what he had to tell him. 'Leo, take a break. You have a visitor.'

Leo was startled. 'Are you sure?'

'Yes, of course I'm sure.'

'My brother Charles! He's come at last.'

Knowing the disappointment Leo faced, the attendant put on a broad smile and said, 'It's your lucky day, Leo. Your visitor is not a he, your visitor is a she.'

41

Tommy was delighted to get an unexpected call from Anna. Not that he needed reminding, but his dad's comments again made him feel how lucky he was to have met Anna, if only on a screen.

'Hi, I just called on the off chance that you would be home. I just want to wish you and your family a Merry Christmas and to thank you once again for all the help you've given my family.'

'Many happy returns, and it's been a real pleasure to help you and to have these conversations. They mean a lot to me. In fact, I've been thinking that when the research is completed we should still keep in regular contact.'

Anna was moved and thrilled but was at a loss on how to respond. She just said, 'Yes, I would like that as well.' Each waited for the other to break the meaningful silence that followed. Anna then said, 'But there's plenty more research to be done.'

'How come?'

'Well, we should try to learn more about Charles Novak and his wife, Alice. We think he was killed in the First World War, and nothing is known about Alice. My dad and his brothers think she died young, possibly a victim of the worldwide flu epidemic after the war.'

'Yeah, you're right,' Tommy answered without enthusiasm.

'Also, I told you my mother's side of the family, the Kellys, came from Ireland – County Wexford she thinks.'

'Oh no!' with mock horror.

'Oh yes!' with laughter.

'Well, I hope there were no bishops in her family?'

'Or police records?' Anna replied.

'I hope we'll talk about the living, about your life and mine and everyday things.'

'Yeah, we'll just shoot the breeze. Merry Christmas, Tommy.'

'Happy Christmas. Talk to you soon.'

* * *

Anna grabbed a coffee from the vending machine in the basketball arena and joined Martha and Jane. They were relaxing on a bench after practice, which they attended as part of their internship. After the usual teasing, Martha said, 'Now, we're not going to depress ourselves are we, by talking about flunking or deadlines and credits and regrets about missed hours of study?'

Jane replied, 'They're difficult to ignore, you have to admit.'

Anna nodded in agreement but quickly changed the subject to Christmas shopping and free time during the break. They talked about an evening at the Crofton Inn and going to one of the live music events in Alessandro's Bar and Grill. Tentative arrangements were made for 27th December and for New Year's Eve.

When Jane had left, Martha said, 'OK, update on your Irish screen idol, please.'

'Nothing much to tell, really. I could update you on our research, but I guess that's not what you want to hear?'

'Right. Get to the interesting part.'

'The only "romantic development" is that Tommy's father,

who's a widower, is getting married again.'

'That's nice, but how about you and Tommy? Any romance there?'

'Well, he wants to keep in touch after the research is completed.'

'Now we're getting someplace, what next?'

'Seriously Martha, could a close relationship be developed on Skype?'

'Wow, so that's what you think of him?'

'I'm not sure what to think. I know I look forward to our chats, especially when we get away from the research, and he's such a sweet guy.'

Martha frowned, took another sip of coffee and said, 'You're going to have to work on it.'

'But how?'

'Make sure that your contact on Skype is more and more about you and him, about interests, plans, etc.'

'Yeah, I'd like that, I'd love that, but what then?'

'If that develops the way I expect it will, you two are going to have to meet – physically, I mean.'

Anna had a very warm feeling about that possibility, but she said, 'Now you're dreaming, Martha.'

'No, no. You and I will go to grad school in Ireland, and he's bound to have a brother or a cousin or friend who will fall madly in love with me.' They both laughed about that crazy idea.

* * *

Deirdre arrived late on the 23rd, too late to get much work done, but Mary set out the duties for the following day, making sure Deirdre noted what was allocated to her.

Tommy, with advice from Mrs Duggan, had purchased the ham in Power's, the butcher. He decorated the kitchen and the sitting room with berried holly and a selection from the frills and ornaments accumulated over the years. He erected a Christmas tree in the dining room, naturally supplied by Walsh's DIY and Hardware, and the established custom would continue of leaving the Kris Kringle presents under the tree when no one was about.

I wonder will there be a present for Orla, but I'm sure Dad will have thought of that.

Deirdre was somewhat surprised when Tommy told her she had an appointment with Alan Manahan for coffee on the morning of the 27th and that he would introduce her and leave them to discuss her career options.

'I thought you'd forgotten about my request.'

'Never. You're so unforgettable.'

'You're so right.'

On Christmas Eve, Tommy decided that the house should be avoided. With Orla and Mrs Duggan on board, he knew he would be in the way, and he spent the day in the shop helping with the last-minute rush on Christmas trees and gifts and batteries, an essential requirement for children's presents. When the shop was closed and made secure, he went upstairs for tea and a sandwich and then to Davy's Hotel to meet a few of his teammates for a Christmas drink or three.

The church was packed before 'midnight' Mass started at 9 p.m. The recently redecorated St Michael's Church looked its best. The crib was sited centre stage in front of the altar with all the statues in place except that of Baby Jesus which would be placed there at the Family Mass on the following morning. The Christmas tree had been erected a few weeks earlier at the back of the church. This year it was designated a 'Prayer Tree' with the parishioners invited to write wishes for their loved ones or other special intentions to be hung on the tree and later included in the Masses in the days after Christmas.

The subdued overhead lighting and the additional candlelight around the Sanctuary showed off the mustard-yellow walls to great effect. This colour was repeated in the mosaic tiled floor in the central aisle. The moulded plasterwork around the Gothic-style windows was painted the same soft peach that decorated the wall behind the altar, and this was enhanced by discreetly placed spotlights. The newly varnished pews matched the exposed roof beams.

Frank and Orla were in the choir that commenced Christmas carols at about 8.45 p.m., and, like all good choirs, their individual voices were blended with the rest and could not be heard.

Jimmy Walker was very familiar with the church, attending there every Sunday, but he felt that tonight it had taken on a special glow. He and Joan had arrived early and, unusually, were seated towards the back. Jimmy enjoyed people-watching on this special occasion. He knew all the regular attendees by sight if not by name, and he decided that many of the others were, by their conduct, either local or visiting irregular Mass-goers who weren't quite sure how to participate. Yet others, he felt, were there because it was part of the seasonal ritual, like Christmas gifts or the Limerick Races on St Stephen's Day. They stood out because of the time they spent in groups chatting loudly or waving at friends in other parts of the church.

Anyway, he thought, it's high time I concentrated on why I'm here. I welcome everyone, whatever their motivation, and I hope they will get as much from the celebration of the birth of Christ as I will. He then switched his attention totally to the altar, to his prayers and to the carols.

O holy night! The stars are brightly shining,

It is the night of our dear Saviour's birth …

When Tommy got home from the pub, at about 11 p.m., Mary

tackled him. 'Come here, I have a crow to pluck with you.'

'What have I done now?'

'It's what you didn't do.' Tommy thought he had forgotten some task assigned by her. 'I expressed concern about your love life, and yet you didn't tell me about Anna.'

'Ah, I didn't know you were interested in her family research. I'll bring you up to date if you like.'

'There you go again. God, you should go into politics. You're very good at answering questions you haven't been asked. I've heard that Anna is beautiful and that you may be smitten.'

'Ah, Dad has been telling tales.'

'Maybe she's the one. If so, don't let her slip away.'

'I'll certainly bear that in mind.'

Mary was silent for a moment and then said, 'Someday, please God, you'll tell me what really is on your mind.'

'Yes, I will. When I know, you'll know.'

He thought, How am I ever going to know, with the Atlantic between us?

42

Tommy had a lie-in on Christmas morning. After breakfast, he lit the fire in the sitting room and replenished the basket of logs and the coal box. Since this required a trip down to the patio, he also put a large bag of logs in the storeroom as back-up. He also checked that the drinks cabinet and the table wine were in order.

Mary and Deirdre were busy in the kitchen so he made himself scarce and went to late morning Mass. He knew his dad worried that he didn't attend more regularly, and he was surprised that his sister wasn't on his case about this too. After Mass, the weather was cold but dry so people lingered. Tommy exchanged Christmas greetings and had a brief chat with friends and neighbours as they stood beside the Celtic cross on the footpath between the church and the priests' house.

As he strolled home, he thought, How embarrassing was that?! A newcomer to the town, asking me how old was the cross and why the street was called Friary Street. I hadn't a clue. I must ask Joe Dunphy. He knows a lot about the town. He said that it lacked a patriot to celebrate or a landlord to berate in song or story.

Orla arrived as invited, at 2.30 p.m. Having assisted with the work on the previous day, she was happy to relax as a guest.

When everyone was assembled, the handing around of Kris Kringle presents began. As the packages disappeared from under the tree, Tommy feared that there wasn't a present for Orla. As he was about to feel embarrassed, Frank produced a small box from his pocket, opened it, took out an engagement ring and placed it on Orla's finger. He was saying something about arrangements for Orla to exchange it, but he could not be heard with the loud expressions of approval and delight. Orla threw her arms around his neck and, holding back tears of joy, said for all to hear, 'Spending the day with you and your family and now this beautiful ring, you've given me two wonderful reasons to remember this Christmas Day.'

The Christmas dinner was as good as ever, and compliments flew in Mary's direction, which she batted away, but you could see that she was both relieved and pleased. Courses were served at decent intervals so it was after six when the group moved to the comfort of the fire in the sitting room. As customary, Tommy and Kevin cleared the table, filled the dishwasher, washed the pots and pans and did anything else that was required – a fair division of labour, or so they thought.

Tommy served post-dinner drinks, hard and soft, and then declared that self-service would operate for the rest of the night. The chat was interrupted for an hour or so while they watched a Morecambe and Wise Christmas Special from many years previously. Towards the end of the night, Deirdre asked her father to sing. Frank and Orla sang 'White Christmas' in perfect harmony. At mid-point, Frank invited everybody to join in, which they did with varying degrees of success. The Walsh siblings could not be said to have inherited their father's singing voice, and Kevin didn't offer much either. When the singing stopped, silence followed as the flames of the fire seemed to grab everyone's attention.

Coming towards midnight, Orla said that she should be getting home, and she asked Frank to walk the few hundred yards with her along Barrack Street and O'Connell Street. When they had left, the remaining four spoke about how much this Christmas was different from previous years and how much would change before another Christmas came around.

Mary mentioned that she hoped to have a chat with Dad about the possibility of taking over the business sometime in the future. Tommy said that if that happened then who lived over the shop would need to be decided.

'Maybe by this time next year,' Mary said, 'Tommy will have an announcement to make.'

Deirdre raised herself upright on the couch, held her arms wide in exasperation and said, 'Would somebody please tell me what's going on around here?'

'You should come home more often,' Tommy joked.

* * *

On Christmas Eve, at home in Center Valley, Anna and Barbara were having a late morning coffee, catching up on all the news since their last phone call.

'Have you seen or spoken to Josh Hamilton?' Barbara asked.

'No. He's in treatment somewhere for his drinking problem. I haven't seen him in months, and I don't expect to see him. I do feel sorry for him though.'

'You've been in regular contact with Tommy, so what's the story?'

'It's kinda crazy. It's only contact on Skype, but I look forward to chatting with him especially when we get away from the research stuff. And, oh, I've met his father. He just interrupted our conversation, much to Tommy's surprise. He seems to be a lovely man, and he just got engaged to be married.'

'Wow, is this getting serious?'

'I'm not sure where it's going, to be honest. We have agreed to keep in touch even when the research is over.'

'Is that a good idea? Can you keep up a long-distance relationship?'

Anna hid her disappointment with Barbara's words. She wanted to keep hope and possibilities alive however remote the chance of a real relationship developing. 'Yeah, you could be right, you could be right. But anyway how is life in Philly?'

'Work is going well. It's interesting and challenging, but there's very little social interaction. Apart from case conferences with my colleagues I work largely on my own.'

'So, anybody special?'

'It's good to be based downtown because I can meet my college friends regularly, but so far there's no sign of Mr Right. It's much easier to meet the wrong type – as you found as well.'

The music on the local radio station was interrupted for a weather alert. 'The National Weather Service has issued a winter storm warning for east central Pennsylvania, including Allentown, Hamburg, Reading, and surrounding areas. Six to twelve inches of heavy snow are expected tonight, tapering to light snow by 8 a.m. Expect wind gusts up to forty miles per hour. Drifting snow will make travel hazardous. Stay tuned for further updates.'

As they were resuming their conversation, Katherine and Peter came through the door laden with Christmas Eve shopping.

'Dad,' Barbara began, 'there's a weather warning—'

'Yeah, I just heard it too. So will we get to church tomorrow? Let's put the cars in the garage, and I'll check that we have everything we might need in my trunk. Looks like we'll be shovelling snow in the morning, so be prepared.'

Christmas morning at first light, a glance out the window told Peter that the forecast was pretty much accurate. It looked serious but not hopeless so he roused his wife and daughters, and, while breakfast was being prepared, he went through his garage and out on the snow-covered ground. He knew from experience that they would need to shovel most of the way out to the road in order for the car to get out of the steep driveway. He hoped the snowploughs would do the rest. It was at a time like this that he was glad he drove an SUV.

After breakfast, he, Barbara and Anna cleared the driveway. As planned, they left immediately, before the falling snow had the chance to undo their good work, and got to the church gingerly but safely as the congregation was assembling for the 11.30 Mass. After the white-out, the rectangular church of wood and brick, standing apart from other buildings, resembled a mountain chalet. Volunteers had been busy making the parking lot accessible.

The priest, Revd Max Lindemann, was inside the door to welcome them and to exchange Christmas greetings. After Mass, coffee and cookies were served in the adjoining room, but, mindful of the weather and the tasks ahead, people did not hang around.

The Novaks sat around the gas fire in the den, drinking coffee and opening their presents. Then they started the preparation of the Christmas dinner, doing the same tasks and following a similar routine as they had done for Thanksgiving.

Peter phoned his brothers to exchange Christmas greetings, and Katherine took time to make one of her irregular phone calls to Clare, her eldest sibling. She said nothing about Leo Novak. Clare would probably never have heard of him but she decided to wait until the full story anyway, whatever that was, was known.

Early afternoon, when it would be about 7 p.m. in Ireland,

Anna thought about contacting Tommy, but Barbara's words of caution took over and she decided to wait a few days.

Next morning, Peter was out shovelling snow again, and Katherine and her daughters were having a late breakfast. When Barbara made a move to clear the dishes, her mother touched her on the arm and said, 'Look, while I have you both here together, I need to tell you about the Kelly family. I know I should have told you this many years ago, so I hope you'll understand.' Barbara and Anna could sense the emotion in Katherine's voice and were apprehensive about what they were about to hear.

'I'm so glad we're creating our family tree because it forces me to talk about something I've avoided since I was a girl. Leo's story has shown me the damage done by keeping family secrets, however well intentioned. Dad knows the story – I felt I had to tell him before we got married, but he's the only one.' Barbara and Anna made eye contact but said nothing. 'As you know, my father, Nicholas, or Nicky as he was known, was a schoolteacher in Pittsburgh. You were never told that he was an alcoholic and that the disease shattered our family. He got worse as the years went on, and before he reached forty he had lost his job and left home, living as a vagrant, dependent on charity. This was in 1965 when I was only six. My brother James was nine, Timothy was eleven and Clare, the oldest was thirteen.'

Katherine had spoken very fast and was close to tears. Barbara and Anna, sensing that she needed to unload, remained silent. 'I was protected from the worst of this. All I remember is that Dad was sick a lot of the time, or at least that was what I thought. I cannot remember what I was told when he left home. I just got used to the idea. My mother took on an evening job as a janitor in offices and factories, and Clare left school in 1968 when she was sixteen. She got a job as an office assistant in order to help

Mom make ends meet. Both my brothers left school early for the same reason and got unskilled jobs but, as you know, did well subsequently. Their sacrifices made it possible for me to finish high school and then go to college.' Katherine drew breath and fell silent, holding back the tears, overcome by having at last lifted a veil of secrecy.

Barbara came to her rescue. 'I often wondered why we knew so little about the Kellys and why you were not close to them. Why the secrecy?'

Katherine moved her hands from her lap to the table. 'That's what I need to explain. Mom died in 1977, when she was only fifty-two, exhausted mentally and physically from coping with an alcoholic husband and from working so hard. She'd been ill and unable to work for about three years before she died, which added to the work and financial problems for Clare. I was eighteen and left for college shortly after.'

Anna, concerned for her mother's apparent feelings of guilt, could not contain herself. 'That was awful for you and for your sister and brothers, and I'm very sorry about that. But Mom, I can't understand why you never told us.'

'It was my way of dealing with it – almost believing it never happened.'

'Oh my God, that must have been stressful,' Barbara said. 'But I agree with Anna: you should have told us; we could have helped you.'

Katherine, looking at the table, dried her tears. 'Silence worked for me, up to a point, but it meant that I never said thanks – to my sister Clare especially, but also to my two brothers, for what they had done for me. They shielded me from my father's alcoholism and made financial sacrifices for me.'

Anna asked, 'Was your mom bitter towards your dad?'

'If she was, she didn't show it. In fact, she never mentioned his name at all. Now that I think about it, subconsciously I probably copied her way of dealing with emotional problems.'

Barbara added, 'Mom, I think I can understand why you didn't talk to us about this as teenagers, but why not in the years since then?'

'When I didn't do it early, my self-criticism and embarrassment grew, and I just felt it impossible to spill it out. In a sense, I treated my brothers and sister in the same way as Leo was treated.' She began to well up as she added, 'I need to make it right with them, to do the right thing.'

Anna and Barbara moved around the table and embraced their mother in a tearful three-way hug. 'We'll help you,' Anna said, and Barbara added, 'Of course we will.'

'Guilty feelings strike every so often, especially in my rare phone calls to Clare, like yesterday. Again, I said nothing about this to her, but when I put the phone down I decided to tell you everything and to ask Clare to forgive me.' Before Anna or Barbara could comment, she added, 'I'll start with invitations to her to spend time with us here. She's on her own in Pittsburgh. When she should have been socialising and dating she was looking after Mom and then supporting me through college.'

Barbara suggested, 'Start with Clare and then invite or visit Timothy and James. I'm sure you'll find that they are dealing with a troubled childhood too.'

Anna said, 'Now I know why you insisted on starting the research with the Novaks. I'm looking forward to getting to know the Kelly side of the family, and, besides, we can talk to them about the family tree.'

'Yes, we will. One last thing. Anna, because of my dad, I was worried sick about you and Josh.'

This concern was anticipated by Anna as her mother revealed

her past. 'I knew you were upset, and you were right. No need to worry any more on that score, Mom.'

'No, thank God for that.'

43

The coffee shop in Davy's Hotel was busy with the town beginning to get back to normal after the Christmas break. Many were still off work and wanted relief from cabin fever. Tommy and Deirdre were chatting, waiting for Alan Manahan to arrive. Deirdre was dressed to impress.

'He's not the world's best timekeeper, so be patient.'

'While we're waiting, I think what I heard about you and Anna is romantic and all that, but I think you're mad.'

'You do? Why?'

'Well, it's like one of those time-traveller movies where two people from different time periods fall in love. You two, separated by distance if not by time, are in the same situation. It's plain daft, if you ask me.'

Tommy was about to reply when Alan arrived. He was dressed in a well-worn tweed jacket, a check shirt with a club tie and scuffed shoes. His hair, dark with hints of grey, reached over his collar. The overall effect made him look much older than his twenty-nine years. In case anyone was in doubt as to his profession, he carried a folder of sheet music, which he dropped on the floor beside the table.

Tommy made the introductions, outlined why Deirdre wished

to speak to him, ordered coffees for them and left.

That afternoon, Tommy met Dave McCarthy and Conor Ryan, who had been re-elected captain for the new season, for an unofficial fitness session. They were joined by a few new members including two Polish men who had come to work in the local joinery. The county championship matches were months away, but they needed to prepare for so-called friendly matches in late February or early March.

The sun was shining, and the temperature was only a few degrees above freezing. They started with a dozen laps of the playing pitch followed by a series of sprints and then thirty minutes in the gym. When they had showered, they went to the nearest pub, O'Riordan's on O'Connell Street, for a few pints, thereby reducing the benefit of the workout – but hey, it was a start.

Conor Ryan looked at Tommy and asked, 'What's this I'm hearing about your transatlantic romance with an American student?'

Tommy looked startled, giving the game away. He tried to recover. 'It's just boring research stuff. You wouldn't be interested.'

'Aren't you the dark horse all the same? You've hidden that power you have over women – who'd have thought?'

The Polish guys were all ears, and Tommy felt a total denial was not going to work so he tried evasion. 'Look, I'm surprised that you are surprised that my sex appeal is so strong. It has been obvious for years, but you're only realising it now.' When this got a jeering response, he added, 'Someone has been telling you tall tales, but to set your mind at rest I'll let you know if any such romance ever develops. Now, are we having another round or what?'

The chat about local people and events went on for another hour, and, with the warmth of the open fire and the good company, they had to resist the temptation to remain longer.

Mary was disappointed that her dad had not talked to her about the business as Tommy said he would. She didn't want to return to Dublin later that day still 'in the dark', so she took the initiative. 'Dad, you told Tommy you would talk to me about your plans for the business.'

'Yes, I did, but before we start I suggest you ask Kevin to join us. He would have a major role to play in this so he should be here.'

The three sat around the kitchen table warmed by the solid fuel cooker. Frank placed writing paper and pens on the table indicating the importance of the conversation they were about to have.

'I have to admit I didn't think you'd be interested. I thought your life was in Dublin or wherever Kevin served. So, sorry, I didn't mean to exclude you.'

'No problem, Dad. I made the same assumption, but Tommy made me think differently.'

'That's a relief. Another thing, I suggest we regard this as a business meeting, not a family meeting, and all decisions should flow from that. So, don't feel under pressure to agree to anything because I'm your dad. OK?'

'Yeah, thanks. That's helpful. As a start, could you tell me in a general way what you have in mind?'

Frank looked directly at Kevin and said, 'Firstly, I'm assuming for this discussion that you could get a transfer to a station convenient to here.'

'Yeah, that should be possible, but it could take a long time.'

'OK. I'm now sixty-three, and in about three years I'll qualify for the state pension. That seems a good time to step back and work part-time, if at all. I would need to talk to my solicitor and accountant on the legal and tax issues involved in transferring the business. I also have to think about Tommy and Deirdre's interests – for example, what financial benefit would accrue to them in due course. One final thing: should this house go with the business. It seems it should, but that's also for discussion.'

'There's plenty of food for thought there. If I returned to work in the business, would I be on a salary or a share of the profits during the years before you retire fully?'

'Yes, of course. It just strikes me now as we speak, my solicitor or accountant might suggest that you would purchase the business so that my financial situation, and Orla's and ultimately Tommy's and Deirdre's would be protected. If we make progress in these discussions you also would need to get independent advice before any commitments are made. So, I expect you have many questions?'

Mary was looking at Kevin when she said, 'Oh, lots of them, but maybe it's best we think about all you've said and talk again another day?'

'Good idea, and let's follow the guideline that nothing's agreed until everything's agreed.'

'We're leaving for Dublin shortly, but I'll call you in a few days.'

'Safe driving, and, as I said, no pressure, OK?'

'It's amazing, Dad. I never imagined myself in this situation and yet here we are. I've no idea what's best, but it's great that we've started this conversation, and I know Kevin feels the same.'

* * *

When Tommy returned from the pub, he found Deirdre on the couch in the sitting room, her legs tucked under her and deeply engrossed in a novel. 'So, how did you and Alan get on?'

'Very well,' she said. 'We're meeting for lunch tomorrow. He's dishy, isn't he?'

Tommy ignored the question and said, 'What I meant was, did he give you helpful advice on career choices?'

'Oh that. Well, he spoke a lot about his career, which was fascinating.'

'He has a certain reputation as a ladies' man.'

Deirdre saw the opportunity to wind Tommy up further. 'Oh, does he now? I'm looking forward to lunch even more.'

'Enjoy your lunch, but remember why you're there.'

'I certainly will,' she replied with a giggle. God, I'm getting good at this.

44

It was past eight on the night of 27th December, and Alessandro's Bar and Grill was packed. To get the crowd in early, a special Christmas karaoke with cash prizes was under way.

Anna, Martha and Jane were with a group of guys from DeSales. By agreement, any reference to student matters was excluded, so the conversation ranged over driving scares and narrow escapes, gossip about fellow students, some ribbing of each other, the best movies to see and how boring it was to be at home over Christmas.

When Martha sensed that Karl Smith was moving in on Anna, she said, for everyone to hear, 'Don't waste your time, Karl, she's spoken for.'

'Gee, tell us more,' Bill Roberts said.

Martha's 'Yeah, she's fallen for a screen idol, but I can't tell you more' was guaranteed to arouse the curiosity of all.

'C'mon, spill,' Bill said.

All eyes turned to Anna.

'Hey, guys, you should all know by now that Martha is pulling your chain.'

'Tell us anyway.' Bill's request got nods and verbal support.

'Very simple, really. I'm doing family research with the help of a guy in Ireland, and Martha Mills & Boon is trying to get you to believe there is some kind of online transatlantic romance going on.'

Anna sensed immediately that this was not going to stop the questioning, so, standing up, she said to Martha and Jane, 'Let's go and do the number we agreed on.'

That worked. The group clapped their support, and, as the trio made their way to the karaoke stage, Anna said with mock sincerity, 'Thanks a bunch, Martha.'

Martha, flanked by Jane and Anna, burst into 'Rockin' Around the Christmas Tree.' After the first two lines, their friends and many others joined in, and when they got to the chorus, the entire crowd was 'rockin''. It was going so well that after the second verse and on a nod from Martha they started over again and finished to wild applause.

* * *

Anna was in her bedroom reading a magazine when Tommy buzzed her on Skype. 'How was your Christmas, Anna? Were you snowed in?' The picture faded in and out for a few seconds as if affected by the talk of adverse weather, but the sound was OK.

'How'd you know about that?'

'The storm in your part of the world was shown on TV here, and I wondered how it affected you and your family.'

'It was no more than a nuisance really. We did everything we wanted to do, but we had to do a lot of shovelling of snow to get to Christmas Mass. How about you?'

'We rarely get snow, but if we do we find it impossible to cope, even in the cities. We just don't have the equipment – we're told the investment couldn't be justified. We get more than our share of rain though, said to be the price we pay for green grass.'

'So you had no difficulty getting to Mass?

'None. My dad would say I don't go often enough.'

'My dad doesn't crack the whip, but he sets a high standard, and I'm OK with that. Tell me about Christmas in Clondore.'

'Much as always, though this year Orla was with us on Christmas Day, and Dad produced the engagement ring.'

'Awesome, how lovely.'

'Please suggest a wedding present? They both have homes, so the usual gift like a kitchen gadget is not on.'

'That's a tough one. Let me think about that. Any other news?'

'Dad has been talking to Mary, my older sister, about handing over the business to her.'

'That's a surprise. I thought the business would be yours someday?'

'No, I think I've managed to get my dad to accept that that won't happen.'

Anna noted that Tommy's future may not be tied to Clondore. 'So, I'll bet you're advising both of them about this?'

'Only in a minor way. Both will take expert advice. Family settlements can be a minefield.'

'You're wearing workout clothes. Has the football season started?'

'A few of us were out for our first training session since October, and I'm feeling a bit wrecked. The county championship doesn't start until early May, but we'll play a few practice matches before then. Now, what have you been doing?'

'My friends Martha Douglas and Jane Taylor and I met some of our college buddies in Alessandro's Bar and Grill last night, and the three of us entered the holiday karaoke contest. We sang 'Rockin' Around the Christmas Tree'. We didn't win, but everyone liked it.'

'I wish I could have been there. Unlike my dad, I can't sing, but I'm an enthusiastic joiner in the singalong.'

'Did you do any more square-dancing or whatever you called it?'

'No.'

Before he could elaborate, she added, 'Do you have a regular dancing partner?'

'No, or any other kind of partner. How about you?'

'No, unattached.'

Tommy thought, that's one obstacle out of the way, at least for now. He said, 'I find that impossible to believe. If I lived in Center Valley I would be calling tonight to your house to bring you out for a romantic dinner.'

Anna was quiet for a moment. 'What a lovely thought. We keep mentioning things we'd like to do together, but I guess they're never going to happen.' First, with Barbara's words in her head, she regretted saying this and then was pleased that she had.

'Let's just keep in touch and see where it takes us. I just don't want to lose contact.'

Anna was relieved to hear these words and felt great warmth towards Tommy. 'Me too, it would be nice just to talk.'

'This is a first for us. We've managed to have a conversation without mentioning research.'

'And I've really enjoyed it.'

'Let's arrange a schedule for making contact that fits with your college and study time.'

'Great. Bye – and, oh, I almost forgot, Happy New Year to you and your family.'

'Same to you and yours. Bye.'

45

Tommy had kept putting off the task of finding some reference to police files on the web. Mindful that Anna's Uncle Adam was a police officer and would have access to any files he could find, he decided to get started. He googled 'Police Files USA' and then 'Police Files Pennsylvania'. After browsing through a list of websites, most of which were about current or recent records, he found a site 'Philadelphia County, Pennsylvania Public Records', which included 'Philadelphia County Criminal and Court Records'.

Under 'Criminal Records' he read, 'Years Available: Criminal records on computer and microfiche from 1969, archived from 1800s; has case records back to late 1980s.' The site also described how information could be retrieved, but Tommy felt that the best route would be through Anna's uncle.

He decided to try a Skype call. When Anna appeared on screen, he said, 'I love seeing you on screen, and if I didn't have a reason to call you I'd invent one.'

'That's made my day. Funny, I was just thinking about you and hoping you would call – telepathic, eh?'

'I'd like to spend more time on these calls to get to know you better.'

'Yeah, me too. Let's have more calls when research is not mentioned.'

'You're on. Right now I need you to get your Uncle Adam involved.'

'Oh?'

'Yeah, I'll send you a site that shows that police records are available back to the 1800s.'

'That's fantastic news.'

'I don't know how much information would be released to you or to me, and that's where Adam comes in.'

'I know he'll help.'

'Good.'

'And Tommy, I know you'll understand when I say that I hope we can find something that helps to restore Leo's reputation, even if it is not good for the bishop.'

'Sure I do.'

Uncle Adam was impressed with Tommy's discovery when Anna contacted him the next day. He offered to come over to her parents' house that evening to discuss the details.

Gathered in the den after supper, Peter suggested that there was bound to be a file on the assassination attempt.

'Let's talk about the next step then,' Adam said, getting everybody's attention. 'I didn't know that our records went back so far in time. As it happens, I know one of the guys in charge in the records office. I worked with John Allen, a senior detective, many years ago. We'd lost touch, and I don't know why he now does a desk job. Anyway, when I phoned him we had a chat about the past, and when I told him our family story he offered to do what he could to help.' Following general murmurs of appreciation, he added, 'Anna, I can give you his number.'

'How much did you tell him?'

'Very little really. I mentioned the mystery about Leo Novak being ostracised and that you found out that he had attempted to kill Bishop Walsh back in 1912 and we wanted to know why he did such a terrible thing.'

'Did he say anything about the chances of finding a record after all this time?'

'He said our timing could be good, and he referred to the reading of files, by detectives and other staff, on cases involving Roman Catholic clergy and the sexual abuse of children. He said he'd tell them what we're looking for.'

'I felt it would be like looking for a needle in a haystack, but now I'm a bit more optimistic. Two more questions: should I meet Mr Allen on my own and would I be allowed to record what he says?'

'You could bring someone with you, but it's my gut feeling that he would prefer to deal with just one person. You could record him, but you would need his permission.'

'Thanks Adam, we couldn't have made these arrangements ourselves,' Peter said, and Anna nodded her agreement.

Anna Skyped Tommy. 'Glad to find you at your desk. How are you today?'

'All the better for seeing you.'

'Now I'm really glad I phoned. I could have updated you by email.'

Tommy was silent for a moment. 'Skype is great, but the more I see you, the more I want to.' Anna's heart took a jump, and before she could reply, Tommy added, 'Anyway, let's make the best of what we have.'

'Yeah, let's do that,' she said, annoyed with her guarded and unintended response.

Tommy's frustration got the better of him. He said, 'You mentioned an update?'

'Yes, with Uncle Adam's help I have made an appointment with John Allen, a former colleague of his who works at a senior level in the Police Records Office.'

'Sounds like he has information.'

'Uncle Adam is optimistic as well.'

Tommy added, 'The major gaps in our knowledge are about the assassination attempt. When, where, how and why, apart from insanity? Also, Leo's escapes, the reaction by the police, the questioning and charging of Leo. You should also check with Mr Allen that you can contact him later with follow-up questions.'

Anna was scribbling as Tommy spoke. She replied, 'Thanks. Good advice. Uncle Adam suggested that I should go on my own, which I am not looking forward to.'

'I would join you if I could.'

Anna, looking intently at Tommy, said, 'I know you would. You'd be very welcome and not just as a researcher.'

46

Anna followed her uncle's directions to the Police Records Office in Philadelphia and found the visitors' car park. She was missing a lecture, but Martha would give her a copy of the notes.

At reception she was directed to a small office on the third floor which had just enough room for a desk and two chairs. There were files on the desk and on every available space on the floor. Some of them looked ancient. A small window at shoulder level and a central overhead light failed to brighten the room.

Detective Allen arrived with more files under his arm, put one on the desk and added the others to the pile on the floor. To Anna, he looked like a college professor with receding hair, glasses and a sweater that had seen better days. He gave her a warm handshake and smile, referred to her Uncle Adam and when they worked together and said that he was glad to have had the opportunity to talk to him again.

He then said, 'Your request is most unusual. Access to files is normally limited to academic researchers who are interested in statistics and trends, not the content of an individual file. However, I am making an exception in this case because the file is a hundred years old and because your uncle vouched for you.'

'Thank you, I really appreciate it.'

He added, 'I'm showing you this file on the condition that it will not be published and will be used only for your family tree. The file contains interviews with Leo Novak, his wife Francesca and their parish priest, Father Clifford. I can't give you copies, but you can take notes.'

'Thank you, of course I will abide by those conditions.' Feeling apprehensive, she added, 'Uncle Adam told you what I'm hoping to find out?'

'Yes, he told me that Leo Novak had been shunned by his family for reasons unknown but thought to be connected with a fight with Bishop Walsh and that you had found out that he had tried to assassinate the bishop sometime in 1912.'

'Yes, the Philadelphia papers didn't cover it, so I am hoping that there is a police file that will help explain what happened and why it happened.'

'Your timing is good. I'm sure you're aware of recent events in the Roman Catholic Church. This has led to a team of detectives examining old files on cases involving clergy.'

'Even those going back to the early 1900s?'

'Yes, a random selection to get an overall picture of common features, for example, the extent, if any, to which the clergy involved the police. One such file was on Leo Novak, so you've been lucky.'

'Oh, fantastic.'

'Well, you might not like the content, and it's unlikely to address all your questions.'

Anna began to speculate where this was likely to lead but then forced herself to concentrate.

Grabbing the file from his desk, Detective Allen stood up, saying, 'Please come with me to a conference room on this floor where you will not be interrupted. You can use the phone there to contact me on extension 3006 if you have burning questions or when you wish to discuss your findings with me here.'

The conference room was windowless with harsh lighting. A rectangular table and six chairs filled the space. A small shelf held the telephone, paper and pens.

Anna, sitting facing the door, skimmed through the file. It was much slimmer than expected and didn't show any signs of being handled repeatedly. Is this the first time it's been read by anybody, apart from Mr Allen and his researchers since it was created a hundred years ago?

She was thankful that all of it seemed to be typed or handwritten in block capitals. I will take notes as I go, reread and prepare questions.

Anna was stunned by the first page.

Sexual Assault of a Minor
Gender: Female
Age: 7 years
Name: Gemma Baudo
Date: July 6, 1912
Interviewee: Francesca Novak
Relationship with victim: Mother
Date of interview: July 26, 1912

Oh God, not Leo, please dear God, not Leo. Anna put her elbows on the table and her head in her hands. Oh Tommy, I wish you were with me now. Then her thoughts went to Gemma and Francesca and how they could have coped. What an almighty shock.

She had to force herself to turn the page and to read Francesca's words.

Francesca: That evening … yes July 6th, I was at home with Gemma. My husband, Leo, was gone to a bar locally to meet friends. At about 9 p.m., our curate, Father Favaloro, a lovely man, called to tell me that my mother, who lived nearby, had taken ill suddenly and that I was required to go to her. Because of the urgency, he very kindly offered to stay with Gemma, who was asleep in bed. I promised to return within the hour or to send someone to replace him. I came back well before 10 p.m. to find Leo sitting on the side of the bed with Gemma in his arms. She was crying bitterly, and when she saw me, she said, 'He hurt me, Momma, he hurt me.' I grabbed her from Leo, she showed me where it hurt, and after I examined her I shouted at him, 'What have you done, what have you done?' He blamed the priest. [Tears and silence]

Interviewer: What did Leo say?

Francesca: He said he had returned only a few minutes before me and that the priest was lying on the bed with his arm under the blankets. Imagine making up a story like that to blame the poor priest. That was disgraceful. I couldn't take any more from him so I shouted at him to leave or I would send for the police. He left.

Interviewer: Did you ever have reason previously to suspect Leo?

Francesca: No. If I did I wouldn't have married him. [Pause – hand-wringing] He always seemed protective of Gemma.

Interviewer: Have you seen him since that day?

Francesca: No, and I don't want to. The policeman called to tell me that Leo had threatened the parish priest. I couldn't deal with it. I told him to call on Charles, Leo's brother, and I gave him his address.

Interviewer: Has your suspicion about Leo changed since July 6th?

Francesca: No, how could it?

Interviewer: Is Leo now living with his brother?

Francesca: You'd have to ask Charles that.

Anna sat back in her chair, light-headed and so sad. Oh my God, Francesca was convinced that Leo was guilty. Three shattered lives. She reflected on this for a few minutes, trying to put herself in the place of any of the three. Despair, how could it be anything else? To try to slow down the whirlwind in her mind and focus on the next interview, she left the room and went to the water cooler on the corridor that she had spotted earlier.

A few detectives walked by, each carrying an armful of files. Judging from the little she had just read, she thought, What a sordid task.

The cool liquid helped. On return, she went to the next page and read a doctor's report confirming that a sexual assault had taken place. Then she thought of her parents. My God, how am I going to tell them? Checking the rest of the file, she saw that it contained an interview with the parish priest and with Leo. She recalled the questions about the assassination attempt suggested by Tommy – the when, where, how and why. She checked again and decided to phone Mr Allen.

'Hello, Mr Allen, this is Anna. I cannot find a report in the file on the assassination attempt.'

'There isn't one.'

'Really? That's what I came here to read.'

'Yes, that surprised us too. The file you're reading was found from a cross-reference in Bishop Walsh's file to this and other reports on sexual abuse, but there was no mention of an attempt on the bishop's life. If the assassination attempt had been reported to the police, I would expect to see a reference to this on the bishop's file and on Mr Novak's file.'

'Looks like a cover-up, doesn't it?'

After a short silence, Mr Allen said, 'Oh, I couldn't comment on that.'

Anna, determined to explore every possibility, said, 'I'm reluctant to give you more work, but is it possible there is another file on the attempted assassination?'

'I'd like to know that myself. It could be an important part of our final report which will be completed soon. I will do another check and contact you in a few days.'

'Thank you. I'll continue reading and will probably have some questions for you.'

'Call me when you're ready.'

What was not in the file now seemed more important than what was, and Anna had to force herself to concentrate.

The interview with the parish priest, Father Clifford, took place in his presbytery on July 27th.

Clifford: Leo Novak arrived here in an anxious state on or about July 13th. He asked to see Father Bruno Favaloro, who he accused of molesting his stepdaughter. I replied that what he was asserting was totally unbelievable, but I promised to question the curate and asked him to return a week later. This he did on July 20th. He was in a very dishevelled state and somewhat incoherent. When I dismissed his story as a total fabrication, he asked to speak to Father Favaloro. I explained to him that he had been transferred to another parish as one of a number of routine transfers. He asked me for the curate's new address. When I refused to give it, he behaved in such a loud, insulting and threatening way that I was left with no alternative but to alert the police. When I told him this, he left abruptly.

Interviewer: Do you wish to add anything further?

Clifford: I should say in fairness to the poor man, on both visits he kept repeating his innocence, saying all he wanted to do was to clear his good name.

Interviewer: Have you seen him or heard from him since July 20th?

Clifford: No.

Poor Leo, all the world is against him. No interview on file with Charles. Was he invited? Did he duck it?

When Anna read the interview again, the implications started to form in her mind. My God, the bishop must have known the full story. Obviously he knew that Leo tried to assassinate him, and now it's almost certain that prior to that he was informed about Leo's accusation of Father Favaloro, his protestations of innocence to the parish priest and that the police had become involved. The bishop could have made it known that Leo was innocent. Did he? Unlikely. If he had, would Leo's insanity have been triggered? Did the failure to absolve Leo result in the attempted assassination and the news embargo by the bishop? It certainly looked that way.

Anna wished she didn't have to read Leo's interview, and expected more bad news, more distress. Leo was interviewed in the police station on July 28th, the day after the parish priest and two days after Francesca. He was described as obviously living rough, straggly beard, dirty clothes, in a very agitated state of mind.

Leo Novak: I'm completely innocent but nobody will believe me. I shouldn't be here. I'm innocent.

Interviewer: Mr Novak, please try to relax and tell us in your own words what happened on the evening of July 6th.

Leo Novak: The evening I went to a bar?

Interviewer: Yes.

Leo Novak: Well, I wish I hadn't – I wouldn't be in the trouble I'm in now. I'm not a drinker. I got home early, and I crept into the house afraid I would wake my wife Francesca or her daughter Gemma. I couldn't believe it when I found a priest lying on Gemma's bed with his arm under her blankets. I shouted something, and he jumped up saying he must have fallen asleep, and he flew from the apartment. Gemma woke, upset, and I took her in my arms to console her. Just then Francesca returned, saw her distress and heard her say, 'He hurt me, Momma, he hurt me.' Francesca thought Gemma was talking about me, and when I tried to explain what I had seen earlier she roared at me, said terrible things about me and warned me to leave the house or she would send for you. [Silence, shifting in the chair, eyes darting around the room as if he was looking for an escape] God almighty, will anyone believe me? I asked the parish priest for help. He threw everything back at me and put you onto me. Will you help me? Please help me.

Interviewer: Gemma is your stepdaughter?

Leo Novak: Yes.

Interviewer: How long have you been married?

Leo Novak: About two years. Francesca's first husband was my good friend Giuseppe Baudo. He was killed in an accident. [Raised voice] But I have known Gemma since she was a baby. I used to mind her when her parents went out ... I would never do anything to hurt her. [Tears and distress. Interview interrupted for 15 minutes]

Interviewer: Thank you for your time, Mr Novak. I now have to caution you about your behaviour with the parish priest and to warn you to stay away from him. You're free to go now, Mr Novak.

A handwritten note on the bottom of the page said:

July 1912. Mr Charles Novak, brother of the above, refused to cooperate with our enquiries.

August 1912: Mr Novak was admitted to the South West Philadelphia Psychiatric Hospital.

Anna dried her tears. Dismissed, nowhere to go, nobody to speak for him, intercede for him, comfort him. Did Charles desert him too?

I wonder if Leo tried to speak to the bishop. In his physical and mental state, that would not have been possible, but did he suffer further rejection? At what point was his insanity triggered? The newspaper reports suggested that the assassination was attempted in August, maybe only days after this interview.

All of this was racing around in Anna's head when suddenly the thought struck her: My God! In the state he was in, how did he manage to get a gun?

She thought of Tommy again and was tempted to phone him but feared that in trying to relay all she had read she would likely dissolve in tears. She left her chair, walked around the room a few times, trying to relieve the tension and to stay focused. She started to read the file again, to check her notes and prepare questions.

As Anna placed the file on Mr Allen's desk, she said, 'I have a few questions. I guess if the answers were not in the file you don't have them either. Your opinion would be helpful though.'

'Go ahead.'

'I take it Leo wasn't charged or prosecuted?'

'Correct. He was cautioned only.'

'Was Father Favaloro ever questioned?'

'It's not recorded, so I doubt it.'

'There's a note on the file that Leo had been admitted to a psychiatric hospital. If that hadn't happened, is it likely that Leo would have been interviewed again?'

'No, I don't think so. If there was any new evidence to justify another interview it would be in the file.'

'Leo escaped twice, in Philadelphia and later in New York.

There's no mention of this.'

'If escapes were recorded, they would be in the file on the assassination attempt.'

'I hope you find that file; it would complete the picture.' When putting her notes in her backpack, Anna added, 'When I discuss all this with my parents, and I'm not looking forward to that, they're going to have questions. If so, may I phone you? I promise not to make a nuisance of myself.'

'Yes, of course.'

As she shook Mr Allen's hand, Anna added, 'Many thanks. I assure you that this information will only be used for our family tree.'

'Glad to help, a pleasure talking with you, and please say hi to Adam.'

When Anna returned to her car, she just sat and stared into space, thinking. *I had expected to learn about an attempted assassination but learned about the sexual abuse of Leo's stepdaughter. I'm upset about a crime against a young girl that happened a hundred years ago. God, what about recent cases? What must the victims and parents be going through, a never-ending trauma?*

Earlier, she had joined her hands to prevent them shaking. Now, to relieve her helplessness, she joined them again to say a silent prayer for Leo, Francesca and Gemma. She then stirred herself to try to be as professional as possible. She made a note of the questions and answers that had ended the meeting and rehearsed how she should break the news to her parents.

Poor Leo. It seems you were wrongly accused of sexual abuse and then, apparently, got no sympathy or understanding from anybody, family members included. Anna was filled with a determination to do what she could to somehow make up for this neglect.

She broke her journey home to have a snack, to try to get her head around all she had learned. When her parents returned from work, she handed them a copy of her typed notes. Her face betrayed her feelings. 'You won't like this, but you should read it. People are still going through this kind of thing today, and I can't imagine how that feels. Dad, maybe Uncle Adam could come over to talk about it?'

With that she went to her room where she emailed a copy of her notes to Tommy, saying, 'The attached is very upsetting. I will Skype you when I have talked to my parents.'

47

Tommy read Anna's report. No wonder she was upset, and I know Dad will be too, no doubt about that. He found Frank downstairs in the kitchen, and together they prepared their evening meal.

Tommy was worried, apprehensive about Frank's reaction. He plucked up the courage to say, 'I got a very disturbing email from Anna. You know she had arranged to visit the police archive. Well, this is the result,' and he handed him a copy.

Frank sat down to read, while Tommy prepared toasted bacon and cheese sandwiches and put on the kettle to brew tea. Glancing at his father, he could see horror registering in his face. Frank finished reading and was silent for a minute or two – a powerful, meaningful silence.

'Oh God, this is the past jumping up to bite us, isn't it? What a tragedy for the Novak family way back then, and here it is again to trouble the current generation.'

Tommy tried to focus on the positive as a distraction. 'The police dropped the investigation. They didn't prosecute Leo Novak. They didn't even question the curate.'

Frank added, 'Not pursuing the curate points to a cover-up by the bishop.' Before Tommy could comment, he said, 'My sisters are not going to like this one bit. For them, it would be like a valuable heirloom being smashed to pieces, that's how they regard the bishop.' Frank was lost in thought. He then said, 'This is helpful to Anna and her family, but at what price to us? Sometimes it's better that things remain hidden. We all know that bishops here and in America covered up child abuse by clergy. I shouldn't be surprised that our relative was among them, but I am. I now know what I wish I didn't know. Right now Tommy, I'm sorry you ever went down this road.'

'Sorry, Dad.'

Tommy tried to take the conversation in a different direction. Pointing to Anna's report, he said, 'Things happened very fast. The sexual assault happened on July 6th, 1912. Leo was interviewed by the police on July 28th, and we know that the assassination was attempted sometime in August.' He didn't wait for a response and went on. 'My gut feeling is that the bishop covered up the sexual abuse by the priest. He regarded the involvement of the police because of Leo's actions as unhelpful, but he didn't try to have Leo blamed for the sexual assault. It's possible that Leo's wife and brother ostracised him because of his attempt to kill the bishop and because of his insanity.'

Frank, with a shake of his head, showed a reluctance to go down this road, but after a short silence, he said, 'God, I hope you're right. I would be horrified, to say the least, if the bishop took advantage of Leo's insanity and his attempt to kill him to falsely blame him for the sexual assault.' He quickly added, as if trying to persuade himself, 'In achieving a cover-up, bishops had cooperation from many sources including the troubled silence of parents. Back then, Bishop Walsh didn't need to transfer blame to a third party to protect the church as he saw it, he had already achieved that.'

Tommy replied, 'Yes, but would removing suspicion from Leo have confirmed the guilt of the curate?'

'Possibly, but apparently all parties knowing that a priest was guilty did not prevent a cover-up, then or since. It was all about preserving the good name of the church and avoiding scandal for the family – everything else was sacrificed for that.'

'A conspiracy of silence?'

'I'm sure there was a huge price to be paid in terms of family rows and turmoil that lasted generations but most of all by the victim who was probably scarred for life. Silence didn't help him or her at all.'

Tommy said, 'Another horrible thought is that the curate went on to reoffend.'

'Very likely, but in fairness to Bishop Walsh, he would have believed that moving the curate away from temptation and sending him for counselling would have brought about a cure. That response didn't apply in the recent deluge of cases in the Irish or American church.'

Tommy was happy that the conversation wasn't just about the impact on their cousin's reputation but felt he had to ask: 'I presume we should keep this to ourselves?'

'My sisters would be better off not knowing any of this.'

'What about Mary and Deirdre?'

'Yes, tell them, but not yet.' Frank went on: 'I know from earlier conversations that Deirdre regarded the bishop as guilty of a cover-up. Mary had also assumed that child abuse by a priest was probably involved but had more to say on the subject.'

'Oh?'

'Yeah, she mentioned that priests and brothers with Irish names have been very prominent in reports on child abuse in other countries. She wondered if we Irish are more prone to paedophilia than others or if it was a case of the disproportionate numbers of Irish among the clergy in those countries – you know, Australia and Canada as well as America.'

'Interesting.'

'She also said that she really felt sorry for the good guys, the priests and brothers who had given their lives to serve others only to be shattered by the revelations and tarred with the same brush.'

Tommy wondered if what he was about to say would upset his dad but decided to risk it. 'What would we do if the *Chronicle* or anyone hears about the police report?'

Frank's face darkened. 'God, I really hope we're not faced with that.'

Tommy said, 'For a start, the report is not ours to release.'

'Yes, but if we refused it would be interpreted as having something bad to hide. Look, this event happened one hundred years ago so keeping the report confidential is not going to put another child in danger. If it did, it would be a different matter entirely.'

Tommy tried to limit the potential damage, saying, 'You recall that the headline in the follow-up report in the *Chronicle* suggested a cover-up and I'll bet many of the readers assumed child abuse was the reason?'

'Yes, you're probably right.'

'Dad, did any of your friends or customers talk to you about the reports in the *Chronicle*?'

'Now that you mention it, I can't recall any serious comment. At the time, a few referred jokingly to having a bishop in the family and made other comments of that kind, but nobody mentioned the attempted assassination or a possible cover-up.'

'Has Father Warren said anything?'

'No, and I met him a few times recently. If anything, he seemed reluctant to have any kind of conversation. Maybe he was afraid I'd raise the subject, and I can't say I blame him.'

'Isn't that strange? What's the expression? The elephant in the room? I had a similar experience. No one stated or queried the obvious. Does that suggest that people assumed the worst about the bishop and were too embarrassed or too considerate to talk about it?'

'Likely, yes. It's not surprising when you think about all the recent disturbing reports and publicity. We Irish have a lot of practice at dealing with things we don't talk about. When you think about the extent of the sex-abuse scandal, there has to be victims and parents in this town, in this parish, who have remained silent over the years, silence as tight as a drum. God, it's awful.'

Tommy said, 'So, God forbid, if the *Chronicle* got hold of Anna's report, it would only confirm for the readers what they already believe?'

Frank answered, without conviction, 'I suppose so.'

Tommy hoped he had managed to ease his father's concerns about public disclosure, but he knew that what the police archive had revealed would be an ongoing hurt for him, a hurt he would want to spare his sisters.

Creating a family tree was intended to distract him from the business takeover. All I've given him is grief. Mary, I'm relying on you now more than ever.

Tommy felt his dad must have been close to asking him to end the research. So, trying to indicate an end of the conversation, he put the sandwiches and a pot of tea on the table. As he did so, he wondered how Anna's parents were reacting.

48

Anna was pleased that Adam was present. She had avoided any detailed discussion with her parents but was well aware that that they were upset and regretful. She hoped that Adam would be a calming influence.

They were chatting in the den. Anna could see that her dad, sitting bolt upright, was uneasy and impatient and wasn't surprised when he interrupted, saying, 'This report reflects badly on the bishop, but it is very bad for Charles and Francesca as well. It's awful, isn't it?'

From her mother's expression, Anna couldn't make out if she shared her dad's view or if she was concerned about the hurt he was experiencing.

Adam said, 'Yes, Peter, it's very sad,' and, turning to Anna, he said, 'Let me have another read of your notes. There's a lot to take in.' When he finished, he said to Anna, 'I'm thrilled about the amount of information you have sourced. It would be impressive if all this happened in recent years, but 1912? A great job. Maybe you should join the police force!'

'Thanks, Uncle Adam, a professional's commendation. Wow!' Anna felt that this eased the tension somewhat.

Adam continued. 'It's horrible for us to read what Leo suffered, but can we take some positives from the report? Is the content good for him?'

Peter, showing annoyance, blurted out, 'How could it be good for him? He was treated disgracefully.'

Adam replied, 'Yes, he was, but let's focus on what we now know. We learned earlier about the news blockage on the assassination attempt. We didn't know why but agreed it wasn't to protect Leo. From Anna's research we now know that it was the priest who was being shielded.'

Katherine said, 'I wish I could be confident of that.'

Adam answered, 'Oh, I think you can. Just think about what Anna has found out: the priest was transferred within days of the assault – a coincidence? Very unlikely. He wasn't even questioned. Leo wasn't charged.' Anna knew from the silence in the room that Adam's words were having a big impact. 'One other point. Back then, the police turned a blind eye to child sexual abuse by clergy. They didn't do so when others were involved. So, if the police thought that Leo was guilty, they would at least have continued with an investigation. As we now know, he was only warned about his fight with the parish priest.'

Peter, now looking less tense, said, 'Maybe, but then why didn't his wife or brother speak up for him?'

Katherine said, 'Peter, love, we need to bear in mind all that Francesca had gone through. She had lost her first husband and was married only two years to Leo. In her eyes, the priest could not have been guilty, and in the circumstances in which she found Gemma with Leo, she blamed him. Then, because Leo threatened the parish priest, the police came to her door. She was in shock, and, as we know, then things went from bad to worse.'

Anna said, 'What are the chances she changed her view later?'

Peter answered, 'Slim. Next came the assassination attempt, and then Leo was sent to a psychiatric hospital, a dark secret.'

Katherine added, 'If I had been in Francesca's shoes, I would want everything kept secret. That's the way things were done at that time. Whether I believed Leo was guilty or innocent I would have cooperated with the bishop in a cover-up. I would not want people to know that my daughter had been sexually assaulted or that my husband tried to kill the bishop or that he was in a mental institution. In other words, the bishop and I would have a mutual interest in hiding the truth.' She was briefly lost in thought before adding, 'Just think about what parents are going through now. They want to keep it a secret but are concerned about endangering other children.'

Adam said, 'It seems to me that for Francesca to change her mind the bishop or a psychiatrist would have had to convince her. Is that likely?'

Anna recalled her earlier thoughts. 'We know that the parish priest did not admit that Leo was innocent. It seems the bishop didn't either. Was this the direct cause of Leo's insanity? The last straw, so to speak?'

Peter said, 'I bet Paul would think so.'

Anna decided she would not raise this with Tommy. It was too hurtful, too worrying. She mentioned that the police report stated that Charles refused to cooperate and said, 'Should we expect the bishop to help Leo when his wife and brother disowned him?'

Adam replied, 'We now know that Francesca told the police that Leo was probably living with Charles. To take him in for questioning they would have sought him there, and so Charles knew the trouble Leo was in.'

Peter was silent, mulling over what he had heard. He then said, 'The Novaks behaved badly, didn't they? Maybe we were better off not knowing anything about them.'

Anna answered, 'Yeah, what we've learned is not good, is it? But look at it with Leo in mind. I don't think Leo molested Gemma, but we don't know if Francesca or Charles believed that then, or later. At least we've cleared his name. At least he's not forgotten.'

Peter replied, 'It seems to me that it's a case of believing what we'd like to believe.'

Katherine responded, 'Even if Francesca and Charles believed that the curate was guilty, they would have disowned Leo because he tried to murder a bishop and because he was probably held in a secure facility for the criminally insane. That must have been bleak and so miserable.'

'God, yes,' Anna said.

Adam, looking at Anna, said, 'Have you heard from Tommy Walsh?'

'Not yet. I wanted us to discuss it first. I wonder how Tommy's father has taken it. His "revered cousin" does this? He must be troubled.' She then added, 'I'm afraid to Skype Tommy, to be honest. We now have more bad news about the bishop, so will Tommy continue with the research?'

Adam said, 'Tommy might be willing to continue, especially when the research must be close to an end, but his father might have other ideas.'

Anna, with a worried frown, said, 'Oh, I hope you're wrong. If Mr Allen produces a file on the assassination attempt, I would want Tommy to be involved.'

Anna's concern was seen by Katherine as more about ending the contact with Tommy than ending the research.

After coffee, Anna saw Adam to his car. 'I'm so glad you were here. Thanks to you, my parents, especially Dad, now know this is about Leo, not us.'

'My pleasure, Anna, and I hope Tommy keeps in touch.' With a smile on his face, Tommy added, 'Would I be correct in thinking there's more than research at stake here?'

Anna, feeling a blush coming on, answered, 'Oh, now, that

would be telling, wouldn't it?'

He laughed as he got in the car.

49

Three days later, when Anna appeared on his monitor, Tommy could see that she wasn't her usual bright self, and he knew why she had delayed contacting him.

'Look, Anna, I'm sorry that you got such disturbing news, and I wish I had been in the archive to help you.'

Anna was moved by his concern and almost became tearful again. She said, 'Tommy, I have to ask you right now: will you continue to help me with the research?'

'Of course, Anna. Of course I will.'

'Oh, thank you, that's a great relief. I spent the past three days worrying that you or your dad would not want to continue, given the implications for the bishop.'

'Anna, I wouldn't desert you in such a difficult time or any other time.'

'Thank you, Tommy. I couldn't do this without you, and even if I could I wouldn't want to do it without you.'

'Anna, the research brought us together, and I'll always be grateful for that.'

Anna asked, 'How has your dad taken all this?'

'He's very upset, said he regretted we had uncovered this awful story and that he's determined to keep it secret.'

'My parents were very upset as well, as I expected they would be. Though he didn't say it, I knew my dad wanted me to wind up the research.'

'Before we go any further,' Tommy said, 'I want to compliment you on your meeting with Mr Allen. You did a great job.'

'Thanks, Tommy. Uncle Adam suggested that I should consider joining the police force.'

'How should I now address you: Sergeant Novak or Police Officer Novak?'

'"Anna", for now, thank you.'

Tommy was glad to see and hear her laugh. 'So, back to your parents. What now?'

'I asked Dad to invite Uncle Adam over, and he made Dad realise that the news was actually good for Leo.'

Tommy replied, 'Yes, at least now we all know why Leo was ostracised, even if we feel it wasn't justified. What do they think now?'

'We're a bit confused. We feel the cover-up was probably because of the sexual assault and not because of the attempt to kill the bishop, but we're not sure if Leo was ostracised because of the assassination attempt and his insanity or whether his wife and brother thought he assaulted Gemma too.'

Tommy said, 'When you think of the sequence of events that Francesca experienced over a few weeks, suspecting Leo of abusing her daughter, his behaviour towards the parish priest, arrest by the police and an attempt to assassinate a bishop, she could hardly have thought anything positive about him.'

'Mom said that as well. Imagine how difficult it would be to even think straight. She says she now feels more sympathy for victims and their families.' Anna continued, 'For Francesca to change her mind about Leo, would the bishop have had to tell her that her husband was innocent, implying, if not stating, that his priest was guilty?'

Tommy replied, 'Dad and I feel that Bishop Walsh would have regarded the attempted assassination as making a cover-up more difficult but not impossible. In other words, he could cover up the action of his curate without implicating Leo. He just needed to avoid unwanted publicity and having to speak publicly about it. That's why he prevented any report appearing in the Philadelphia press.' Tommy was quiet for a moment and then added, 'Of course, we may be biased in favour of our cousin.'

'That's helpful.'

Tommy said, 'When we started out on the research, we never anticipated such a sad story, did we?'

'God, no.'

'If Mr Allen doesn't find a file on the assassination, we'll have reached the end of the road, don't you think?'

'Only the research, not our chats.'

'Of course, we have the best reason to stay in touch.'

'You bet.'

A week later, Tommy got an email from Anna. 'I called Mr Allen. He told me he had asked someone to search for a report on the assassination attempt but they couldn't find anything. We have to draw our own conclusions from that. What a pity, but at least we can now just chat about us. Good news, eh?'

Tommy replied, 'Looking forward to it.' He was disappointed to leave unfinished business and 'what ifs', but then he thought that the file would likely give them more unwelcome information for their family. We have enough of that already. Dad would not want any more bad news for himself or for his sisters.

50

Frank looked across the table at Orla with feelings of great affection which he knew he should voice more often. They were at dinner in a manor-house restaurant about fifteen miles from home on the Birr to Roscrea road. 'You look terrific – that's a beautiful dress.'

'Thank you. Glad you like it.'

'Mary will be asking me about the restaurant and the food and what you were wearing.'

'Tell her it's a knee-length dress made of fine wool.'

'Hope I remember. Colour is dark red, right?'

'Burgundy.'

'Close, but I'm learning.'

Orla placed her hand over his and said, 'Don't worry, I'll teach you.'

Frank asked himself again, Why didn't I propose sooner? Anyway, no point in trying to undo the past. Count my blessings: a second beautiful woman says she loves me.

The restaurant was quiet. They liked to eat early and then linger. He returned to their earlier conversation about the business. 'I think the accommodation over the shop should go with the business. I don't know how they could ever be sold separately. If Mary and Kevin want the business but don't want to live over the shop, it could complicate matters. I need to get legal advice from your boss and from my accountant. Another issue is how do I try to ensure fairness for everyone, including you. How do I divide things as equitably as possible?'

'Frank, please leave me out of it. You know I'm not marrying you for your money,' Orla said with a wide grin.

'Just as well, then, isn't it? OK, let's discuss more important things like setting a date for our wedding and where we'll spend our honeymoon.'

'When you say that, I think I'm dreaming and I'll soon wake up.'

'No, it's not a dream. It's a wonderful reality.'

'Well, the things we need to consider are what dates are available in our parish church, what hotel would be suitable and available, when you and I can get holidays, whether my brother and his wife will travel from New York, what dates would suit your children.'

'You've obviously been thinking about this.'

'Nothing else.'

'Would you like to elope?'

Orla laughed, saying no. 'Why don't we have a discussion with your children. They're more clued in to the modern way of doing things.'

'OK about the wedding, but let's decide on our honeymoon ourselves. Just a thought: if your brother doesn't come home, how about a honeymoon in New York?'

'Lovely idea.'

* * *

Tommy had come home for one of Mrs Duggan's lunches and joined his dad in the kitchen.

'So, how are you and Anna getting along?'

'Skype is great, but for building a relationship it certainly has its limitations. Deirdre said that I'm daft, that the whole thing is daft and it's bound to fizzle out.'

'Well, Tommy, if the attraction is there I'm sure you'll find a way to overcome the problems. Remember: "Fortune favours the brave".'

'Her priority for now is to concentrate on her studies, and that's as it should be.'

'Well, I'm not so sure about that, but keep battling against the odds. You need to be as determined as you are on the football field.'

'I hear you, I hear you.'

Mary phoned, and after the usual chit-chat she mentioned the discussions with Dad. Tommy decided he shouldn't push too hard or encourage Mary to make a decision she might later regret. Am I passing the buck? But if she declines, what then? The pressure's back on me.

He said, 'You and Kevin have had a lot to think about. Can I help in any way?'

'Thanks Tommy, I'm sure you can. In some ways, the decision is easy: Kevin will support me in whatever decision I make, I'd like to work in the business again, and I'd like to return to Clondore.'

'So, what's the difficult part?'

'I don't want to be a grabber. Why should I get everything?'

'I'm sure Dad will want to look after everybody, including Orla. Anything else?'

'The transition. I wouldn't want to push Dad out, but I would be afraid of uncertainty.'

'You're right about that, so you and Dad should regard all of this as a business decision rather than a father–daughter decision.'

'You two think alike. He said that too, and he also said I should get independent advice.'

'That's wise. If you don't know a solicitor, I recommend you talk to my friend Dave McCarthy, here in Clondore. You'll remember he's on the football team. He'd know the various types of family settlements, and that would be a good place to start. Dad will be consulting Tom O'Donnell, I expect. I don't know an accountant, but maybe your better half does?'

'We'll have a chat, and I'll talk to you soon.'

'Bye, Mary. Call me if I can help.' Relief, relief, he thought, blessed relief.

Just after 7 p.m., Anna answered his Skype call. When she appeared on screen wearing a white T-shirt under a plaid flannel shirt, he was reminded again how easy it appeared to be for her to look beautiful. He assumed that she had a busy morning in college and had just finished a snack lunch, but she looked serene, unruffled and breathtakingly gorgeous.

'How do you manage to always look so beautiful?'

Anna was surprised and pleased with this forthright comment. 'Thanks Tommy! I'm not sure about that, but thanks. Hey, you know what? I've only ever seen you sitting down. How tall are you, anyway?'

Standing up, his upper body disappearing from the screen, Tommy replied, 'Five eleven in my stocking feet,' and sat down again.

'I'd be looking up to you then. I'm five inches shorter.'

Tommy stood up again and moved his computer monitor in an arc around his bedroom, showing his large old-style mahogany wardrobe, his single bed beside the wall and behind the door, a more modern chest of drawers, an easy chair and back to his desk in front of the only window in the room. He had acted on impulse and wondered if Anna thought the room was old-fashioned and in need of upgrading. It brought home to him that the whole house lacked a woman's touch and probably needed a total makeover. I'll leave that to Orla or Mary, he thought. He was relieved that quite by accident the room looked reasonably tidy. 'Now,' he said, 'You've seen my bedroom.'

Anna burst out laughing, 'Hope your dad never finds out.'

'If it was daylight I could show you the outdoor area of the shop where gardening, farming and heavy goods are displayed. Nearby to the right are my school and Gaelic football club, and the rest is rural and wintry County Offaly.'

'Gee, I'll be trying to picture all that in my mind. For now, my parents said thanks for continuing to help us.'

'Looks like the research is over, so what's the best way to stay in touch? How about we Skype each other once a week? You suggest the day and time that suits you to receive a call. Your call to me can be flexible.'

'Sounds good. I'll let you know the best day.'

'We can have longer conversations about us.'

'Yes please.'

51

Jimmy was packing winter-flowering bedding plants, a bag of compost and two large plant pots into the boot of a customer's car when Tommy arrived in the shop. Jimmy was dressed in his usual full-length dustcoat and broad-brimmed hat. Tommy noted that Jimmy always dressed this way, winter and summer, while his dad always wore a tweed sports jacket over collar and tie. Their attire, he knew, had nothing to do with their roles as owner and employee. It was just what they felt comfortable in.

When the customer left, Jimmy joined him in the shop and said, 'I'm about to place an order with one of our suppliers for gardening equipment. Should I do anything differently?'

'No, do as normal for all three suppliers. Get Dad to witness the order. When the goods arrive, do not let the delivery man distribute the various items around the shop. Use some excuse if you have to, say you are reorganising, and get him to drop the delivery in one place, preferably inside the shop. When he has left, you and Dad together check the items delivered against the delivery invoice and then against the original order. If my suspicions are correct, this should show up the fraud. If not, I will have to dig further.'

'Thanks Tommy. I'll do exactly as you say, and then I'll wring the guy's bloody neck.'

Tommy laughed at Jimmy's bravado and said, 'If I'm correct, you won't get the chance – you'll never see him again.'

'More's the pity.'

On Sunday night, when Tommy was packing his briefcase for the following morning, he received an unexpected call from Anna.

'Hi! Glad you're at home, there's someone here who wants to meet you.'

Tommy expected her dad to appear on screen, something he was not prepared for. 'Who?'

'My friend Martha.'

'Oh, one of your singing group. Am I going to hear "Rockin' Around the Christmas Tree"?'

'Sorry, no. Jane isn't with us today.'

'Pity.'

Martha's face appeared on the screen. 'Hi, Tommy.'

'Hello, Martha. I'm very pleased to meet you.'

'Thanks, Tommy. When are you and your football team going to visit us? All the girls in college would love that.'

'Well, if I could tell my team that all the women in your college are as beautiful as you two, they would book their tickets tomorrow.'

Tommy could hear Anna and Martha laugh off screen followed by whispering. Martha's face reappeared. 'Well, you've met the two most beautiful women at DeSales.'

'In that case, I won't invite them – I wouldn't want all that competition.'

More laughter, followed by Anna's appearance. 'We're supposed to be studying, but Martha made me call you. Back to work!'

'Thanks for insisting, Martha. Great to meet you and to have an unexpected time with Anna.'

'Bye, Tommy.'

'Bye, Anna; bye, Martha.'

Martha said to Anna, 'I'm going to be here this time every Sunday. It's the best excuse I know to interrupt study.'

'You like him then?'

'I'm surprised how well you could contain yourself when talking about him.'

'It's the distance thing. You know, how do you get excited when confined to a screen?'

'Anna, he's cute, he's funny, charming, and he seems crazy about you. What more do you want?'

'I want him here in Center Valley not thousands of miles away. I look forward to seeing him on screen even when we are just talking about the research. We're getting closer, but I wonder if anything will come of it? I mean, if we met, would we still like each other?'

Martha was unusually quiet then said, 'It's very romantic and all that. You know, like a novel or a movie where two people meet just before he emigrates or goes off to war, and she's left wondering if letters will keep their relationship alive and will she ever see him again. Except in your case you have never actually met the guy so it's doubly frustrating and a pain in the butt.'

'What should I do?'

'Nothing for now. From what you've told me, the research is coming to an end, and if Tommy is the kind of guy I think he is, he'll think of something.'

'I want that to happen, but I'm scared that it will. Does that make sense?'

'Yeah, it does.'

* * *

When Tommy saw the name 'Martha Douglas' in his inbox, he

worried that something may have happened to Anna and opened the message immediately.

Hi Tommy,

I'll bet you are surprised to hear from me. I managed to get your email address when Anna wasn't looking.

I know you and Anna have a shared interest in family research but I also believe that a warmer relationship is developing and that you two should meet.

Is there any possibility that you would visit this part of the world in the near future? I know this is a big ask and I guess it's impossible to forecast what would happen between you and Anna if you did come.

Please do not tell Anna I contacted you. She would kill me.

Finally, please forgive me if you feel I have misread the situation; otherwise please depend on my willingness to play Cupid.

Best wishes,

Martha Douglas

Tommy read the message twice. Here's the opportunity I've been hoping for. Martha is acting independently, but she must be reflecting Anna's feelings. If our relationship is to develop, we have to meet.

He replied immediately.

Dear Martha,

Many thanks for your surprising and very welcome message.

You've been reading my mind. For some time I have been thinking should I, and how could I, arrange to meet Anna. Now, with you as an ally, a visit is more achievable.

I expect to have about a week's holiday around Easter, in late March/early April. How would this fit with Anna's college schedule? The alternative is to wait until exams are over. My summer holidays begin in early June. The sooner, the better, but even if it is months away, a visit arranged for then would be better than the current frustrating uncertainty.

Until you and I decide the most suitable time to visit, please keep Anna in the dark.

Thanks again for your initiative, and I look forward to hearing from you.

He wondered how a trip to Pennsylvania would fit with his schedule for football matches, his dad's marriage plans or his work commitments in the business during holiday time. He had no doubt what his priority was, and for now he would not disclose his plans, such as they were, to anybody at home.

52

Anthony Dudek's kitchen table was covered in assorted documents, photos, letters, certificates of births, marriages and deaths. Anthony was relieved that his son, Edward, who was due any minute, had agreed to create their family tree from all this information. He had no idea how this would be done, but in an effort to be useful he put a sticky note on each document and wrote the event and the year to which it referred.

While doing this, he was also keeping an eye on the frozen dinners he was preparing for the two of them. It was Edward's day off, and he wanted to save him the time of cooking for himself to make up for the time he was spending on the family tree. Anthony thought about his other son and his daughter who said they were interested in the research but had not offered to do any of the work.

Anthony regretted selling his house and moving to an apartment when his wife died eleven years earlier. His children assured him that it would be much better for him, but he never felt that way. I really miss the old place, and sometimes I wonder if I left many of my memories there. At least I'm still in the same neighbourhood near my friends, and I'm glad Edward lives nearby. But I don't want to be a burden.

Edward arrived, carrying a large brown envelope from which

he took another set of documents. 'You need a bigger table, Dad,' he said with a smile.

Anthony was wondering how chaos could be avoided. 'Are they more of the same?'

'Yes, mainly certificates confirming what we already know and one major surprise.'

'Did you find a skeleton in our cupboard?' Anthony said this jokingly but was apprehensive at the same time.

'Well, something like that.'

'C'mon, you have my full attention.'

'When I searched for your grandma's marriage certificate, I found two.'

'Two certificates?'

'Yes, but for two marriages.'

'C'mon, that has to be a mistake. No way, that couldn't be. It must be two people of the same name who happened to marry at the same time.'

Edward was apprehensive. He didn't want to upset his dad. 'That's what I thought initially. I found the record of the second marriage first and assumed, like you, that it was for a different person, but, having checked more than once, I believe Francesca got married for a second time.'

'I was in my early teens when she died, and if she had married twice, I would have heard about it. Was this second marriage before or after she married my grandfather?'

'After. About eight years after.'

'All the more reason I would have known about it.' He took out his reading glasses, saying, 'Let me see the certificates.'

Anthony glossed over the certificate for the marriage to Giuseppe Baudo in 1902. He knew all about that. He then read the certificate of the marriage between Francesca Baudo and Leo Novak in 1910. He just looked at Edward in disbelief.

Edward said, 'Did you notice that Francesca's address is the same in both documents?'

'Could there be two people of the same name, for example a cousin of Francesca's?'

'The age given for Francesca matches with her birth certificate. We also know from other sources that she continued at that address right through her life.'

'My mother would have been about five in 1910. I just can't believe that she had a stepfather she didn't tell me about.'

'Well, that's the situation we're in.'

They were both lost for words. Anthony broke the silence. 'I'm astounded. There's no other word for it.'

Edward was anxious to soften the blow. 'Do I smell something nice for dinner? Let's discuss it as we eat.'

'OK, but your news has certainly blunted my appetite.'

They left the kitchen table undisturbed and moved to the dining room.

Edward had thought a lot about the unknown second husband but didn't want to burden his father with it. However, after a period of silence, Anthony said that his head was full of questions.

'Who is this Leo Novak? What happened to him? Why were we not told about the marriage, and how did my grandmother and mother manage to keep it a secret?'

'Well, they certainly succeeded. We have no clue about him.'

'I wonder …'

'What?'

'It may be nothing, but it might give us a clue. When my mother died, I found a letter addressed to her that I think was intended to remain hidden.'

'So?'

'It was signed by someone named Leo. Now, will I remember where I put it?'

Edward didn't comment but hoped that he could complete the family tree soon and without any further research.

53

Deirdre phoned, a rare event. She enquired about the discussion Mary and Dad were having.

'It's going well as far as I can tell, but why don't you ask them yourself? I'm sure they would welcome a call.'

'I'll phone Mary. I'll leave Dad alone; he may think I want a slice of the action, and I don't want to complicate things.'

'Phone him anyway. He'd welcome a surprise.'

'I will. Now do you have Alan Manahan's mobile number?' Deirdre knew that this would rattle Tommy, and this was part of her plan, but only part. She had begun to think that long term she would really like to teach music at university level, but she had no intention of disclosing that to Tommy or to Alan Manahan. They would think she had 'ideas above her station'. She continued, 'I'm wondering whether I should be a music teacher or a teacher who teaches music, if you follow my drift? I need to talk to Alan to get his advice.'

'Yeah, the more versatile you are the more employable you'll be, and I don't have to tell you how difficult it is to get a teaching post, with all the cutbacks.' Tommy read out the number, wondering did she really need to talk to Alan again about this.

'Thanks Tommy, I'll see you, and I'll see Alan soon.' Mission accomplished.

The shop got busier with people preparing for seasonal planting, garden maintenance and the DIY tasks that had accumulated since the autumn. On Saturday from mid-morning to closing time at 6 p.m., Tommy helped out in the shop, compensated later by his regular get-together with his pals in O'Riordan's pub.

* * *

Anna was working alone in the bookstore during the morning slack time, doing the jobs she was supposed to do: restocking shelves and general tidying. She had her back to the door when she heard, 'Hi, Anna, I was hoping to find you here.'

She recognised the voice, but Josh Hamilton was the last person she expected to see. Before she could respond, he continued, 'I won't take too much of your time. I'm here for two reasons. Listen, I'm sorry about the way I acted. It was unforgivable.'

Anna tried to interject. 'Josh, I—'

But Josh went on: 'I also want to thank you for trying to help me.'

'Glad I was of some help.'

'More than you could know. I've been having treatment in a clinic in Philly, and I'm doing a lot better.'

'Well, good for you. It's not easy to admit to having a problem.'

A three-way conversation approached the door, students she did not recognise. Josh said, 'I've said what I came to say, Anna. I hope you're fine. Thanks again.' And he was gone, leaving Anna confused and troubled.

She tried to concentrate on the customers, and, when they departed, her head was full of Josh, of first dates, first kisses, and exciting possibilities. Josh's expressions of repentance and gratitude were as impactful as they were unexpected. She would have felt it easier to deal with the addicted Josh, to confirm that he was no longer part of her life, but was the old Josh now back?

It must have been difficult for him to come back to apologise. Feelings of compassion were competing with a reawakening of physical attraction. He looks great, younger and fitter than the last time I saw him … Yeah, he sure does.

Hold on a minute, she told herself. Why am I getting worked up about this? He just called to say thanks. Let that be the end of it. It's over.

It didn't convince.

She thought about phoning Martha but changed her mind, not because personal calls were prohibited during working hours but because she needed to get her head straight.

Over the next few days, she thought of little else. She was reaching a conclusion that because Josh's return had such an impact on her that she must still have strong feelings for him.

She was in her bedroom when her sister Barbara phoned for her usual update.

'You won't believe this, but Josh Hamilton arrived in the store to apologise and to thank me.'

'Will he contact you again?'

'Not sure, and not sure if I want him to.'

'Anna, you closed that book months ago. Don't feel you have to open it again.'

'Yeah, I hear you.'

'Just be careful. Don't rush things.

'Right.' She's my caring sister, my protector, but …

Anna exchanged texts with Martha.

'He's back.'

'Josh?'

'Yes.'

'Oh, tell me more.'

'I'll see you in class tomorrow.'

'You're so mean making me wait.'

Anna and Martha went to a coffee shop at Saucon Valley for a private chat. Anna described Josh's apology.

'Well, you seem pleased that he's back.'

'I'm all over the place. I cannot think straight.'

'That suggests you still care for him.'

'That's how it looks to me as well, but what should I do now?'

'Nothing. As far as you know he could be madly in love with someone else.'

'Yes, I suppose. What if he phones and asks me out?'

Martha thought for a minute and said, 'You could refuse him first time, make him beg a little, but then there's no harm in just meeting him, is there? But I suggest somewhere very public so that he doesn't get the wrong idea.'

'I knew I could rely on you. I'll be careful. That's if he does contact me. Maybe I've scared him away for good.'

'Anna, there's something you seem to have forgotten.'

'Oh? What?'

'Where does Tommy fit into all of this?'

'God, I wish I knew.'

Anna's thoughts, which she didn't dare disclose to Martha, were that Josh was flesh and blood, here and now, while Tommy was a face on a screen that she would never meet or touch.

Martha, believing Anna would avoid or resist any advances from Josh, decided to maintain her effort as a dating agency. She emailed Tommy.

Hi Tommy,

Glad my intuition was correct.

The timing is tricky. The timing of the spring break doesn't suit. The Easter vacation is just for the weekend from Friday March 29th to Monday April 1st inclusive, and the semester exams begin on Tuesday May 6th. This is the cramming time.

Would a brief visit be possible at Easter to be followed by a second meeting here or possibly in Ireland when your school term finishes? That's the expensive option. Alternatively, postpone a visit here until, say, June, but announce it soon. That's the practical option, but maybe it's not the time to be practical?

Let me know what you think.

In the meantime, my lips are sealed. I do enjoy the intrigue.

Best wishes,

Martha

She sat back and exhaled to relieve the tension she was feeling. God, did I do the right thing? What if Josh comes back?

54

Anna and her mother were having a chat over a cup of coffee. 'How's Tommy these days? I haven't heard you talking about him.'

'Tommy is fine, Mom. We agreed that we would keep in touch when the research is completed, and in the meantime I have a lot to do at school.'

'Very wise. So, you two are getting along OK then?'

'Of course, Mom. He's a lovely guy, he's sweet, he's fun, and you know how much work he's done on our family tree.'

'So, what does he look like? Describe him for me.'

'He's tall, almost six feet, sandy-red hair, fair-skinned with grey-blue eyes. It's difficult to be sure about colours on screen.'

'Tell me more.'

'His face lights up when he smiles, which he does often, and, oh, he has a lovely Irish accent. I wonder what he thinks of mine.'

Katherine looked at her wide-eyed and said, 'Tell me how you know his height.'

'I asked him.'

'It's like that, is it? Too bad he doesn't live here.'

'Yeah,' said in a way that Katherine found difficult to read.

* * *

Mary, knowing that Tommy would be on his coffee break, phoned looking for Dave McCarthy's contact details. She then asked, 'What about the living accommodation over the shop?'

'It would be a problem later if the accommodation and the business were under separate ownership.'

'Yeah, it would be difficult to sell them separately.'

Tommy added, 'I've been thinking that whoever moves in, Orla or yourself and Kevin, would want to upgrade. I would move out. It's time I had a house of my own anyway, and because of the recession it's a good time to buy.'

Mary replied that he was probably right on both counts and then said, 'Now, Mr Best Man, what arrangements have you and Dad made for the wedding?'

'None that I'm aware of.'

'Now I call that dereliction of duty. Did you know that by law a three-month notice is required of the intention to marry and that the church likes the couple to do a pre-marriage course? I could go on.'

'Dad may be working on it, but I doubt it. Perhaps Orla has everything in hand? I'd better get moving. You recall that he mentioned the possibility of being married at Easter, but it looks like he's already late for that. Just as well you called.'

'You'd better google "marriage plans". Phone me if you want any advice or suggestions.'

'Sure will, thanks.'

Tommy's embarrassment was balanced somewhat by the realisation that an Easter wedding was now unlikely and that he'd be free to visit Anna but concluded he needed to help his dad and get clarity on plans for the months ahead.

55

Anna's reaction when she saw Josh's number on her cell phone was as if she had been hoping for a first date. It was two weeks since he came to the bookstore, and she had begun to think she would not hear from him again.

'Hello, Josh, how is your course going?' She was about to say 'treatment' but decided to be more diplomatic.

'Fine, thank you, getting better every day.'

'That's wonderful. I'm happy for you.'

'Thanks Anna. It's you I have to thank for my recovery. I'll be home next weekend, and I'm hoping you will come over Saturday night. I guarantee that my mother will be there this time. Please say yes.'

Anna was surprised given the previous experience at his house and was mindful of the advice from Barbara and from Martha, but her heart ruled her head. She answered, 'OK, what time were you thinking?'

'Say, 7 p.m.?'

Anna decided not to tell Martha about the invitation. She knew she'd say not to go.

* * *

Josh's mother was not what Anna expected. Yes, she was well dressed, but she was warm and down to earth. 'Hello, Anna, I'm Lucy. It's lovely to meet you. Josh has told me a lot about you.'

Just as Anna was thinking what Josh could have told her, she added, 'Thank you for knocking sense into his stubborn head.'

They sat in the kitchen, where dinner was already on the table. Anna took one glass of wine because she was driving but then felt she should have declined since Josh obviously would not be joining her.

When the meal was over, his mother said, 'I have to head to the club. Hope you have a good night.'

Anna wondered if she had any inkling of what had happened the last time she came to this house – probably not. She said, 'Thanks for supper, Mrs Hamilton.'

Anna then offered to tidy up and stack the dishwasher, which Josh was pleased to accept. Josh made a second pot of coffee, and they lingered at the table chatting about this and that. Josh then said, 'Let's move to the sitting room. It will be more comfortable there.'

He went straight to a CD player on a cabinet, saying, 'These CDs belong to my parents, but let's see if there is anything here we could listen to.'

Well, she thought, he hadn't planned a seduction, otherwise he would have selected the music earlier.

Anna joined him, and they spent a few minutes without success making the same type of comments that each generation makes about their parents. Anna picked up a Peggy Lee CD and said, 'Oh, I've heard of her. She's one of my parents' favourites. Let's see.' She went down the list of songs, then said, 'I've heard of this one: "Fever." You could try that.'

'Yeah, I think Michael Bublé recorded it, Beyoncé too. Anyway, let's give it a go.'

When she heard Peggy Lee sing about fever brought on by love and kisses, she blushed inwardly. Oh God, what must he think of me?

Josh took Anna's hand, drew her close and started to move in rhythm with the music. She was startled but in a nice way and tried to follow his movement. She soon began to relax and to enjoy being held by him. He put his hand on the back of her neck and kissed her, using the other hand to hold her body closer.

As the song ended, he drew her towards the couch where the physical contact continued and former passion was rekindled.

Anna extricated herself from Josh's embrace, smoothed her clothes and her hair and stood up saying, 'I gotta get going, Josh. Thanks for a lovely evening.'

'Well, it's certainly been better than the last time you were here. Anna, I have to go back to Philly for three weeks. Will you join me for dinner when I return?'

She was tempted again to ask about his treatment but thought better of it. She just smiled and said, 'Text me when you come back.'

When Josh escorted her to her car, she gave him a friendly peck on the cheek, thanked him again and drove away. On her way home, she reflected on the last time she had made the same trip. Who would have thought that the old Josh would return?

She was happily confused, at least for that moment, wondering if her plans for grad school would now depend on where Josh lived. She decided her parents would be kept in the dark and then thought, Now what do I say to Martha?

56

When Anna opened her email, a quick glance told her that her inbox did not include a message from Tommy, but then she noticed the name 'Edward Dudek' in the list. She quickly opened it.

This email is made possible by the 'Member Connect' facility in the software programme which we both used to create our family tree. Leo Novak is the link between our families.

I prepared our tree, but my dad, who is eighty-two, was the instigator. He knows very little about Leo Novak who was the second husband of Francesca, my great-grandmother. He disappeared early in the marriage. My dad and I are hoping that you will be able to tell us more.

I live in Philadelphia, and it would be great if we could meet up to share information. With this in mind, could we arrange a telephone call to discuss this?

Best wishes,
Edward Dudek
Tel: 215-825-4066

Anna was amazed that the system had worked for her again, first with Tommy and now with someone listed on Francesca's family tree. On impulse, she dialled the number. A female voice answered: 'Good evening, St Petroc's Parish. How can I help you?'

'Oh … ah … ah … could I speak to Edward Dudek please?'

'Father Dudek is saying the evening Mass, but if you call back in about forty-five minutes he should be here. Who shall I say called?'

'Anna Novak. Please tell him I'm responding to his email.'

'Of course. Goodbye.'

Anna sent a copy of Father Dudek's email to Tommy with a short comment celebrating the connection and promising to keep him posted.

When Katherine read the message, she said, 'So, will we be meeting Gemma's son?'

'God, I hope not. It would be very stressful for an eighty-two-year-old.'

Further conversation was cut short when Father Dudek returned Anna's call. After an exchange of pleasantries, Anna confirmed that a meeting was indeed possible and that she and her parents would travel to meet him in Philadelphia. He gave her directions to his church and presbytery, referred to the location map on the parish website and the car parking space available. They agreed to meet at 11 a.m. on Saturday of the following week.

'Please join me for lunch after our discussion.'

'Thank you, Father, that would be nice. When we started the research we knew nothing about Leo Novak, but we found out quite a lot which we will share with you. You need to be aware that you and your father might find some of the information upsetting.'

'Have we skeletons in the cupboard?'

'No, no. It's a case of someone having a very bad experience.'

'Right, I won't pry any further, but I'm now intrigued about what you are going to tell me.'

'The other important point is that I was given information from police records in confidence and with the limitation that it would be used only for our family tree, so we will be sharing it on that basis.'

'Now I'm doubly intrigued, but of course I'll abide by the same conditions.'

'We're not talking about state secrets here, just family stuff.'

'Despite your warning about the upsetting nature of some of the information, I'll invite my dad to join us. Is that OK?'

Anna hesitated briefly then replied, 'Of course. My parents Peter and Katherine and I look forward to meeting both of you.'

* * *

Tommy just watched and waited as Jimmy and Frank checked the goods delivered and then checked them again. At first glance, all the different products listed on the original order had been delivered, but on closer examination they found that they were left short in five of the eighteen items.

'A very clever theft,' Frank said. 'Up to now I never did a detailed count of the items delivered, and I expect this is common practice in the business.'

Jimmy made a note of the missing items: garden rakes, bales of chicken wire, lawn feed and weed, gardening gloves and patio cleaner. 'Tell me, Tommy,' he said, 'does being a genius become boring?'

'Now and again, Jimmy, now and again. I suppose I'll just have to get used to it.'

All three shared the light relief.

'So McLoughlin's is the culprit. Well, doesn't that take the biscuit?' Frank said.

Later, Frank telephoned Hugh McLoughlin, assuming he would be shocked, but the reply he got was, 'Oh God, not you as well. We're investigating this, and it seems that the delivery man we took on last year is the thief. We think he's been running his own wholesale business with our supplies.'

'Sorry you have this mess to clear up, Hugh.'

'Thanks. You'll be hearing from me.'

Jimmy, who was listening to this conversation, said, 'Fair dues to Tommy. He's the man for this business, no doubt.'

'Very true, Jimmy. I'll thank him for his detective work.' As he said this, Frank was reminded to phone Mary.

* * *

Anna was studying in her bedroom when Barbara phoned out of the blue, not her routine weekend chat, no pleasantries. Anna sensed bad news.

'Hi, Anna. I'm now going to tell you something that I'd have to deny later if it became known. When you told me about Josh calling to see you I figured that you and he might become an item again, so I asked around about him. He seems to have done well in the treatment centre—'

'Yeah, isn't that wonderful?'

'Let me finish. Yes, he did well there, but sadly he has just swapped one addiction for another. Little or no booze, but not only is he now doing drugs, he's dealing as well – not in large amounts but dealing all the same.'

'But if—'

Barbara cut her short, saying, 'I think you know what you have to do. Bye.'

Anna felt that if her sister had not spoken so abruptly, she might not have spoken at all. She had wanted to say that if

Josh could recover from one addiction, he could do the same with drugs. She spent some time optimistically considering that possibility but couldn't avoid the conclusion that rehabilitation was unlikely and that even if he succeeded he would relapse. She knew that sharing such a life would be hell.

Does Barbara think I'm one of those women who think they can rescue a guy like Josh? I'm not, definitely not. God, what was I thinking? It's less than six months since I could have – and maybe should have – reported him for assault. I should have listened to Martha, played it cool. Instead, I rushed back in his arms. What a fool!

Her mind then jumped from grieving for him and for the end of a relationship that once promised so much to the hurt caused by his repeated duplicity and breach of trust. A flood of tears, a silent expression of grief, increased her distress.

When she recovered, she felt relief that her parents had remained in the dark. She stayed in her room so that they would not see her troubled face, and she tried in vain to return to her studies.

57

Anna was waiting for Tommy's scheduled Sunday Skype call with her head and her heart full of him and her increased awareness, in the light of recent events, of just how much he meant to her. Right now, she thought, I'd love to hug him and be hugged by him.

When his face appeared on screen, she said, 'You're so reliable and punctual.'

'Well, I try to be. I'd hate to miss seeing you even if only on a screen.'

'Me too. I'm trying to stay focused on my studies and avoid distractions, but you're the exception.'

Skype's limitation and frustration caused a short silence, broken by Anna. 'Tell me about your work on career guidance – I cut you short on a previous call.'

'In our system, the fourth year in secondary school is a transition year. Maybe you would call it a gap year. One of my jobs is to plan and coordinate the programme of activities for that year.'

'So, what's the purpose?'

'It's intended to help the students to discover and develop their own individual talents and strengths.'

Anna just wanted to keep talking about things not connected with their research. 'Give me a couple of examples.'

'Each pupil prepares their own plan for the year in consultation with the teachers, and these are evaluated and scored. In addition, there are group events such as fundraising for charity or an information evening in Limerick Institute of Technology, which we attended recently.'

'Wow, sounds good. We do things so differently here.'

'Anna, tell me about your college schedule. Do you get any midterm breaks, any downtime?'

'We get a week in early March and the Easter weekend, and that's about it. It isn't downtime. It's when the cramming gets done.' Anna then added, with laughter in her voice, 'Why are you asking? You're not thinking about coming to see me, are you?'

'Well, I am actually.'

'Oh, I was just joking Tommy. Oh, that's wonderful news. Please visit, Tommy, please, please. Just before you phoned I was thinking about how much I wanted to hug you. Now I look forward to it happening and to the chats over coffee or a beer we talked about so often, and to being together, and to learning more about each other, and am I excited or what?!' She then blurted out, 'Why are you coming to see me?'

'Because I can't wait to be with you.'

'That is a really good answer.'

They both laughed and relished the moment.

Tommy, captivated by Anna's response, said, 'I didn't intend mentioning it until I could suggest a definite date, but now I'm glad you asked. I'm thinking of a short visit around the Easter weekend, and I can't wait.'

'My head's whirling. This is awesome.'

'What will your parents think?'

'I know they'll look forward to meeting you.'

'One more thing: no pressure, no obligations. Let's enjoy a few days together and take it from there.'

'Relax, Tommy. We'll have a blast.'

'Looks like the research has come to an end, unless of course your contact with the Dudeks suggests other lines of enquiry.'

'Now you've broken the spell.'

Anna was anxious to get back to discussing the visit. 'Tommy you've made my day, my whole year, and please do come for Easter, and please book your trip as soon as you can. I'll concentrate on my studies much better when I know for certain that you're coming. So, there's your incentive.'

'This is a special day for us, isn't it?'

After a short but potent silence, Anna said, 'Yeah, really special.'

Tommy was quiet for a moment, suddenly shy. 'In a way, Leo brought us together.'

'What a wonderful thought. I wish we could tell him.'

'Yeah, he had very little good news in his life.'

'I look forward to seeing you at Easter,' Anna said. 'Really seeing you, if you know what I mean.'

'Me too. Now how can I think straight?'

'Make it happen, Tommy, please.'

'Will do. Talk to you soon.'

Anna reached for her phone. She just had to tell Martha. 'Hi, you're not going to believe what has just happened! Tommy is coming for a visit at Easter.'

'Oh, awesome, but I'm not surprised really. When I saw him on Skype I just had a hunch he would do this. Any chance a few of his football team would come too?'

'He didn't mention that, but who knows? Maybe the next time, eh?'

'I'm very happy for you, I really am. A face on a screen is never enough. I look forward to meeting him, and I promise I will disappear at the appropriate time.'

'Thanks Martha. Your support has been terrific.'

Martha thought, Wait until she finds out, but said, 'How are you going to concentrate on your classes? Even I'm distracted.'

'I expect my dad will say the same, but it's the most wonderful distraction imaginable.'

'Lucky you.'

'Yeah, lucky me.'

* * *

Tommy received a message from Martha telling him that when she met Anna the following day she intended to disclose her role 'firing Cupid's arrows'. He replied, saying how the proposed visit at Easter had come about and requesting that the emails they exchanged be given to Anna so that any possible misunderstanding would be avoided.

Tommy joined his dad in the kitchen and was relieved to be told that no firm date had been set for the wedding but that late May was the target time. Tommy expressed relief and confided that he was planning a visit to Pennsylvania during his Easter holidays. His dad reached across, shook his hand warmly, saying, 'Good on you, Tommy. I'm delighted you are taking the brave step, and I hope you'll be as lucky in love as I've been – not once, but twice.'

'Thanks, Dad.'

'Get Anna to come and visit us during the summer.'

'Yeah, I hope that'll happen,' he answered, with the unspoken possibility that Anna might do a postgraduate course in Ireland. They both knew the implications for the business succession, but nothing was said.

* * *

Anna departed from the agreed schedule and Skyped Tommy midweek. 'So, I now have to deal with two conspirators.'

Tommy was relieved that she laughed as she said this. 'I hope Martha showed you the emails we exchanged.'

'Yes, she did, and I know you were already planning a visit.'

'What she said encouraged me to think that you would welcome a visit even at this very busy time.'

Anna had a fleeting thought about Josh as she said, 'I don't know how you could have doubted it. I'll show you when you get here.'

'Is that a promise?'

'A very definite promise.'

'Wow. I'd like to be there right now.'

'You're saying all the right things.'

Each savoured the silence.

Anna said, 'As you say, back to business: my parents and I are meeting Father Dudek and his dad in St Petroc's presbytery in Philadelphia on Saturday. It's bound to be upsetting for Gemma's son, but I guess it can't be avoided.'

'Pity I can't help you. I wish you well. This hopefully will bring the research to an end and allow you to close the file. My timing for the visit looks good now.'

'Yes, indeed. Skype me on Sunday at the usual time and I'll tell you how it went.'

'Great, bye for now.'

On Friday evening, Anna and Katherine were chatting as they prepared dinner. As they were about ready to eat, Peter joined them. 'I'm glad to be home early on Friday for a change. I expect you both are looking forward to a rest.'

Anna replied, 'Sure, relaxation and some study.'

'Glad to hear it,' her dad replied. He had talked earlier to Katherine about the impact Tommy's visit would have on class or study time, but she said it was just for a few days.

As if prompted by this, Katherine asked, 'Any word from

Tommy on his travel plans?'

'No, not yet, but I expect to hear soon.'

'Will he stay with us?'

'I assume Barbara will be here for the holiday weekend so he'll probably share my room.'

Peter looked startled but Katherine just smiled.

Anna went on, 'Seriously though, you both know he's special to me. We've become close – well, as close as Skype will allow.'

Peter said, in a serious tone, 'Take it slowly – that's what I want you to do, Anna. A relationship on Skype could be very misleading, and you need to check that out. Don't get me wrong, Tommy seems great, but don't rush it, OK?'

Katherine supported him, saying, 'Yes, I agree, but I hope you and Tommy have a wonderful few days together. You both deserve that.'

'Thanks, Mom, and yes, Dad, I won't rush things. You'll be relieved to hear that Tommy said something similar. He said that neither of us should feel under any obligation or pressure, that we should just enjoy the few days and see where that takes us.'

Katherine and Peter exchanged expressions of relief.

58

St Petroc's Roman Catholic Church was located in the inner suburbs of Philadelphia, on the junction of Belvedere Place and Putland Street. Built in the 1870s, its appearance was enhanced by being set back from the road. A line of ten three-storey row houses was located left of the church, and a further ten to the right, separated by Putland Street. One could be forgiven for assuming that a number of these row houses had been demolished to create a site for the church, but, according to the parish history, one of the many garment factories in the city operated there before the houses were built. When the archdiocese purchased the factory, the house to the left of the church, the home of the factory manager, was part of the deal. An alley gave access to a garden at the rear and also provided space for parking six cars.

Father Edward Dudek had seen them parking their car and was at the hall door to meet and greet them. He thanked them for taking the time to come to Philadelphia, hung their coats on the old-style hallstand, and ushered them along the hallway and into a formal dining room. His father, Anthony Dudek, rose from the chair on which he had hung his tweed jacket, with his hand outstretched. Anna noticed that the far end of the long dining table, which could seat twelve, was already set for their lunch.

Katherine focused on their two hosts, who were very different in appearance. Father Dudek was low sized, broadly built with a florid complexion and receding dark hair. He wore a dark-blue cardigan over a grey shirt and a Roman collar. His father was tall and slender and, for his age, very erect. They took the chairs at the top of the table, facing the window, and motioned Peter and Katherine to their left and Anna to their right.

Father Dudek welcomed them again and said, 'I should explain that the priests' apartments on the upper floors are a bit cramped for five of us and the parish meeting rooms in the basement are somewhat uninviting.' Smiling at his guests, he immediately added, 'Isn't the internet amazing? We would never have made the connection without it. Anna has cautioned us about some of the information you've uncovered, but we're looking forward to hearing what you have to say.'

He then invited the Novaks to take the initiative, saying, 'We've very little to tell you about Leo Novak. In fact, neither of us ever heard of him until we stumbled across a marriage certificate a short time ago, one of the final pieces of our research. Leo was the stepfather of Gemma Baudo, my dad's mother. Leo's wife, Francesca, referred to herself as Mrs Baudo, the name of her first husband, as if Leo never existed. We are intrigued as to why she did this so I suggest you start by telling us what you know.'

Anna, confident that she could provide the explanation they required but apprehensive on the impact it would make, answered that since she was most familiar with the research she would do the talking and added that she had brought a copy of the key documents for them. 'Please stop me if you have any questions as I'm talking.' In saying this, she hoped she could deliver the upsetting information as sensitively as possible.

'Thank you, please go ahead.'

'We started with the Novak side of our family with little

information and virtually nothing about Leo Novak, my dad's great-uncle. We believed that he had been ostracised. We had no record of any reason for this. One of Dad's brothers said he understood that Leo had a fight with a Bishop Walsh, an Irishman based in Philadelphia; another brother said he understood that the fight was not trivial.'

The Novaks could sense unease, especially in Father Dudek.

'I checked the website for the archdiocese and found that Bishop Richard Walsh served from 1906 until his death in 1926. This period seemed to fit the timescale. The only thing I could think of doing then was to include Bishop Walsh in our family tree, which I posted on Ancestry.com. So, father, in the same way that you found us, we found Tommy Walsh in Ireland. His great-grandfather was a cousin and similar in age to Bishop Walsh. I sent him an email in a million-to-one chance that in his research he had come across some information on this not-trivial fight. By an amazing coincidence, he had only recently located a news story in the New York Times and the Washington Post dated February and June 1913 that referred to Leo Novak and Bishop Walsh in the most dramatic and upsetting way.'

Anna handed a copy of the news items to Father Dudek, who placed them on the table so that he and his father could read them together. Anthony reached back and took reading glasses from the pocket of his jacket.

Anna and her parents exchanged eye contact, signalling their concern about the impact this would have on the two men.

'Good God,' Anthony said. 'I never expected anything like this. An attempt to assassinate a bishop! No wonder the marriage didn't last long.'

'This is amazing and must have been distressing for you,' his son added. 'Were you able to get any explanation for this awful event?'

'Yes, we were, but we could not have done it without the help from Tommy Walsh in Ireland.'

'Please continue,' Father Dudek said. 'We need to be patient and hear you out.'

'No, please stop me any time, and maybe Mom and Dad will add comments as well.'

Peter leaned forward, resting his hands on the table. 'Yes, well, we learned by instalments over a few months, and it took time to absorb and come to terms with each new bit of information. You, on the other hand, are hearing it all at once so please take as much time as you need to comment or ask questions.'

'Thanks Peter,' Anthony said. 'We'll do that and maybe take notes to be raised later on.'

Anna resumed. 'Tommy Walsh had earlier received information on Bishop Walsh from the archive operated by the Philadelphia archdiocese so he sent them a copy of the newspaper clippings and asked for more detailed information. I think it's fair to say that the response really surprised us. They had never heard of an assassination attempt on Bishop Walsh or any other bishop. The archivist said he checked an index for the period, which covered all sorts of news stories in Philadelphia, major and minor, but could find no record of the event. So the attempt to kill the bishop and Leo Novak's two escapes from captivity were reported in New York and Washington but not mentioned at all in the Philadelphia press.'

Peter could see the impact this news was having on their hosts, so, in an effort to give them time to absorb it, he said, 'We had a long talk about this. Anna also discussed it with Tommy Walsh by email and on Skype. We could not avoid the conclusion that a cover-up had taken place and that this was unlikely to have been done to protect Leo.'

'Yes,' Father Dudek replied. 'It certainly looks that way. I'm wondering where this story may be heading, but I'll keep my thoughts to myself for now.'

Anthony looked very uneasy but remained silent.

Katherine said, 'At this point we thought that Tommy Walsh would want to stop the research because it might show the bishop, and not Leo, in a bad light. But no, he stuck with it. He's a wonderful young man.'

Anna, very pleased with her mother's comment, resumed the story. 'We were upset about all of this, and I recall Dad saying that it might have been better to have left the past in the past, but our overall feeling was that we owed it to Leo to do everything possible to find out what had happened to him, if he spent the rest of his life in a psychiatric hospital.' She let that question hang and then continued. 'From the Census, Tommy learned about Leo's marriage to Francesca, and that she had a daughter, Gemma. Tommy also found a website on historical police files and Uncle Adam, who is a police officer, arranged access for me to the police archives where I read a file, created in 1912. What we learned is even more upsetting than what went before.' As she handed over a copy of her report, she added, 'As I mentioned on the phone, father, we were asked to treat this information as confidential.'

Katherine felt compelled to interject. 'Anthony, Father Dudek, you have a very close connection with the people mentioned in Anna's report. I hope you won't think we are behaving insensitively towards you.' She continued, 'Could I suggest that if you want some time to talk about this alone when you have read the report, just let us know.'

They didn't comment. It took several minutes to read the report, and then, after an uncomfortable silence, Father Dudek said, 'Now I know why you warned us about what you had learned. Maybe my mind has been conditioned by more recent events, but when you told us about the attempt to kill the bishop I wondered if child abuse might be a cause. I would like to read the report again before saying any more. Perhaps, Dad, you may like to comment at this stage?'

Anthony was visibly stressed. Father Edward rose from his chair, placed his left arm around his dad's shoulder and held his right hand. 'It's upsetting to hear what happened to my mother. I would never have guessed that she experienced such a frightening and traumatic event.' After a short silence, he added, 'I also now realise that the little information I have about Leo Novak is more revealing than I could have imagined. Yes, it would be helpful to read Anna's notes again.'

With a whisper to Katherine and a nod to Anna, Peter suggested that they leave the table and move to the window at the far end of the room, which overlooked Belvedere Place. They chatted about the view and the traffic and kept their conversation going to give their hosts the privacy to exchange views and to absorb the disturbing content of the report.

Less than ten minutes later, Father Dudek joined them. 'Thanks for giving us time and space. This is really hard for my dad.'

Katherine, trying to control her emotions, said, 'Our hearts go out to him and to you.'

Father Dudek sighed, expressed his thanks and said, 'What we would like now is that you would give us your views on all of this since you have had the time to discuss and debate it.'

'Of course,' Peter replied. 'We want to be as helpful as possible.'

When they resumed their places at the table, Anna responded to the request. 'Both families have talked about this, and we think Uncle Adam is right. The police would not have hesitated to arrest Leo Novak if they regarded him as guilty. He noted also that the priest was not even questioned. Our conclusion is that Bishop Walsh was trying to avoid publicity and embarrassing questions about the assassination attempt. That's why the press didn't cover it. As you will have read, a file on the assassination attempt did not exist. Mom and Dad, does that cover it all?'

'Yes, I believe so,' Peter said. 'Another thought crossed my mind just now. Tommy drew our attention to the sequence of events. Anna, do you have the dates in your file?'

Anna searched for the relevant page. 'Yes, here it is. The assault took place on July 6th. Francesca was interviewed on the 26th, the parish priest on the 27th and Leo on the 28th. Based on the newspaper reports, we estimate that the attempt to kill the bishop happened sometime in August. So things happened very fast, and for that reason alone it must have been bewildering for Francesca.'

Peter added, 'Leo failed to show Francesca he was innocent. This led to insanity and his attempt to kill the bishop. Even if he had been subsequently exonerated of child abuse he would likely have ended up in a psychiatric hospital anyway.'

Katherine then said, 'We wondered if the bishop or his representative told Francesca that Leo was innocent or if Francesca changed her mind about him or kept in touch with him subsequently. We believe that Leo was disowned by his brother, Charles, Peter's grandfather, but we hoped this was because of Leo's attempt to kill the bishop and because of his insanity and not because he believed he was guilty of a sexual assault.'

Peter felt that Anthony and Edward should be given time to respond. 'We do know what happened to Leo subsequently, but perhaps we should stop now and listen to what you have to say.'

Father Dudek took up the offer. He leaned back in his chair and made brief eye contact with each of his guests. 'We're all only too well aware of the recent scandals in our church about the cover-up of child abuse by priests. I've been trying to support individuals and families in my parish who were victims of this disgusting behaviour, and even when assaults happened many years ago the pain and the trauma continues. Having listened to what Gemma, Francesca and Leo went through I can now empathise even more with my parishioners who are suffering.'

Peter wondered if a response was expected, but after a brief silence Father Dudek continued. 'I can understand why a conspiracy of silence was commonplace a hundred years ago and maybe for many years since then. That was how society operated. I mean, think about the secrecy surrounding unmarried mothers, around the adoption process, around marital infidelity and mistresses, even around insanity and some other illnesses. Child abuse and not just sexual abuse was also "swept under the carpet" so to speak. The advice from medical specialists at that time was that priests, or anyone else who sexually assaulted a child, could be cured by removing them from the location of their temptation and by counselling and redirection. So, I believe it's against that background that we should judge what happened a hundred years ago.' Before anyone could respond, he said, 'Look, I'm sorry if I appear to be giving you a homily.'

'No. No,' Katherine said. 'I agree with you. People are too quick to judge past events by today's standards. The recent awful behaviour of the hierarchy, right up to the Vatican, is a different matter though.'

'Yes indeed, I agree fully. The treatment I described did not apply in more recent times. I can't put an exact date, but maybe from the 1960s and certainly from the 1970s the hierarchy knew very well that paedophilia was incurable and that priests transferred to another parish were likely to reoffend. Priests I trained with, priests I worked with, now stand accused. This cover-up was nothing less than a criminal act.' For a few seconds, he seemed lost in thought. 'Look, I don't want to go on about this, but if I was working in another organisation the revulsion

I feel towards my former colleagues who are paedophiles and towards my superiors would force me to look for another job.'

A long uneasy silence was broken by Anthony. 'Maybe this is the right time for me to tell you the little I know about my mother Gemma and Leo.' Turning towards Anna, he said, 'Prior to today I didn't place much importance on what I'm about to tell you. From an early age I began to notice that my mother used to go away on the odd occasion for most of a day but never said where she was going. When I kept quizzing her, she eventually said that she was just visiting a friend but told me that it was a secret and that I wasn't to tell my Grandma Francesca anything about it.' Katherine sat forward in her chair, looking like she was about to comment, but Anthony went on. 'The other piece of family history that will interest you is a letter I found when I was sorting out my mother's affairs when she died in 1976. When I was putting her collection of books into containers, I dropped one on the floor and a handwritten letter fell out from under the dust cover. When I was replacing it, I found an envelope inside the front cover. These were clearly meant to be hidden. They are in a very poor condition, so I brought you a typed version.'

As he handed this across, Anna joined her parents at the other side of the table.

Letter from Leo (Novak?) to Gemma Dudek, April 20, 1928
Address of sender not stated.
Addressed to Mrs Gemma Dudek,
C/O The Accounts Department, Ellenmount Insurance Company, Kenneth Place, Philadelphia

Dear Gemma,
Thank you for the letter which came yesterday.
Delighted that your wedding was a happy day, and why

303

wouldn't it be when you married a Polish man? I hope he'll be very good to you because you should have the best.

I said it many times, and I say it again, that your visits mean the world to me, and I look forward very much to your next one. The problem at home makes it difficult for you to come, and because of that I am two times grateful.

The doctors tell me I shouldn't be thinking of the past and my troubles, but sometimes I can't stop myself. I know it shouldn't be happening, but it's the truth. I also know that I'm blessed to be allowed to work outdoors in this fine weather. With the season that's in it, I'm very busy. We had a lovely display of daffodils again this year, and each day brings new growth in the hospital grounds and in the garden.

Please tell Edmund about me if you think it's a wise thing to do. I know that married life will make you more busy, but I hope you'll be able to steal away to come here.

Thanks and best wishes,

Leo

Anthony added, 'Only a few weeks ago, when I learned about Francesca's second marriage, I assumed the Leo who wrote the letter was her husband, and you have now confirmed my hunch.'

Katherine, drying her happy tears, said, 'Anthony, you have no idea how relieved this letter makes us. We have been very upset about Leo, who went through so much trouble and pain without family or friends to support him. What you said about Gemma's visits and this heart-warming letter now tells us that he had a loving friend in your mother. It also tells us that she must not have thought he committed an assault. I've no doubt her visits helped his recovery. Oh, this is a wonderful relief.'

Father Dudek gave a guarded response. 'It's difficult to be certain of anything that happened so long ago, but my grandmother's visits to Leo do suggest that she, and maybe she alone, felt he was innocent. I was only a teenager when she died, so I'll find it difficult to make any judgement. We'll need to reflect on all we're learning today before arriving at a firm conclusion.'

Peter then explained that they had learned that Leo spent the rest of his life in the psychiatric hospital, so knowing now that he had even one friend to visit and show affection for him was great news.

Anthony was deep in thought. I can't make sense of it. My mother cooperated with Grandmother Francesca in removing any mention or record of Leo Novak from their shared lives while at the same time she secretly visited him on a regular basis. How could they have maintained this pretence? This is crazy. Did my dad know anything about this? How come I'm only learning about it now?

He decided to follow the line taken by his son. 'I'm so glad the letter means so much more than I imagined. However, as you saw, the letter was addressed to my mother at her workplace. That, and my mother instructing me to keep her visits to Leo secret, suggests that Francesca was still estranged from him, and it seems likely that her attitude remained that way to the end.'

Anna put forward a different interpretation. 'Another angle struck me just now as you were speaking. Gemma visited Leo regularly, so, as Mom said, she must have believed he was innocent. She either had a memory of the awful event of July 6th, 1912, when she was seven years old, or her mother told her that Leo was innocent. Either way, her visits to Leo suggest that Francesca also knew he was innocent.'

'Why then did my mother keep her visits a secret?'

'Maybe Gemma did so because Francesca would fear that the stigma of insanity and Leo's crime against the bishop would become known. Maybe Francesca would also have worried about her personal safety when visiting a deranged man.'

Katherine wondered if Anthony and Edward, given all they had just heard, would conclude that Francesca had decided to bring her marriage to an abrupt end.

Anthony decided not to offer an opinion. He said, 'We need to reflect on this and many other aspects of what you have learned.'

Peter was concerned about the pressure that seemed to be building on Anthony and his son. 'I agree fully. As I mentioned earlier, we had months to consider and debate all we've told you. It was a painful experience, and it required all that time to arrive at conclusions. Besides, you, Anthony, must have known Francesca very well, so you'll have a different perspective on all of this.'

'I was about fourteen when Grandma Francesca died, but I couldn't claim to know her very well. However, I take your point.'

Anna said, 'You both must be mentally tired from all the upsetting information we have given you. I've just one final piece about how Leo spent the rest of his life. After his arrest, he was an inmate of the South West Philadelphia Psychiatric Hospital, and in 1915 he moved to Webster House. So, that was his address when he wrote the letter. He was discharged in March 1931, to immediately become an employee, tending to the grounds and the garden. He lived in the gate lodge. So, he never left the hospital and died there in January 1940 and was buried in the nearby Roman Catholic cemetery which, we were told, has not been used for many years.'

'So, a happy ending of sorts,' Katherine suggested. The thought struck her that since Charles was killed in the First World war and Alice probably also died young, it is likely that only Francesca or Gemma could have given him shelter and support. She decided not to mention this.

Peter added, 'We were saddened by the news that apparently Leo felt unable to leave the hospital, unable to face the outside world. He paid a heavy price, didn't he? But so did all the victims of sexual abuse as you mentioned earlier, father, and this included Gemma. I want to thank you both for the interest you have shown in my great-uncle. Having listened to our story, you may now be regretting that.'

'No, indeed not,' Anthony replied. 'I'm glad to know that my mother's letter means so much and that, given the circumstances, she was very considerate and kind-hearted towards Leo who, at least for a short time, was also part of our family.'

Anna then asked, 'When do you think Gemma started to visit Leo?'

'Difficult to say. Maybe about 1922 when she started her job in the insurance company. She was about seventeen years old then. Of course that is only a guess. My father worked for the same company, and that's how they met.'

'So,' Anna replied, 'Leo probably didn't have any visitor for his first seven years in Webster House.'

'Yes, but my mother may have written to him during those years.'

Peter, prompted by the information Anna had given on Webster House, said, 'Maybe Leo had a history of mental illness prior to trying to shoot the bishop, and, if so, this could have contributed to Francesca's decision to disown him – the last straw, so to speak.'

'An interesting possibility,' Father Dudek replied, 'but it's unlikely that we'll ever know the answer to that.'

'That reminds me,' Anthony said. 'The three of you have done a wonderful thing for Leo. As you spoke about him, I recalled the French philosopher who wrote that to be forgotten is to die twice. Because of your kindness and dedication you have rescued him. Leo is now remembered; he's no longer forgotten.'

Anna wished Tommy had been there to hear this.

'Thank you, Anthony,' Katherine replied. 'That's a wonderful thought to cling on to.'

Father Dudek then said, 'It would be useful for us if you wrote down your conclusions about all you have learned. Oh, I meant to say this much earlier: I'm amazed that you were able to find out so much about Leo. I mean, the central event happened a hundred years ago, and yet you were able to dig out the whole story.'

'Yes,' Peter said, 'Anna and Tommy did great work. Yes, of course we'll give you a summary. We'll prepare it later and send it to you.'

Father Dudek expressed his thanks and said that they would read all the information again, copy it for other members of their family and come back with comments or questions. 'Now, I'll bet you won't say no to some refreshments.'

The invitation received an enthusiastic yes, and they made their way to the end of the table while Father Dudek went to fetch a tray of coffee and sandwiches.

59

Tommy was very moved by the letter from Leo Novak to Gemma and by how much it must have meant to Anna's family. He read the summary prepared for the Dudeks, which was attached to Anna's email, a summary of a sad life.

It was 7 p.m. on Sunday in Clondore, the scheduled time for the weekly Skype session, and right on cue Anna appeared on screen. Tommy's reaction was the same as in all previous sessions. He just looked at her in silence, admiring her beauty, which he had learned was matched by her warmth and absence of any hint of vanity.

'Please tell me you've booked your flights.'

'Yes, flights are booked, and I have applied for my visa. I'll be on a US Airways direct flight on Wednesday, 27th March, departing Dublin at 11.35 a.m., arriving in Philadelphia at 2.05 p.m., returning on the evening of Tuesday 2nd April.'

'I don't want to think about the return flight – meeting you at the airport is getting all my attention.'

'How romantic is that? Just like in the movies, Meg Ryan and Tom Hanks!'

They both silently enjoyed the thought.

'Mom and Dad want you to be our guest. They will insist.'

'Sorry, too much, too soon, I don't want to be any trouble.

Please suggest a hotel.'

'OK, six nights, right? Maybe I could do a deal with a hotel or motel.'

'Any place within walking distance of your home?'

Anna laughed at this thought, saying, 'Americans don't walk anywhere if they can help it. You will have to put up with my beat-up old Beetle.'

'Oh, wonderful.'

Anna did not want to break the spell of this conversation, but she needed to get Tommy's reaction to her email about the meeting with the Dudeks on the previous day, so she asked if he had read her message.

'Yes, your dad's summary seems good to me. You could include it as an appendix to your family tree.'

'Good idea.'

'The letter from Leo to Gemma must mean so much to your family. It just shows that little things can mean a lot.'

'Yes, the letter was a wonderful surprise, a declaration of Leo's innocence, a breakthrough really.'

'How did your meeting go?'

'I was very conscious that Gemma's son was sitting in front of me and of how the information would impact on him. I felt there was no easy way to tell him. Father and son were upset, of course, but despite this they responded very positively and were very appreciative of the research work that you and I had done.'

'Were you tempted to withhold information?'

'Not really, except I didn't mention that the researchers in the police archive were busy reading old files on paedophile priests or that my Uncle Paul's view was that the bishop incriminated Leo to protect the priest and that he probably deserved what happened to him. I felt they had enough disturbing information to deal with.'

'I wonder if the curate's name turned up in any of those other files. Anyway, let's not go there. You made the right decision. Did they have any other information for you?'

'They had never heard of Leo Novak until they found a marriage certificate recently, and only then recognised the significance of the letter to Gemma that Anthony had found. Neither Gemma nor Francesca had ever mentioned his name. How incredible is that?'

'The poor man. Both families banished him from their lives. Thank God, as we now know, Gemma was both brave and compassionate.'

'Yeah, she was.'

'There's a lesson there for all of us.'

'You bet. Keep a line of communication open, no matter what.'

'Will you keep in touch with the Dudeks?'

'Our talk over lunch was good, considering the information we'd just shared. They said they'd think about it, share the information with other family members and then contact us.'

'Good. They need time, don't they?'

'Dad says he is going to suggest to Father Dudek to say Mass in memory of Leo, Francesca and Gemma and Bishop Walsh as well, which both families would attend.'

'Great idea. I would love to be there, but that's not—'

'Sorry to interrupt, but there's somebody here who wants to talk to you.'

Anna moved from sight, and Tommy could hear a muffled conversation going on. He was expecting to see Martha, but then a different face appeared.

'Hello, Tommy. I'm Katherine, Anna's mom. I just wanted to say how much we appreciate all the research you've done which made it possible to bring Leo back into the family fold, so to speak.'

'It's been a real pleasure. I have to confess that I'm not sure I would have persevered if I hadn't been dealing with Anna. That's been really special.'

'That's nice to know, and I'm looking forward to hearing your travel plans and to welcoming you to our home.'

'I've given the details to Anna, and I'm counting the days.'

'Bye, Tommy.'

Tommy could see the mother–daughter resemblance but waited to see her dad before final judgement.

'Now you've made another conquest. She's nearly as excited as I am – well, not quite.'

'Two weeks from Thursday! I can hardly believe it.'

'I hope you realise how difficult it is to focus on my work when I'm thinking about your visit, but the more I get done in advance, the more time we'll have together. Now, isn't that mature and wise?'

'You said it. Bye for now.'

'Bye, Tommy.'

* * *

Frank and Tommy were standing in the shop in a lull between customers, discussing Anna's latest email. Frank enjoyed these lulls when they were short and seldom – otherwise they were bad for business.

Frank said, 'Isn't it sad the way people can be made to vanish. Everyone deserves to be remembered, even if their life is very ordinary. Francesca and Gemma never mentioned Leo, so Gemma's children and possibly her husband never heard of him. I wonder if Leo had more siblings. Would they also have disowned him?'

'Maybe a sister would have been more compassionate.'

'I can understand that someone who was insane and who tried to murder a bishop would not be mentioned among friends or neighbours, but I would have thought that visits or letters to him would have been the norm.'

'That was then, Dad.'

'Yes, you're right. Anyway, it's wonderful for the Novak family that Gemma broke ranks, as it were, and that the letter referring to this survived. It must bring closure of a sort.'

'Yeah, that's how I see it. And Anna's mum said that because of the work Anna and I did Leo has been brought back into the family fold. Of course I have benefited too – I wouldn't have met Anna otherwise.'

'As they say, virtue is its own reward. So, you'll be singing "For I'm off to Philadelphia in the morning!"'

'Easter in Pennsylvania, who'd have thought? That reminds me, how are your wedding plans progressing? Anything I can do?'

'Not yet anyway. Jimmy is bending my ear with suggestions and offers of help. Orla has everything under control, but when you return I'm sure you'll be conscripted.'

'Fine by me.'

Tommy's curiosity about the curate continued to play on his mind. The New York Times certainly won't tell me if he assaulted another child, but maybe he was newsworthy for a different reason. God, I hope he wasn't made a bishop. He decided to check. He repeated the previous search instructions, inserted 'Bruno Favaloro' and '1912–1932'. He found a few references to Favaloro's presence at liturgical events and then,

MAFIA KILLING IN THE BRONX?

March 28, 1924, New York Times

The body found on waste ground on Sunday morning was that of Bruno Favaloro. It is suspected that he had been a bag man for a crime gang. The police are investigating and looking for witnesses. The victim was formerly a Roman Catholic priest in the Philadelphia diocese.

So, did he leave the priesthood or was he defrocked? While this doesn't prove anything, it certainly supports the belief that he was guilty of assaulting Gemma. Tommy printed a copy to bring to Pennsylvania.

He decided to phone Mary before she got to him. 'Hi, Mary, are you visiting here during Easter?'

'Not sure.'

'Well, I won't be here.'

'Yes, I know.'

'You've been talking to Dad then?'

'Yeah, we've had a few conversations.'

'Any conclusions, decisions?'

'No, not yet.'

'Maybe you just have to take a leap of faith?'

'God, you should know, going across the Atlantic to visit a woman you've only met on Skype. I know I've been on your case, but I never expected this bold move.'

Tommy laughed at her reaction. 'You see, I've been taking your advice to heart.' He wished he felt as confident as he sounded. Mary is saying what I've been thinking. But then, I know I'm attracted to Anna because of her personality, her warmth, as well as her beauty, and that's encouraging. I know I should leave Clondore, but could a few days with Anna mean moving permanently to the States? A change from claustrophobic familiarity to the totally unknown? Is that what I want to do? Would I teach or do something totally different? Don't be such a wimp. One day at a time – best not to think too far ahead.

Mary added to Tommy's doubts. 'If you think I'm surprised,

wait until Deirdre gets you.'

'Yeah, I could guess. She's already told me I'm daft just getting to know Anna on Skype.'

'Could this be love?' Mary said, without any hint of amusement in her voice.

Tommy hesitated, not sure how to respond. 'Ask me when I come home.'

'Dad says she's beautiful, so that explains a lot. She must be some woman to move you. I wish I had that effect on men.'

'I'm sure Kevin would say that you have.'

'I must ask him, just as a tease.'

Tommy took the opportunity to change the subject. 'Seriously, if you and Kevin are happy with the general idea of taking over the business, why not make a commitment for an agreed period, why not "taste and see"? Kevin could commute during this period and you could revert to your present life in Dublin if it didn't work out.'

'We thought about that. Would Dad go for it?'

'I'm sure it would suit both parties. Also, remember, your decision has a bearing on where Dad and Orla will live.'

'I tend to forget that, thanks Tommy. I hope everything works out well for you in the States, I really do, but I'm worried you may decide to live there.'

Tommy wondered if the possibility of him living in America, however tenuous that might be, had increased the pressure on Mary to take over the business, but he decided not to mention it. 'Who knows? I'll introduce you on Skype the next time you're here. Say hi to Kevin for me.'

'Of course. Bye, Tommy, and safe travelling.'

That night, Tommy had a weird dream. He was in Philadelphia, playing American Football in a packed stadium, but he was wearing his Clondore club strip of white shorts and blue and green jersey, with cowboy boots, and instead of a helmet he wore a Stetson. A fan in the crowd roared, 'He says he's Irish but he speaks with an American accent.'

* * *

Anna couldn't wait to get on the phone to Martha to tell her the good news. 'He's coming on the 27th.'

'Wonderful! Oh, how romantic. I'll be at the airport with you to meet him.'

'No, you won't.'

'Just testing. Will I be allowed to meet him while he's here?'

'Of course, but your time will be strictly limited.'

'Meany. When does he return home?'

'I'm trying not to think about that, but it's Tuesday, April 2nd.'

'So what are your plans? The Crofton Inn is a must.'

'I'll see you for coffee tomorrow and please have plenty of suggestions.'

'Apart from a romantic walk in the woods?'

'I knew I could count on you! Bye.'

* * *

As the weekend approached, Tommy asked Jimmy Walker to tell his stepson, Sean Maher, that he would be away for Easter and wouldn't be available for the trial football match on Easter Sunday. He didn't say where he was going, but he knew Jimmy would soon find out.

He went through his travel checklist again. Visa documents, passport, flight tickets, all in order, check-in arrangements noted, dollars to be collected at the airport, credit and debit cards in date, weather forecast checked for the Center Valley area of Pennsylvania and appropriate clothes ready for packing. He decided to wear rather than pack a light sports jacket with a tie in the pocket in case he was asked to any kind of formal do. I should have bought a present for Anna and a present for her parents. Maybe I'll pick up a bottle of Bailey's Irish Cream in the duty free? He made a mental note to find out Anna's birthday.

Getting to Dublin Airport was presenting a problem. He would need to catch the 5.43 a.m. train from Tullamore on the Wednesday morning which would mean leaving Clondore an hour earlier to be on the safe side. It would also take an hour by coach from Heuston Station to the airport. The schedule was too tight for comfort. Deirdre, who would be on her Easter break, had offered to drive him to Tullamore despite her restated misgivings about his trip. He decided to travel on the Tuesday evening with Deirdre's help and to stay overnight in an airport hotel. His final task was to research any special offers available from the airline or the hotels.

All his thoughts and efforts had been focused on getting to Pennsylvania and seeing Anna. Now that he was ready to go, he looked in the rear-view mirror of life and wondered about what he may be leaving behind.

60

It took about an hour to get through customs and passport control. When Tommy approached the Arrivals Hall, he saw Anna before she saw him. The impact was even greater than he had imagined. When she saw him, she hurried towards him, calling his name, and was in his arms as soon as he came through the doorway.

They hugged, and when they separated, Tommy said, 'God, you're even more beautiful off screen.' Their eyes met, and a silent meaningful message passed between them.

'I'm so glad you're here, so glad. I've been dreaming and thinking about this all week, and now I'm speechless.'

They both laughed as they hugged again, this time with deeper meaning and intent.

Acknowledgements

The starting point, the 'what if', of this novel was as described in the prologue. The finished product was made possible by the assistance of editors Robert Doran, Bernadette Kearns and Liz Hudson who recommended, persuaded and supported. I am very grateful to them.

Thanks to Clare Tuohy and Tom Conlon, very accomplished members of the Genealogical Society of Ireland, who guided me on the online sources of family research.

I prevailed on family members and friends, in some cases more than once, to read my manuscript. They did so with competence and diligence. These included Virginia Gill, Kieran O'Driscoll, Mary O'Driscoll, Ursula Quinn Ryan, Frank Quinn, Denise Watt, Bess Barry and the late Oscar Barry.

I am indebted to Joe Ryan and Barbara Stack who provided technical services and very helpful advice.

I was also greatly assisted by the Irish Writers Union, the author Olive Collins and Carrowmore Publishing.

I may have failed to include others who helped me along the way and to these I ask forgiveness.

Dublin
September 2019

South Dublin Libraries

www.southdublinlibraries.ie

Printed in Poland
by Amazon Fulfillment
Poland Sp. z o.o., Wrocław

53336286R00190